About the Author

Claire Boston is a contemporary romance author who enjoys exploring real life issues on her way to the happily-ever-after. She writes heart-warming stories, with resilient heroines and heroes you'll love. In 2014 she was nominated for an Australian Romance Readers Award for Favourite New Romance Author.

When Claire's not writing she can be found creating her own handmade journals, swinging on a sidecar, or in the garden attempting to grow something other than weeds.

Claire lives in Western Australia with her husband, who loves even her most annoying quirks, and her grubby, but adorable Australian bulldog.

Also by Claire Boston

The Texan Quartet
What Goes on Tour
All that Sparkles
Under the Covers
Into the Fire

The Flanagan Sisters
Break the Rules
Change of Heart
Blaze a Trail
Place to Belong
Take a Chance

The Blackbridge Series
Nothing to Fear
Nothing to Gain
Nothing to Hide
Nothing to Lose

The Beginner Writer's Toolkit
Self-Editing

Break the Rules

The Flanagan Sisters #1

Claire Boston

BANTILLY
PUBLISHING

First published by Claire Boston in 2016

Break the Rules: The Flanagan Sisters 1
EPUB format: 978-0-9945528-0-8
Mobi format: 978-0-9945528-1-5
Print format: 978-0-9945528-2-2
Large Print format: 978-1-925696-30-1
Cover design by Amygdala Design
Edited by Dianne Blacklock
Proofread by Laura Cook

Dedication

To my sister, Jane

Chapter 1

Bridget Flanagan's head thumped in time to the booming dance music. She shouldn't have let her best friend Tanya convince her to go clubbing.

She sighed. Who was she kidding? Tanya could convince her to do almost anything, and the promise of a girls' night to dance, drink, and forget her troubles sounded like just what she'd needed.

But her head had begun to throb almost immediately and Tanya had found a new friend. It was a shame Sally and Trish hadn't been able to come out tonight. At least then she'd have someone to talk with. Bridget scanned the dance floor, spotting Tanya dancing with the guy she'd picked up. So much for the girls' night.

She shouldn't be surprised. Tanya did tend

to forget everything when a cute guy walked by. Knowing better than to try to drag her out of the club, Bridget headed for the bar and ordered a glass of water. When it arrived, she moved away, taking a sip and willing her headache away. Tanya looked like she was going to dance all night.

"Is that your friend dancing with my brother?" The male voice was loud but sexy and his breath tickled her ear.

Bridget jumped and turned so she was face to face with a man who did not slow her pulse rate at all. He was slightly taller than she was, with thick brown hair and dark eyes that smiled. Yum.

He pointed toward Tanya and leaned closer to be heard over the music. "Is your friend the blonde in the red dress?"

Bridget nodded. "That's Tanya."

"I don't suppose she'll turn into a pumpkin by midnight?" He had a hopeful look on his face.

Bridget grimaced. "Not a chance. I wish she would." She put the glass up to her forehead and sighed at the coolness. "What about your brother?"

"His motto is 'all night long'." He frowned. "Perhaps we can convince them to go somewhere quieter at least, somewhere with some seating."

She was intrigued. Why had he come out if he didn't want to dance? "You don't feel like partying?"

"I moved back to Houston from Australia two days ago. My body hasn't quite adjusted yet."

The mention of his body had Bridget checking it out again. It looked perfectly fine to her. His blue jeans fit in all the right places and the button-down black shirt clung to his well-defined chest. She cleared her throat. "There's a bar around the corner. The music is quieter but they can still dance if they want."

"Shall we give it a go?"

"Sure." Bridget put her glass on the bar and followed him to where Tanya and his brother were dancing. She couldn't hear what he said but they nodded in response. As he turned back to her, Tanya gave her a very unsubtle thumbs up. Bridget ignored her. All she wanted to do was find some quiet and get rid of her headache.

Outside the club, her ears adjusted to the blissful reduction in noise and she took a deep breath.

"Bridge, this is Hal," Tanya chirped.

Hal was slightly taller than his brother, maybe six foot two, with the same thick brown hair and dark eyes.

Bridget forced a smile. "Nice to meet you."

Tanya raised her eyebrows, waiting expectantly. "Who's this?" she nodded to Hal's brother.

Bridget shrugged apologetically. "We didn't swap names. I'm Bridget."

"Jack." He smiled at her and she forgot her pounding head for a moment. It was some smile, lighting up his eyes and sending a lovely warmth through her body.

"Great. Now let's find something to drink," Tanya said, and keeping her hand tightly in Hal's, she led the way to the bar. Hal didn't seem to mind.

Bridget walked alongside Jack, not sure what to say. Now she was out of the noise she realized she'd effectively been picked up. Was this some kind of scam the brothers had going? Find two girls and take them somewhere quieter?

She snuck a look at Jack. No, he really did look as tired as she felt.

They walked past a drugstore. "Wait a second, I've got to grab something." Bridget dashed inside, found the painkillers and bought a packet. When she went back outside, Jack was the only one waiting for her.

"Where's Tanya?"

"They went on ahead. I thought I'd wait."

Bridget tamped down her annoyance.

They'd only just met these guys, and while they seemed nice, they could be anyone. Tanya should be more careful. "Thanks."

Inside the bar, they found a table away from the music. It was quieter than the nightclub and they could talk without shouting. Bridget ordered a glass of water and a coffee, and took two pills. Hopefully they would kick in quickly.

Tanya put her drink on the table and grabbed Hal's hand. "I love this song." She pulled him away to the small dance floor.

Bridget slid on to a chair next to Jack who was nursing his cup of coffee. She had to say something, otherwise this was going to get awkward fast.

"So you've just moved back from Australia?" she asked. "How long were you there?"

"Three years. I was ready to come home and the perfect job opportunity came up."

Bridget did *not* want to talk about work. She wasn't sure she'd be able to keep the frustration out of her voice if she spoke about her job. "What did you do for fun?"

"I did a lot of surfing, a bit of diving, and was roped in to play cricket and Aussie rules football."

"Is their football much different from ours?"

He laughed, a warm, rich sound. "Yeah,

completely different. It took a bit of getting used to."

Bridget couldn't help smiling back at him. He had one of those laughs that made her want to laugh as well, made her want to make him laugh so she could hear it again.

"Have you ever been to Australia?" he asked.

"No. I was born in El Salvador, but since I moved here I haven't done a lot of traveling. I've been focused on work." Which had turned out to be a waste of time.

"When did you move here?"

A stray curl floated in front of her face and she brushed it back impatiently. Her hair did its own thing when she left it out. "I was five."

"It must have been hard, moving somewhere you didn't speak the language."

"My father was Irish so he used to speak English to us at home." She remembered it was like a secret language because her mother couldn't speak English. She'd always thought it was her special thing with her father. "I was lucky because I was starting school and it didn't take long for me to pick it up."

"Do you still speak Spanish?"

"*Sí*. My family still speaks a lot of Spanish at home."

"I only know high school Spanish and I'm not

going to embarrass myself by attempting it now. Do you have any siblings?"

"Two sisters – one older, one younger. What about you? Is it just you and Hal?"

Jack glanced over at the dance floor where Tanya and Hal were still dancing. "Yeah."

"You must be close to go out clubbing together."

He shrugged. "I'm staying with him until I find my own place. He lives closest to where I'll be working from Monday. He said we had to celebrate my return to Houston."

She smiled. "I see he's pleased about your homecoming."

Hal was bumping and grinding behind Tanya.

Jack laughed again. "What about you and Tanya? Having a girls' night?"

"Supposedly." Bridget sighed. "Tanya said I needed to dance my worries away." At his raised eyebrow she added, "I got passed over for a promotion yesterday."

"That's rough. What happened?"

She shook her head. "I don't want to talk about it. I'll get all bitter and you'll think I'm a scary shrew."

"That's not likely to happen." His gaze sent warm tingles through her body. "How's your head?"

She blinked. "It's dulled to an ache."

"It's a start."

It was. If she made no sudden movements she could mostly ignore it. She was enjoying talking to Jack. It wasn't the usual slightly sleazy pickup she was used to. She felt she could actually get to know him. When was the last time she'd been able to do that? She frowned as she tried to remember. There'd been no one since Lionel. She was still recovering from *those* burns and had thrown herself into her work to prove herself. Then in the last six months she'd been temporarily reassigned to a managerial role which came with even more responsibility and a greater workload. When her boss had finally retired, she was sure she'd get the role permanently – he'd recommended her.

Someone obviously hadn't agreed with him.

Bridget pushed the thought aside. She wasn't going to let work mess up her evening. She wouldn't think about it until Monday, when she met her new boss. In the meantime she was going to enjoy the night.

"So no work talk. What do you do for fun?" Jack asked.

It was a good question. She'd been so busy at work she hadn't had time for fun. Sometimes Tanya would convince her to go

Claire Boston

out dancing, or they'd go for drinks with a couple of girls from work, but more often than not it ended with her friend finding a guy and Bridget hanging in a corner, waiting until Tanya had had enough. Bridget wasn't willing to leave her by herself. Often Tanya drank too much and didn't make the best choices. At least Bridget could keep her from doing anything too silly.

"I read when I get the time," she said in answer to Jack's question. "I go to the movies, have drinks with friends, you know the usual stuff."

"What do you read?"

She hesitated. She was always getting ribbed by the guys at work for her choice of reading material. "Romance." She loved the happy endings.

"Can't say I've read much of that," Jack admitted. "I'm more into action and suspense."

"There are some great romantic suspense books out there. You should give it a try."

"I might."

"So what about you? Now you're back in Texas, there'll be no cricket or Australian football."

"I heard about a cricket league around Houston, but I didn't love the game that much. I'd like to check out local dive sites though. But

9

the first thing I need to do is find somewhere to live. As much as I love my brother, he's not the tidiest of roommates."

She grinned, thinking of Tanya. "I've always wanted to learn to scuba dive. It must be amazing to stay underwater for so long."

"It is. You should definitely try it." His eyes lit up and his enthusiasm was palpable. "Once you've dived you'll be hooked. I know I was."

"Maybe I will." She should have a bit of free time now she was going back to her old job. She deserved to do something for herself.

Tanya and Hal came back to the table and Tanya flopped on the chair next to her. She took a deep swig from her cider. "You two should dance. Get your bodies moving." She raised her eyebrows up and down.

Bridget suppressed a groan. Tanya was in her "I've had enough to drink to think I'm being subtle but I'm not" mode. Next she'd start making sexual innuendo, because she'd decided the solution to Bridget's worries was to get laid.

"You two are doing enough moving for the both of us," Jack said.

"Tanya knows how to dance." Hal grinned.

Tanya beamed at him. "You've got some moves yourself." She took another sip of her drink and sighed. "You guys have the most glorious hair. I'd love to have you in the shop."

They exchanged a confused glance.

"She's a hairdresser," Bridget explained.

"Well, you can run your fingers through my hair any time you want," Hal told her.

"Oh, good. Turn around." When he did, Tanya dug her fingers into his hair.

Bridget turned to Jack. "Tell me more about diving. Did you go to the Great Barrier Reef?"

"No, I was on the west coast, but the Ningaloo Reef is an amazing dive. In places you don't even need scuba gear, you can walk straight off the beach with goggles and snorkel and see fish and coral with the most amazing colors."

Bridget didn't even know how to use a snorkel. The only swimming they had done as children was at the municipal pools, when their mother could afford to pay, which wasn't often. These days she liked to swim to keep fit, but she didn't get a chance very often.

"There were also a number of shipwrecks to dive," Jack was saying. "The ocean takes over the man-made structures so quickly. The fish and eels move right in and make themselves at home. When you swim by they watch you as much as you watch them."

Tanya giggled at whatever Hal whispered in her ear. "It's getting late. We should probably head home."

Bridget's headache had disappeared and she was enjoying talking to Jack. Wasn't that just typical?

"Bridge, Hal's offered to show me his place. Are you all right getting home on your own?"

So that was the real reason. Not sure whether to be amused or annoyed she simply said, "Sure."

* * *

The cab pulled up in front of Bridget's house and nerves tickled her stomach. "This is me," she said and paid the driver.

"I'll walk you to your door," Jack said, before asking the driver to wait.

After Tanya had left with Hal, he'd insisted on accompanying her home, saying he wanted to delay his return so he didn't cramp Hal and Tanya's style. Bridget could totally understand that and it gave her an opportunity to decide what she wanted to do about him.

"Nice place," he said as he followed her up the path to the front door.

"Yeah." The front light came on and she turned to face him, her hands clasped together. She was tempted to invite him in, but that was against her dating rules.

He took hold of her hands. "I had a nice time

tonight."

"Me too." Her body tingled in response to his thumb lazily brushing the back of her hand.

He pulled her closer and she tilted her head, her lips parting slightly. Something in her chest fluttered. He was going to kiss her and she wanted him to. He bent his head and his lips met hers. The fluttering stopped as her senses took control. His lips were firm and he tasted like coffee. When his tongue flicked over hers she couldn't suppress a quiet moan. It had been a long time since she'd been kissed like this, since her body had reacted like this. She had to stop this now before it went too far.

Bridget broke the kiss and took a step back, her breath unsteady. She swallowed. "I have two rules to dating," she said. "And one is never to sleep with someone on the first date."

"What's your second rule?" His tone was light and he was smiling.

Her lips twitched in response. "I don't date people I work with." She wasn't going to make *that* mistake again.

"Fair enough." He shuffled his feet. "Want to be a rule-breaker tonight?"

The hopeful look on his face was sweet. She grinned at him. "Yes," she admitted. She kissed him again needing one more taste before he left. He gathered her close, and ran his hand down her back to her butt. Her body heated and she leaned closer. Damn she wanted him. She broke the kiss. What the heck, she deserved some fun. Playing by the rules hadn't got her anywhere. "Want to come in?"

"Hell yes."

She laughed as she unlocked the door and Jack dashed back to tell the driver he wasn't needed.

Anticipation stirring, she led him down the hall to her bedroom. It was way past time she did something spontaneous, and Jack was the perfect guy for it. She turned, drew him into her arms and claimed his lips.

It had been too long for Bridget to take things slowly. Her body was on fire and she wanted him naked. Her fingers worked busily on the buttons of his shirt, while his hands snuck under her top. She shoved the shirt off his shoulders and then lifted her arms so he could rid her of her own top. Her brown hands contrasted against his lighter skin as she ran them over his chest, enjoying his muscle tone. She needed more. She wanted to forget her responsibilities and just feel. And damn he felt good.

Quickly she unclasped her black cotton bra and threw it to the floor. His thumbs brushed her nipples and she threw her head back as glorious sensations flooded her and pooled between her legs. They had to get to the bed.

She moved backwards, her hands tugging on his jeans to draw him along with her as she undid his button and zipper, pushing his pants and underwear down. He was sexy as hell. She couldn't stop running her hands over him, and the sound that came out of her mouth as she stroked his manhood sounded like a purr. She wanted him inside her now.

His eyes darkened as he pushed her on to the bed. She fell willingly back onto the mattress, and then fumbled with her own jeans until he grabbed the waistband and pulled them off.

She couldn't get any hornier. Her mound pulsed with desire, and when he brushed his fingertips lightly over her belly and down between her legs she had to have him, now. Lifting herself onto one elbow, she reached into the drawer of her bedside table and handed him a condom. "Jack, now," she panted.

He quickly sheathed himself and then his body covered hers. It wasn't enough. His hardness pressed against her and she kissed him, needing to taste him.

Slowly he entered her, filling her, and her

brain short-circuited. All she could do was move and feel, moaning his name.

Sensation built quickly like a tidal wave. She was on the edge, and then they both went over, calling out each other's names.

* * *

Bridget lay on her back, her arms outstretched, and a huge grin on her face. That had been incredible.

"Wow," Jack breathed.

Wow didn't really begin to cover it. She just nodded, not able to form a coherent word.

He leaned over and kissed her long and deeply. "I'm glad you broke your rule."

Bridget gazed up at him. "So am I." It was past time that she had some fun, that she lived a little and tonight she'd lived a *lot.*

"Got any plans tomorrow?"

Shoot. She did. "I've got lunch at my mom's."

"That sounds nice."

"Yeah, we get together every other week."

He stretched and glanced at her. "Should I call a cab then?"

Bridget hesitated. As much as she would have liked him to stay, it could get awkward in the morning. She sighed. "Yeah, my sister is picking me up early."

He reached to the floor, pulled his phone out of his jeans pocket, and ordered a cab. She couldn't resist running her hand over his back and down to his luscious bottom.

He glanced over his shoulder and grinned. "Can I see you again?"

"I'd like that." She rattled off her mobile number and he saved it in his phone.

"What about dinner tomorrow?"

Her chest squeezed. He was as keen as she was. "I won't get back until late. How about later in the week?"

"Sure. I'll call."

She was a little disappointed that he didn't offer an alternative, until she remembered he was starting a new job on Monday.

Jack got up and pulled on his pants and shirt. It was a shame to see him cover up that gorgeous body.

Outside a horn tooted. "That'll be my ride," he said.

Bridget stood up, threw on a T-shirt, and followed him to the door. She kissed him again, not really wanting him to leave.

"I'll call," he promised.

"You'd better get going, otherwise the cab might leave." She stepped inside and put a hand on the door. "I'll look forward to your call."

Break the Rules

She shut the door and grinned.

She'd have to thank Tanya for making her go out.

Chapter 2

Bridget's cell phone rang, waking her. Groaning and reaching over to check the display, she saw the time and swore.

"Morning, Carly. Are you on your way?"

"I'm at the front door. Are you still asleep?"

Bridget suppressed another groan and sat up. "I was. Sorry, late night. I'll be right there." She hung up, threw on some clothes and walked to the front door to let her older sister in.

Carly stood on the doorstep, immaculately groomed as always. Her naturally curly brown hair was straightened to perfection and hung just short of her shoulders. She was wearing a knee-length gray skirt and a white blouse, and her feet were clad in a smart pair of four-inch gray pumps.

Bridget leaned in to hug her shorter sister.

"We're going to Casa Flanagan, right?"

Carly gave her a look. "Yes. I've come from a business brunch."

Bridget frowned. "It's Sunday, sis. You shouldn't be working." She turned and led her into the kitchen, where she switched on the coffee maker.

"It was a charity thing," Carly said. "I'll make the coffee. You go take a shower."

Bridget smiled her thanks and headed for the bathroom. Tanya's bedroom door was open and she was lying face down on the mattress, still dressed in the clothes she'd worn last night. Bridget closed the door. She was sure Tanya would give her all the details when she got home tonight.

Her thoughts drifted to Jack. She'd had such a great time with him. She was glad she'd broken her rule and invited him in. It had been ... well, amazing was too soft a word to describe it. She'd never experienced such overwhelming passion before. She'd been consumed with lust, and the only words in her head had been the mantra – *now, now, now.*

Bridget turned on the shower, then stripped off and stepped under the spray. As much as she'd wanted him to stay, she was glad he hadn't. It would have been totally awkward to have him still here when Carly arrived.

She hoped he'd call her today.

After a quick shower, she dressed and met her sister in the kitchen where she had a travel mug of coffee ready to go. "Thanks, Carly." Bridget took a sip and sighed with pleasure. "You're not having one?"

"No, I've had my coffee for the day. You ready? You know how Mama gets when we're late."

"Zita will let her know." Bridget grabbed her phone and sent her younger sister a text saying they were running late.

The response arrived moments later. *Late night, huh? Can't wait to hear about it!*

Bridget grinned and locked the front door behind her. Carly was already getting into the driver's seat of her brand new silver BMW. Bridget closed her eyes as she sank into the rich leather interior and took another sip of coffee.

"You going to tell me about your night?" Carly asked.

She opened her eyes. "Tanya wanted to go dancing. Said it would take my mind off not getting the promotion."

Carly glanced at her. "They didn't give you the job?"

"Nope. They didn't even bother to tell me. I ran into the HR manager as I was leaving on

Friday afternoon and asked him when I would hear. He said the new safety manager was starting on Monday." The familiar irritation bubbled up inside her. "They must have known for weeks and they didn't tell me."

"I can't believe they could be so stupid," Carly said, her tone indignant. "You work your ass off for them. You know that oil refinery inside out and all of the guys respect you. You were the natural choice."

Carly was right. Bridget had been working as group leader of safety for two years and everyone had expected her to get the promotion. "I know. Doesn't matter. I don't know if it's my age or my gender, but something isn't working in my favor."

"They can't discriminate on either of those terms. You should go after them for equal opportunity."

"There's no point. I can't prove anything. All it would do is make me less popular with senior management, and I've ticked them off too many times telling them truths they don't want to hear."

Carly opened her mouth to say something else.

"Just leave it," said Bridget. "I want a whole day when I don't have to think about work."

With that in mind, she turned off her cell

phone. She wasn't on call this weekend, but the guys on shift often called anyway for her opinion. Today they could contact the designated person instead. Bridget needed the break.

* * *

The drive out to their mother's property took just over an hour. Carmen lived on five acres that Carly had bought for her after making her first million. She was fairly self-sufficient – growing her own food and with a coop full of chickens. She always said farming reminded her of El Salvador.

Carly pulled into the long driveway and slowed as Zita's two dogs came bounding out to greet them.

"She has got to train them to stop doing this," Carly said, her knuckles white on the steering wheel as the dogs darted around the car.

"You know Zita," Bridget replied.

Their youngest sister was all about animal rights. She was too kind-hearted to discipline her rescue dogs. Aside from rushing out to greet visitors, the two animals were actually well behaved.

Carly stopped the car close to the house and they got out. Carmen was already at the door.

"There you are! I thought you'd found something better to do." She spoke in rapid Spanish.

Bridget resisted rolling her eyes. Her mother loved to joke about their busy lives. She said the same thing whenever they didn't arrive on time. It didn't matter if they'd sent a text to say they were running late.

She kissed her mother on both cheeks. "I'm sorry. I slept in."

Carmen tutted at her as she greeted Carly. "Have you been out partying?"

"Tanya took me out."

Carmen sniffed. "That girl never stops."

Bridget walked through into the kitchen where spicy smells hit her. Zita was stirring something in a pan. "Hey, Z," she said, pinching one of the *pasteles* from the table. She was starving.

"*Hola.*"

She broke her *pastel* in half, careful not to let the stuffing drop out, and gave some to Mario, one of the young foster children her mother was looking after. Bridget winked at him and he grinned back.

"Where did you go last night?" Her mother puttered around the kitchen getting them a drink, while simultaneously giving Bridget *the* stare. "Were there boys involved?"

"I hope they were men," Zita said, and grinned at her mother's shake of the head.

Bridget smothered a smile. "I met a nice man and gave him my number."

Carmen glanced at her. "What does he do? Where is he from?"

"Mama!" Holy hell, she always wanted details. "His name is Jack, he's from Houston but has been living in Australia, and I don't know what he does. I didn't want to talk about work because I didn't get the promotion."

Carmen slapped a glass of *horchata* on the table in front of her, spilling some of it. "Oh, baby, why are you working for such fools?" She stood with her hands on her hips.

As Bridget had hoped, she'd distracted her mother from more questions about Jack.

Zita lay a hand over Bridget's. "I'm sorry."

Bridget shrugged. "There's nothing I can do about it. They obviously didn't think I was ready for the position."

"But you have been doing the job for six months!" Carmen gestured emphatically.

"That doesn't seem to matter."

"You should quit. They'll be begging you to stay."

"It doesn't quite work like that, Mama." Changing the subject, she asked, "What's for lunch?"

* * *

After Bridget had eaten far more than she should have, she followed Zita outside to pick some fruit to take home.

Her little sister had inherited her looks from their Irish father. Her strawberry blonde hair was naturally straight and she often tied it back in a ponytail. She always wore the most colorful clothes she could find. Today it was a bright red skirt, matched with a white T-shirt and sequined flip flops. Zita didn't remember much of El Salvador, being only three when they'd left, and Bridget sometimes thought she was making up for it by wearing traditional festival clothing.

As soon as they were clear of the house, Zita said, "Tell me about Jack."

Bridget laughed. "There's not a lot to tell."

Zita pushed on. "Where did you meet?"

Bridget sighed. "Tanya dragged me out dancing last night and hooked up with Jack's brother. Neither Jack nor I wanted to be out, so we convinced them to go to a quieter bar where they could keep dancing. We chatted for a couple of hours, then he took me home. I gave him my number." She shrugged. "We'll see if he calls." She really hoped he would.

"Sounds like a gentlemen if he took you home and nothing else."

Bridget wasn't going to discuss it with her little sister. "He was nice." She entered the large greenhouse to pick some mamey and jocote, her mother's favorite fruits. "So what's the story with the new girl?"

The farm was a foster home for refugee children, mostly from Central America. Their mother had insisted on helping when she heard how the situation had worsened over the past few years and unaccompanied children were fleeing to the United States. It worked well because she and Zita spoke Spanish and there were no men around, so it was generally the abused girls who were sent to them.

"I don't know the full story yet," Zita said. "She's been raped."

It was tragic that didn't surprise Bridget. It was all too common for the girls to have been sexually assaulted either before they'd left their home or by the people smugglers who took them across the border. "Where is she from?"

"El Salvador. We only know what she told immigration, and that's not a lot. I'm sure she'll open up when she gets to know us." Zita placed another fruit in the basket. "She's part of the new trial."

"That's great." It was a big deal. Zita and Carmen had been fighting for many years to stop children being imprisoned in detention centers. It could take months, if not years to process them, and the incarceration was hard on them. The trial was to test whether the children could indeed be fostered out in the community while their applications were being processed.

Children who were granted asylum and had no family in the United States inevitably stayed at Casa Flanagan and became part of their family. The house had eight bedrooms, plus there were multiple small self-contained units on the property, where the girls moved as they got older and more independent. Celebrations were always huge in the Flanagan household.

"What about Mario and Jacinta?" The brother and sister had been living with Carmen for two months now while the search for their mother continued.

"We've got a lead. Their mother might be in Wisconsin. We should know in the next week or so."

"That's great."

The situation in Central America was uncertain for many people. Mario's mother had fled the country for the United States in the hope of finding work, leaving her children with her own mother. As she'd earned enough money, she'd sent it back to help get her children out of the country, but because she wasn't a legal citizen, she never included her address.

"It is great," Zita said with a sigh. "But I'll miss them. Mario is so cheeky."

Bridget gave her sister a hug. Zita had the softest heart of all of them. She always got too attached. "You'll stay in touch. You always do." She picked up the basket full of their harvest. "Come on, let's get this inside."

Chapter 3

On Monday morning Bridget arrived at work early to catch the six o'clock shift. She always made an effort to meet with all the operation technicians before they started to discuss any safety issues they might not be aware of.

She walked into the supervisor's office, placing her hard hat on the table. "Morning, Joe."

Joe, the outgoing shift supervisor, looked up from his computer. "Howdy, Bridge. Why'd you have your phone off last night?"

"Out of range," she lied. "Any problems?" She'd turned her phone on this morning and had listened to the messages. The only good one was from Jack, asking how her lunch had been. She hadn't wanted to call him back so early, so she'd saved his number and would call him this afternoon.

"A permit problem, but Ken helped out."

"Great." She'd follow up with Ken, one of the safety officers.

Joe handed her a report. "The incidents for the shift."

Bridget glanced through the short list. A twisted ankle and a level transmitter that was sticking, which meant a tank could potentially overflow. She sighed. So much of the plant was rundown and needed replacing. She had her own project to replace relief valves on the crude tower that were venting to atmosphere.

"I hear the new safety manager's starting today," Joe said.

"That's the rumor."

"What's he like?"

She looked up. "No idea. I don't even know his name."

"It's tough they didn't give it to you. We all wanted you to get it."

Bridget smiled. He was genuinely upset for her. It was nice to be appreciated. "It is what it is. Anything else I need to know?"

"Nah. That's about it."

"Great. Why don't you go home?"

"Hallelujah to that."

Bridget chatted with the incoming shift supervisor and made sure he knew about the sticking level transmitter.

"Bridge, that thing always sticks. It's the nature of the stuff. It's murder on equipment. It usually unsticks itself."

"If the tank overflows we could be in serious trouble." The likelihood might be low but the consequences were very high.

"All right. I'll get one of the guys to raise a work order."

"Thanks." She'd have to remember to check it was done. Part of the problem was the guys on the plant were so used to its quirks, they didn't recognize the potential incident. "Don't forget to remind your guys not to cut through the units."

Each section of the plant was a separate unit, surrounded by a concrete containment area. Roads divided the units and workers were meant to use those roads, but too many of them took shortcuts to save time. It was also bad practice, as everyone had to sign on to the exact unit they were working in so they knew exactly where everyone was if an emergency occurred.

"Sure thing." He turned to his computer.

Bridget sighed. She'd been dismissed. Most of the guys thought she was overly safety conscious to the point of being pedantic but she couldn't help it. She knew what it was like for someone not to make it home from work.

"Have a safe shift." Replacing her hard hat, she strode across to the administration building where her office was located. She had another hour or so before her new boss arrived and she wanted to write some notes so he knew the current status of safety at the plant.

Stopping by the breakroom, she poured another coffee, greeted a few co-workers who were early starters like herself, and then retreated to her office and turned on her computer. She opened her email, scanned quickly to make sure there was nothing urgent, and then began to type a report for the new manager. Management might not think she was capable of doing the job, but she wanted to give her new boss a good first impression.

A knock on her door had Bridget glancing at the time. Already half past nine and she hadn't left her computer. She turned around to find Anthony, the human resources manager, standing at the door.

"Bridget, I want to introduce you to our new safety manager, and your new boss. I thought the two of you could have a chat, and then you could call a department meeting and introduce him to the team."

Bridget stood. "Sure, Anthony."

He turned to gesture the person into the

room. "This is Jackson Gibbs."

Bridget's stomach dropped and she gasped. She blinked quickly, hoping her eyes were playing tricks on her.

They weren't. Jack was standing there, with the thick brown hair she'd dug her fingers into on Saturday night, and those brown eyes looked as stunned as she felt.

Holy hell.

The disappointment felt like a heavy brick in her stomach. The one guy she'd connected with since Lionel, and he was her new boss. In one carefree moment she'd broken both her dating rules. This was why she had the damned rules in the first place.

Pushing aside her shock and regret, Bridget stepped forward. She didn't have time for self-pity now. She needed to act professionally, and the minute she got Jack alone, she had to swear him to secrecy. Saturday night never happened.

She smiled, her hand outstretched. "Nice to meet you."

* * *

Jack took Bridget's hand automatically, shaking it as he tried to process what he was seeing. The gorgeous, feisty woman who had captured his thoughts all of yesterday was now standing in front of him, and she was part of his new team.

"Likewise," he replied.

Her hair was tied back in a messy bun and she was wearing a high-visibility yellow long-sleeved shirt with cargo pants and steel-toed boots. Not the sexiest attire, but she made it look good.

In the next breath he remembered part of the conversation they'd had on Saturday night. She'd been angry about not getting the job she'd applied for. His job.

Shit, this was messy.

Why hadn't Anthony mentioned that one of his team had applied for the job? Surely he knew there could be disgruntled feelings Jack should be aware of.

"I'll leave you to bring Jack up to date with the safety department," Anthony said. "And I'll see you at the manager's meeting this afternoon, Jack."

He acknowledged Anthony with a nod as he left and then turned back to Bridget. She brushed past him and closed her office door.

"You can't tell anyone about Saturday night," she said. Her eyes were fierce.

"No, of course not." He wasn't the type to kiss and tell.

"Good. It never happened. We need to

pretend we don't know each other."

He frowned. "Why?"

"It won't work. People talk."

"It's all right, Bridget. Colleagues get involved all the time."

"Not me. I have my rules."

That's right. Her second rule was not to date co-workers. Jack hadn't given it much thought, hadn't imagined it would be a problem. He smiled, trying to make it as relaxed and casual as he could. "You broke one rule on the weekend."

"And look where it got me." She took a deep breath. "I'm sorry, Jack. I won't deny I enjoyed Saturday night, but it can't go any further. I won't break my second rule." As if sure of his acceptance, she indicated the small meeting table in her room. "Have a seat. I've written a short report on the latest issues." She handed him a document before opening her door and calling, "Ken, department meeting in half an hour. Can you book a room and tell the others? I'll introduce our new boss then."

"Sure thing, Bridge," came the reply.

Bridget came back inside and closed the door behind her. "If I leave it open, we'll get disturbed."

She was very businesslike, not at all like the woman he'd met on the weekend, the woman he hadn't been able to stop thinking about.

He couldn't be quite so businesslike. "I think we need to talk more about the other night."

"There's nothing more to talk about. I won't date a colleague."

"What if I'm not happy with that?"

She frowned at him. "Then you'll have to learn to deal with it. We didn't know we were colleagues at the time. It can't happen again."

But that was the problem. He *wanted* it to happen again.

"Now let me explain what's been happening in the department."

Jack had no choice but to let the matter drop, for now. He would find out the reasons behind her rules later. At the moment he had to focus on his new job.

* * *

By the end of her overview, Jack felt sick. The safety situation in the plant was appalling. The company safety audit had issued a number of corrective actions at their last inspection, some of which were now urgent. The problem was they only had a set amount of funds with which to fix the issues, and they all seemed to be priority one to him. But despite the audit occurring several months ago, Bridget hadn't started any of the main actions. As annoyed as she was about not getting the promotion, it was obvious why she hadn't: she'd clearly not been effective.

He could hardly say that though. He'd have to raise the issue and find a way to resolve it immediately. It was not how he'd hoped to start his new job. No, when he'd applied, he'd just wanted to get back to Houston. He wasn't completely qualified for the role – sure his safety skills were top notch, but he didn't have the official university degree, and his knowledge of training and environment – the other two sections of his responsibility – needed to be improved. He had no experience working in an oil refinery, only mine sites and processing plants. He'd hoped to be surrounded by staff who knew the plant and knew their areas so he could learn from them.

He'd never been responsible for so much and Jack suddenly felt he was in way over his head. He'd have to fake it until he made it.

"We'd better get to the meeting so you can meet the others," Bridget said. "I'll find out which room we're in." She disappeared across the hallway and he glanced at her report. His brain was too overwhelmed to make sense of the words.

"We've got time to grab a coffee," Bridget said, returning to the room. "I'll show you to the breakroom."

The administration building was a maze of hallways and Jack took note of the locations Bridget pointed out. They eventually made it to the meeting room where his team was assembled. As safety manager he had responsibility not only for safety, but also environment and plant training. He had three safety officers, a fire officer, two trainers, two environment officers, and Bridget, who would now return to her original role as group leader of safety.

After the introductions had been made, Jack stood at the front of the room.

"I'm really looking forward to working with you," he began. "Bridget has given me a good overview of the department, but I'd like to hear a little about what you're working on. We'll go around the table and you can tell me your top two priorities."

The environment officers went first, and as each person spoke, it was clear most were enthusiastic about their job. There were a range of ages and experiences. A couple of his safety guys had been at the plant for over ten years and Jack was hoping they would have a good understanding of what was required – though with the current state of the plant, maybe he was being too hopeful. Aside from Bridget, there were two more women on his team, one in environment and the other in safety.

Jack took notes and asked questions, and when they were done he gave a spiel about how important safety and the environment were to him and how he was always open to suggestions for improvement. There wasn't much more he could say at this point because he didn't know enough. This week would be a getting settled and fact-finding week.

Then he would work out what to do about Bridget.

* * *

Bridget returned to her office and closed the door. She shook her arms, trying to release the tension that had taken hold from the moment Jack had walked into her office. There was no way she was going to open herself up for that kind of gossip ever again. It had ended *so* badly last time.

She slumped down on her chair and rested her head on her arms. She should have stuck to her rules on the weekend. She'd been foolish to get caught up in the moment, to not assess the risks. This was worse than awkward.

But at least it proved she was right to have

her two rules – if only she'd followed them.

A knock on her door had her getting to her feet. She didn't have time to feel sorry for herself. There was a lot of work that needed to be done and little time to do it.

When she opened the door one of the planners was standing there. "There's an issue with the upcoming shutdown. Can you come take a look at the paperwork?"

She grabbed her hat and safety glasses. "Sure. Lead the way."

* * *

Bridget arrived home from work and poured herself a glass of white wine, before flopping on the couch.

What a day! After the meeting with Jack she'd spent the rest of her time fighting fires – not literally, thank goodness, but figuratively. She was still wrestling to get her capital project approved so she could do some of the urgent safety repairs the audit required. Every time she checked its status she was told it had been moved to the next person. There were just too many people in the line who needed to sign off on it. Currently it was sitting at head office, probably invisible in the mass of emails in someone's inbox. But she wasn't allowed to contact any of the people directly. She could only speak to the accountant on site who would follow it up. It was so damned inefficient.

Tanya breezed into the living room. "You're home finally!" She poured herself a glass of wine and sat on the sofa next to Bridget. "I've been dying to tell you about my weekend."

When Bridget had arrived home from her mother's yesterday Tanya was out, and there was no way she would have been up this morning before the sun like Bridget.

Pleased her friend was excited about something, she settled in for the tale. "All right. Regale me."

Tanya clenched her hands together and squeezed her eyes shut. "Hal is an absolute sweetie. I think he might be the one."

Bridget smiled. She'd heard that before. "So you had a good time?"

Tanya rolled her eyes. "*So* good. And he has stamina."

Bridget held up a hand. "I don't need to know any more."

"All right. So anyway, on Sunday he called and took me out to dinner. We talked for hours and just gelled, you know? He's busy tonight, but tomorrow we're going to the movies."

Bridget raised her eyebrows. That was unusual. Generally by this stage Tanya had scared off any guy with her enthusiasm. It appeared Hal was as into her as she was into him. It was nice.

"Sounds great," Bridget said. "I'm happy for you."

Tanya grinned and took a sip of her wine. "So, what happened with his brother – what was his name again?"

"Jack. He insisted on seeing me home and I broke my first rule."

Tanya grinned. "You go, girl!"

Bridget shook her head. "Not so good," she said. "Turns out, he's my new boss."

Tanya had her wine glass halfway to her mouth and she stopped, mouth agape, wine splashing on to her top. "You're kidding?"

"I wish I was."

She brushed at the wine. "He's the schmuck who stole your job?"

"He didn't *steal* it."

Tanya waved away her protest. "When did you find out?"

"This morning when the HR manager brought him into my office to introduce him."

"Oh, that sucks. How did you take it? How did he?"

"It was a shock to us both but I handled myself all right."

"I'm sure you did. Nothing shakes you, Miss

Unflappable."

She grimaced at the nickname Tanya had given to her at college.

"So are you going to see him again?"

"I'm pretty sure I'll see him every day at work."

Tanya gave her the look. "You know what I mean."

Bridget took a sip of her wine. "Rule number two."

Tanya placed her glass of wine down on the coffee table. "You can *not* let the Lionel affair affect every potential new relationship. He was a jackass, he treated you badly, but not all men are Lionel."

"He almost ruined my career," Bridget reminded her. "I could have handled breaking up and still working with him, but he blamed the whole incident on me. I lost my job and my reputation. I'm lucky Jeremy convinced Dionysus to give me a chance." Jeremy was the fire officer at Dionysus but had worked with her and Lionel previously. It had been a horrible six months and she'd had to cope with a broken heart, betrayal and a potential lawsuit all at once. She was not going through that again.

"That's not likely to happen again. Love is a risk, Bridge. You've got to open yourself up to it."

Bridget shook her head and got to her feet. She didn't want to talk about this now. "It *is* a risk, and while the likelihood is low, the potential consequences are far too high. It's not worth it." She put her empty wineglass on the kitchen sink and said, "I'm going to take a shower."

It wasn't until she was standing under the cool spray that she unclenched her fists. She was right, no matter what Tanya said. Relationships at work were a bad idea and one with her boss was even worse. She needed to be one hundred percent focused, had to make sure she didn't miss any safety issues, had to ensure that each person who came to work left in the same state. A relationship would distract her. Bridget was sure she was right.

The only problem was going to be ignoring her attraction to Jack. When he'd been in her office, her whole body had been aware of his presence. She'd doggedly run through her report, ruthlessly ignoring her physical reactions. It had been a relief to escape the small space and head to the meeting. After she'd introduced him, she'd moved to the other side of the room so Jack could take control of the proceedings. She'd admired the way he'd spoken to the team and could see they were already taking to him. He said the kinds of things you wanted to hear.

But then again, she'd heard it all before. The real test was if he delivered on his promises.

Chapter 4

Jack's first week at Dionysus proved to him what an enormous job he'd taken on. So much of the equipment they used was outdated and the corrective actions loomed overhead like a cloud threatening rain. He wasn't sure what he was going to do, and it weighed heavily on him. Did he really have the skills required? Was he kidding himself?

He shook his head. There was no point getting down on himself. It wouldn't help. He needed to concentrate on the main problem, which was the audit actions.

What had Bridget been thinking? She'd prioritized the actions but had barely begun fixing them. He was not looking forward to his meeting with her this morning. Hoping he'd misinterpreted the information, he'd spent the weekend reading reports, checking and cross-checking the data. It had taken him hours.

In the end, every way he examined it, the plant desperately needed to address safety. He had to get to the bottom of why, and it was going to be a hell of an awkward conversation. From what he could tell, the staff loved her. Perhaps that's why she'd been left unsupervised.

Working with Bridget had been harder than he expected. Her laugh echoed down the hall and he often heard her calling out greetings to people. There was something about her voice that warmed his body. He had to get a grip.

But right now, he had to deal with her from a work perspective. He looked up at the knock and gestured Bridget into his office. He ignored the way his heart sped up at the mere sight of her. "Shut the door behind you."

A frown flitted across her face but she did what he asked and took a seat at his meeting table.

"I want to talk to you about the safety audit and the corrective actions list," he began.

"Sure, I brought all of my notes."

Jack swallowed, bracing himself for the unpleasant task. "From what I can see, only two corrective actions have been completed. They were the least important items."

"They were the quick wins. We didn't need

money to fix them."

"These issues are very troubling. There could be a major incident if we don't get them fixed. Shouldn't they have been a priority?" He couldn't prevent his tone from being accusatory. This was a big deal.

She arched an eyebrow, tilted her head and glared at him as if he was a piece of dirt. "You don't think I know that?"

"There's no evidence of it." He crossed his arms and leaned forward.

Bridget sifted through her papers. "*This* is the complete action plan and project outline I wrote within two days of getting the report." She handed him a couple of documents. "*This* is a copy of the capital expenditure request I submitted after management *finally* agreed the changes needed to be done. It took me a month to convince them I knew what I was talking about and wasn't just spending money for the sake of it." Her eyes flashed and her spine was rigid. "Here are the quotes for all of the expenses, and I could show you two dozen emails I've sent chasing up the capital expenditure request, not to mention the number of times I've raised it in management meetings. I can't get the *damned* funds to fix the problems." She was breathing heavily by the time she finished.

Shit, maybe he'd missed something when he'd read all those documents. "We're waiting on funds approval?" he asked, unable to believe management could be that ignorant of the problem.

"Yes." She let out a deep breath, obviously trying to regain control of herself. "I can't convince anyone of the seriousness of the issue. The general manager, Kevin, is certain it's not a big deal, just the company wanting to cross every t and dot every i, and the funding request is sitting somewhere at head office awaiting approval. No one will tell me who has it, and when I suggested I'd call myself and ask, I was told in no uncertain terms I wasn't allowed to. There are processes to follow and no one wants to ruffle feathers at head office."

"This is ridiculous."

She nodded. "I know. Even if we get the funds tomorrow, we're going to have to hire people to be able to complete the work before the next audit. It's going to cost far more than I originally budgeted and we don't have a hell of a lot of money to begin with."

Jack closed his eyes. He'd heard about these kinds of issues at other companies, but that was generally when head office was in another country. When it was less than an hour down the road he didn't think there'd be a problem.

"All right. I'll raise it in the meeting this afternoon," he said.

"Good luck."

He ignored the doubt in her tone and turned to the next issue. "What's the problem with replacing the fire equipment? Some of it has expired."

"Same problem. Budget was approved, but getting the expenditure signed off is proving difficult."

"Why?"

"They're saving money wherever they can. They don't consider it essential as the equipment is working, it just doesn't fully comply with the standard."

Jack made a note to bring that up today as well. He was going to be really popular with his peers.

"Did you really think I was that incompetent?" Bridget asked, tilting her head to the side and meeting his gaze.

Shit. What was he supposed to say to that? "I couldn't comprehend how something this serious could be ignored. There didn't seem to be a good explanation." He felt about as big as ant.

"There isn't a *good* explanation," she said curtly. "Now, can I help you with anything else? I've got work to do."

Her posture was stiff and her eyes dared him to raise any other issues. There were a couple of things he wanted to ask her about but they weren't important right now. He would leave it until she'd had a chance to calm down and wasn't feeling so hostile toward him. Not that he blamed her.

"No," Jack said finally. "I'll let you know how the meeting goes."

"Thanks." She left the room.

He ran a hand through his hair. He didn't have time to worry about Bridget's feelings, though he knew he would anyway. He had a couple of hours to figure out how to convince the management team of the urgency of the situation and to give him the money he needed.

* * *

Bridget headed out to the plant. She was not in the right frame of mind to speak to anyone and at least she could do her inspections undisturbed while she cooled down.

Jack thought she was incompetent.

She'd given him all her reports, documented the status of everything, *including* that they were waiting for finance, and he still thought her inept. Wasn't that typical?

It was just as well she had her two rules. She couldn't date someone who didn't respect her skills. She'd tried every way she knew to get people to listen to her: she'd emailed, called, gone to speak to them one-on-one, raised it in management meetings and discussed it with the managers separately. The problem was that they all had projects they wanted funded, projects they thought were more important than hers. Plus no one wanted to disrupt the production schedule, and part of Bridget's project would require a line shutdown. Even emphasizing it was a *safety* issue didn't matter. She didn't know what else she could do.

Stopping at the edge of the administration boundary, Bridget took a few deep breaths to calm herself. It wasn't safe for her to be so distracted going into the plant. She had to clear her head and be mindful of the potential hazards. She checked her personal protective equipment, that her radio was switched on to the correct channel, and she had her inspection clipboard, and then swiped on to the section of the plant she was going to.

Her ear plugs blocked a lot of the noise but there was still a rumbling hum of the machinery around her and a bad egg smell in the air from the sulphur pit. Each step made her aware there was a lot around her that would be dangerous without the proper controls. But that was her job – to make sure the controls were in place and being followed. It was her task to make sure everyone went home at night.

She started in the plant administration hut, examining a couple of jobs that were on the go and making notes.

"On the prowl, Bridge?" one of the guys asked her.

"As always. Got to make sure everyone's doing what they should."

"No one dares to do otherwise when you're around."

Bridget smiled, but she wished it wasn't the case. She wanted them to be safe *all* the time, not just because they didn't want to get caught. It was often pure laziness that caused the minor incidents, or else a lack of training. While she'd been acting safety manager, she'd made sure all training was up to date.

However, the laziness was a problem she hadn't been able to resolve so far.

* * *

By the time she'd finished her inspections Bridget was calm. Back in her office, she called the accountant at head office to check if the approval had been forwarded. It was her weekly task before the management meeting and she figured she could give Jack an update before he went in.

"David Randall."

Bridget took a second for her mind to adjust. She'd been expecting the site accountant to answer. She glanced at the phone display to check she'd called the right number, while trying to work out who she was speaking to. The name was familiar. "Hi, this is Bridget from the plant. I was after Laurel."

"So am I." His tone was slightly annoyed.

That's when it clicked. David Randall was the Chief Financial Officer for the company. He was one of the signatories she needed. "Maybe you could help me," she said quickly. "I'm chasing a capital expenditure request I submitted a couple of months ago. It's for some safety improvements on the plant." She held her breath.

There was a pause. "I know the one. Have you finally refined the scope? Can I approve it yet?"

Bridget's mouth dropped open. "Sorry. What do you mean refine the scope?"

"Kevin called me and asked me to hold off on the approval. Said someone was going to refine the scope and he'd get back to me."

She was lost for words. What the hell was he playing at? He'd not mentioned anything about refining the scope. He'd simply said head office was busy and she couldn't rush them. Bridget had had enough. "Of course. I thought someone would have called. You can approve the request."

"Sure thing. I'll do it as soon as I get back to my desk."

"Thanks." She hung up. How much trouble was she going to get in for that? She pushed her unease aside. It didn't matter. What mattered was the safety of the staff. She should tell Jack though.

"Bridge, you coming to training?" Jeremy poked his head into her office.

Bridget checked the time. She was the backup fire officer, which meant weekly training sessions to ensure each shift knew what to do in an emergency, particularly a fire. It was the one part of her week that she loved. There was a real sense of camaraderie between the operation technicians and a real purpose to what they were doing.

"I'm right behind you," she said, grabbing her gear. She stuck her head into Jack's office but he wasn't there. She would have to tell him about the approval afterward. She headed for training.

* * *

At the end of the day Bridget stopped by Jack's office.

He looked up and raised an eyebrow. She glanced down at her shirt which was plastered to her skin and covered in grime. They'd been practicing confined space rescue and she'd been the "injured party". It had been hellishly hot in the vessel and none too clean.

"How was the meeting?" she asked. She wanted to know what excuse Kevin had given him before she told him about her conversation with David.

He shifted in his seat. "I explained how urgent the situation was and Kevin told me to call the CFO. I was just about to."

Her jaw dropped. For three months she'd been explaining how urgent it was. She let out a deep breath. It didn't matter. "About that ..." Bridget recounted her phone call and what David said. "I couldn't let the opportunity pass."

He frowned at her but nodded. "Let me know if the approval hasn't come through and I'll call."

"Thanks." She paused. "Are you happy for me to run with the project?" He might still doubt her capabilities.

"Absolutely. You run into any problems you

tell me. Keep me updated with weekly reports."

She nodded and returned to her own office. Checking her email she saw the approval sitting there, along with the expense code. She grinned. Grabbing her project notes, she found the phone numbers of the suppliers who had been waiting for her call. She called the first one. "We're finally good to go."

* * *

Jack turned back to his computer after Bridget left. He'd been shocked by the management team's response when he'd raised the issues. Kevin had waved his hand dismissively. "That's just Bridget," he'd said. "She tends to get passionate about most things. It's not necessary to spend so much money."

Jack had outlined just how *necessary* it was and by the end of his presentation, which had mostly been taken from one Bridget herself had done, Kevin was telling the team it was their number one priority.

It made no sense. OK, Bridget was passionate about safety, his own conversation with her that morning had proved that, but surely they could see she knew what she was talking about? Why had they not approved the funds in the first place? Could it be something as simple as a personality conflict? Jack hoped not.

The doubts he had about the company swarmed around in his mind. He had to ignore them, but it was difficult. Bridget was highly competent, possibly more than he was, yet they had chosen him as the new manager, someone untried in a managerial position. He was going to have to work so hard to prove he was as good as Bridget – at least to his team. The rest of management didn't seem to see it.

He sighed. The contract he'd signed had ensured Dionysus paid all of his relocation costs but as a result he had to stay for a minimum of a year. Besides, he wasn't willing to give up yet. He just needed to figure out how to solve the mess the plant was in.

* * *

Jack arrived home looking forward to a cold beer, sitting on the couch and relaxing. But Hal ambushed him at the front door.

"Good, you're home. We're going to be late."

Jack squinted at his brother. "Late for what?"

"Dinner. Tanya's invited us both."

"It's Monday night," he protested. After the day he'd had, the last thing he wanted to do was go out and be sociable.

"I knew you wouldn't have plans. Tanya's

had the day off and has been cooking all day. Hurry up."

Hal had been out with Tanya almost every night since they'd met. Jack couldn't remember him ever mentioning a girl when they spoke while he was in Australia, but now every other word from him was about Tanya. He was smitten. It was kind of sweet.

"Let me take a shower."

Standing under the cool spray he closed his eyes and let the water wash the tension of the day away. He didn't know what to do about Bridget on either a work or a personal level. She was good at her job and so obviously frustrated by the lack of support she received. He could hardly believe Kevin's attitude himself. If he'd been in Bridget's position he would have quit long ago. Why did she stay?

Then there was his reaction to her. It didn't matter if she was furious with him, there was that spark, that passion that drew him to her. He wanted to explore it further.

But she had her stupid rules.

He sighed and turned off the water, grabbing his towel from the rack. Tonight he needed to apologize for his assumptions. He'd insulted her and he understood she was mad, but hopefully they could have a truce. She would be an asset to him at work.

Claire Boston

As for the personal side, well he'd have to see where it could go.

Chapter 5

Tanya met them at the door wearing a floral sun dress with an apron that said, "Have you kissed the cook today?"

"I don't believe I have," Hal said and swooped in to kiss her.

Jack stood back and waited for them to finish.

He waited a while.

Finally they broke apart and Tanya invited them in. "Bridget isn't home from work yet, but she shouldn't be long."

Jack frowned. She should have left work before he did. Perhaps she had some errands to run on her way home.

"Let me get you a drink."

He followed Tanya and Hal down the hall to the kitchen and living room. The barbecue aroma grew stronger and his stomach rumbled.

"Beer?" Tanya asked Jack, holding up Hal's favorite brand of beer.

"Thanks." He took the bottle she offered, before sitting on the sofa.

"What's for dinner?" Hal asked. "It smells sensational."

"You mentioned you liked barbecue ribs, so I've made you some."

"You're the best," Hal said, picking her up and spinning her around while she shrieked.

Jack examined the label of his beer. The sweetness of those two was getting a little sickening. He'd never seen Hal like this before.

At the front of the house the door slammed shut. His body tensed. Bridget. He hadn't quite figured out what to say to her. Footsteps came down the hall and as she walked into the room, she saw him and stared. She was still wearing her high-vis gear and her eyes were shadowed with fatigue. He hoped she hadn't come straight from work, otherwise she was working far more hours than she was supposed to.

"Hi Bridge. Dinner's almost ready. Why are you so late?"

Bridget blinked. She glanced at Tanya. "I had to chat with a couple of guys on night shift."

"Why?" Jack wanted to know.

"They'd asked me to follow up on an issue. These guys never check their email so I needed to tell them in person."

"Isn't email a standard communication tool?"

"Not to the guys in the plant," she said. "They're barely indoors."

"Then it's something we need to address with the production team," Jack told her. There had to be an effective way of communicating between shifts. Bridget shouldn't be working such long hours to combat that.

"I've tried. Though you might have better luck." She turned to Tanya. "I'll take a quick shower." She turned on her heel and left.

Jack winced at the bitterness in her tone. He couldn't blame her. If management thought it was just Bridget making a fuss, she'd never get anything achieved.

Tanya turned to him. "Don't mind Bridget. Safety is her passion." She checked the doorway to make sure Bridget was gone. "Her father went to work one day and never came home."

Jack's mouth dropped open. "What happened?"

Tanya shrugged. "She's never told me the details. She just says she won't let anyone else go through that if she can help it. She can be a little intense, but her heart's in the right place."

"Does she often work late?"

Tanya nodded. "She's gone before I wake up in the morning, and she comes home after me. They tend to call her after hours and on weekends too, whether she's on call or not, because they know they'll get the help they need."

That wasn't fair to Bridget. Jack had to talk to her about it. He wasn't sure whether the site had a fatigue management procedure, but if it didn't, he was going to implement one. Everyone needed enough downtime to rest and relax, no matter what their job was. And if the plant was in as bad a state as he suspected, it meant Bridget was constantly working. This was something he could definitely fix.

* * *

Bridget returned to the kitchen as Tanya was serving. Her hair was damp and unrestrained, her curls already forming, and she wore three-quarter length pants and a pink top. Her feet were bare and her toes were painted the same shade of pink as her top. It was sexy as hell. Lust shot through him. How was Jack going to keep that image out of his head while he was at work? He would constantly wonder if her toes were painted under the steel-toed boots. Like he needed any more of a distraction.

"Smells great, Tanya," she said, taking a seat at the dining table. She gave him a tentative smile.

The fact she acknowledged him at all was a good sign. It was difficult with the work thing hanging between them. Would they ever be able to have the easy conversation they'd had in the bar? He hoped so.

It turned out he needn't have worried about what to say. Tanya and Hal started the conversation with their plans to go to Jamaica.

"When are you going?" Bridget asked. She seemed as surprised about it as he was.

"As soon as we can get the time off work," Tanya said. "You know what my boss is like. She hates to give us leave."

Bridget nodded. "What is it that you do, Hal?"

"I'm a graphic designer," he said. "I'm considering branching out and going freelance. There's a lot of work out there, and a number of websites where you can submit for jobs. That will give me the flexibility to be my own boss."

Jack frowned at his brother. He'd never

mentioned anything like that to him. As far as Jack knew, Hal was happy in his work. He couldn't imagine him being organized enough to go freelance.

"How long have you been thinking about that?" he asked.

Hal looked at him and then Tanya. "For a while now. Tanya thought it was a great idea."

She nodded. "I want to start my own mobile hairdressing business," she explained. "That way I can work when I want to and have the flexibility to travel. We can see the world together." She and Hal shared a smile.

Jack choked back a cough. They were getting serious fast. How were they going to find clients if they were constantly on the move? He glanced at Bridget who appeared as amazed as him.

"You never mentioned anything to me," Bridget said.

Tanya shrugged. "It was always a pipe dream until I met Hal." She put a hand over Bridget's. "But don't worry, we'll probably save for another six months until we do anything. You won't need to find a new roommate immediately."

Wow. They were completely serious about it. Jack was pleased for them, of course he was, but his brother had never struck him as the responsible type. He hoped Tanya was better.

Bridget opened her mouth and then shook her head and let out a small sigh. He suspected she'd be talking to Tanya after they left.

Jack changed the subject. "These ribs are delicious, Tanya." The meat fell right off the bone and was beautifully tender.

"They've been cooking for hours," she said.

"I'll have to get the recipe from you."

"You cook?" Bridget asked.

"Sometimes."

Hal laughed. "He collects recipes, but he hasn't cooked since he arrived."

Jack smiled. "Mom loaded us up with frozen meals that we're still working our way through."

"Yeah, the prodigal son has returned." Hal said it with a good-natured grin.

"How's the house-hunting going?" Tanya asked.

Jack smothered a grin at the abrupt change of subject. He suspected she was ready for him to move out. She'd stayed over a lot during the last week.

"I've found a couple of places, but the fact I've just started a new job doesn't sit well with the banks." He'd been to several to ask about loans, because he was ready to buy, ready to settle down. It didn't seem to matter that he had a very healthy down payment, they were reluctant to give him the money.

"What about renting?" Tanya asked.

She definitely wanted him out. He'd have to talk to Hal about it. He could always move in with his mom or his dad if they wanted the place to themselves. His parents had divorced after he and Hal left home and they both had room for him, though his mother lived closer to the oil refinery than his father. It would mean a longer commute but Jack didn't mind. Especially if he didn't have to wear ear plugs to bed anymore.

"I'd prefer to buy," he said. "I'm ready to settle down." He ignored the pointed look Tanya gave Bridget.

As they cleared the table, conversation switched back to the Jamaican holiday and Tanya pulled out some travel brochures she'd picked up. They moved over to the sofas and with Hal and her engrossed in their conversation, Jack sat next to Bridget. She shuffled slightly away from him and he acknowledged the sting of hurt.

"If you could go anywhere in the world, where would you go?" he asked.

She held herself stiff, upright, as if she didn't

want to relax. "For fun?"

"For any reason."

She was quiet for a long moment. "If it was safe, I'd take Mama back to El Salvador," she said finally. "She misses it so much, even though she has some bad memories."

"Does she still have family there?"

Bridget nodded. "Her mother, a sister, and two brothers, plus all the nieces and nephews."

Jack knew nothing about the political situation in El Salvador. "Isn't it safe?"

She shook her head. "There's too much violence."

He couldn't imagine it. Growing up in the United States made him take certain things for granted. All the time he was in Australia, he'd been secure in the knowledge he could leave whenever he wanted and return to his family.

"Does your mother keep in touch with her family?"

"She calls my grandmother every week, and at least one of her siblings."

"She must miss them."

"She does." Bridget's posture had relaxed, but now she seemed sad.

"So where would you go for fun?" he asked, hoping to distract her and cheer her up.

She frowned as if the question was difficult.

Surely she had locations on her bucket list. There must be places that inspired her or intrigued her.

"I'd love to trek the Inca Trail, and maybe go to the Galapagos," she said.

"Ugh!" Tanya scowled at Bridget. "Sounds like too much hard work. You don't know how to relax."

Bridget flushed. She looked away and waved her hands. "It's only hypothetical."

Jack could tell Bridget was getting uncomfortable. "Everyone has their own ways of relaxing," he said. "There are some great dive spots in the Galapagos. I'd love to go there myself someday."

She smiled at him. "What about you? Where would you go?"

"Antarctica." His answer was instantaneous.

"Why? There can't be much to do there."

"I'd love to dive under the ice. It would be incredible."

"Wouldn't you freeze to death?"

"You can get special suits," he explained. He'd watched documentaries showing the underwater world of Antarctica and it fascinated him. It would be the ultimate dive. "Imagine being under all of the ice and seeing things no one has ever seen before."

"It could be interesting," Bridget said.

"Have you thought any more about learning to dive?" he asked. Maybe that was a way he could get to know her away from work. He could help her get her dive certification.

She shook her head. "I haven't had time to look into it yet."

"You should. It's a great experience. I'd be happy to buddy up with you for a dive when you've got it."

Her face closed down immediately. "Thanks for the offer, but I'll be fine."

Jack debated for a moment whether he should push the subject. He wanted to hold her hand, tell her it was OK, there was nothing to be afraid of. But he didn't know how she would react. He leaned closer to her so Hal and Tanya couldn't hear. "I know you felt a connection with me the other night. Why should working together prevent us from exploring it?"

Her eyes turned to stone and she got to her feet. "I'm tired. I'm going to bed." She strode out of the room.

No. She didn't get to hide. Jack wanted an explanation. If she wasn't as attracted to him as he was to her, he deserved to be told so he could move on. He walked after her and caught up as she was shutting her bedroom door.

"Wait." He put a hand against the door to stop her from slamming it in his face. "Don't run away from me."

She flung the door open again, her eyes flashing. "I'm not running away. I don't have to discuss this with you."

"Tell me you don't feel anything and I'll drop it," he challenged.

She glared at him. "It doesn't matter how I feel. I don't do work relationships." She bit off the last words.

"They can work. I've seen it." There had been a couple at his last job.

"You have *no* idea." She ran a hand through her hair. "You're a man. Your actions won't be questioned. At worst you'll get a slap on the back and a 'good for you'." She took a breath. "*I'll* get accused of sleeping my way to the top, of getting my projects approved because I'm dating my boss, and if anything goes wrong, I'll be blamed for it."

She was so fired up, so sure of herself.

"You've been through it before," he guessed. That put a whole different spin on things. It must have gone really wrong.

Her mouth dropped open. She closed it and nodded once. Then she closed the door.

Jack sighed. It was complicated, but he wasn't willing to give up yet. She was too

73

intriguing, too fiery. He'd just take it slower. He needed to get to know Bridget away from work and perhaps Hal and Tanya's relationship could help him. They could have more dinners like tonight, which would show Bridget he wasn't like her ex.

He was tempted to ask Tanya about what had happened, but it didn't seem right. He wanted Bridget to trust him enough to confide in him.

But he didn't know how long that would take.

* * *

Bridget flopped down on her bed and put her head in her hands. She was a fool.

She'd overreacted and blown things out of proportion. If she'd had her wits about her she wouldn't have panicked when Jack suggested helping her with her dive certification. The urge to say yes had been so damned strong. He had a way of slipping through the cracks in her defenses and making her relax.

But she couldn't do that. Not with him. There was too much at stake, too much to lose, too much that could go wrong.

And then he hadn't had the decency to leave her alone. He'd followed her to her room, made her mad, and made her say things she shouldn't have said. He didn't need to know she'd been burned in the past. Though he was sure to hear about it sooner or later. Everyone in the industry knew about the Lionel affair. All Jack needed to know was she wasn't interested.

But Bridget didn't have the nerve to say it. She couldn't lie to him, couldn't say she felt nothing. It was easier to run away.

If he wasn't her new boss … she shook her head. No. It didn't matter. There was no point playing "what ifs". She had her two rules for a good reason and breaking the first one had got her into this mess.

Jack would just have to deal with it, like she was.

Chapter 6

The next few days were stupidly busy. Now that her project had been given the green light, Bridget had a mountain of work to do. She worked long hours, collaborating with the guys on the plant.

Bridget avoided Jack where possible. She had to keep reminding herself that he was her boss and she had to concentrate on her job – keeping the site safe.

"Bridget, I've got the latest results from the line scanning."

She looked up at Mike, the plant inspection engineer. His expression was somber. "Bad news?"

He nodded.

"We'd better get Jack." She went next door and knocked on Jack's door. "You got a minute?" Her skin warmed as he glanced up and met her eyes. She ignored it.

"Of course."

She motioned Mike inside. "Mike's our plant inspection engineer. He's got the latest results for you."

She stepped back while they shook hands.

"Take a seat." Jack gestured for Bridget to join them.

She was curious about what Mike had found. The last time they'd scanned that section of the pipeline it was thin in places, but it was difficult to judge how quickly it was thinning. The previous inspection records had been lost.

"We've got a bad case of corrosion," Mike began. "The pipeline is corroding faster than I predicted. We need to do something about it ASAP. It's not going to last until the next turnaround."

Jack swore. "What are our options?"

Mike outlined the few choices available. "I've set up a meeting tomorrow with production and maintenance and thought you'd want to be in on this."

"Yes, please," Jack said. "Is it just this section, or are there issues elsewhere?"

"The inspection was postponed and we're a few weeks behind, so I can't tell for sure. Priority is the areas where the records have gone missing. In my opinion, I think that whole line is going to have to go. It wasn't made from the right material in the first place." Mike stood. "If that's all, I'd better get back to it."

"Of course," Jack said. "Can I have a word before you go, Bridget?"

"What's up?" she asked as Mike left the room.

He ran a hand through his thick hair and she itched to do the same. It was luxurious. Then she noticed the dark rings under his eyes and the worry in his eyes.

"Is everything all right?"

"No. It's not." Jack picked up the report Mike had left and then tossed it down on the table in disgust. "This whole plant is falling apart. It's ludicrous. We deal in flammable and highly dangerous substances and yet no one realizes disaster could be only moments away."

Bridget felt his disbelief and frustration. She'd been feeling the same way since she started here.

"Dionysus is going through a period of rapid expansion," she said. "They've bought several companies in the past two years, and are consolidating their assets. They're focusing on systems and processes across the company worldwide and letting each plant run itself." She wasn't sure how much Jack had been told before he'd started. "They bought this plant two years ago. It was built in the fifties and much of it is due to be upgraded, but head office doesn't want to spend any money. As long as we keep pumping out the gallons, we'll be fine." Bridget sighed. "When I started here, I searched for the old records, tried to figure out what safety systems they had in place because the documentation was abysmal. Record-keeping wasn't a strong requirement of the previous owners."

Jack shook his head.

"Since I've been here, the number of incidents per month has decreased from ten to two. Most of those are minor or insignificant, but our disabling injury rate is still too high."

"That's an impressive decrease."

She acknowledged the compliment, ignoring the warmth that spread through her body. "It's why management believe everything is fine, but there's still so much more to be done. If I'm not visibly seen keeping an eye on safety it's ignored."

"How much staff turnover was there when Dionysus bought in?"

"Not a lot. There was an organizational reshuffle that laid off a few people, but a lot of the guys working here have done so their whole lives."

"So they don't think there's any need for change."

He understood. Bridget let out a deep breath and nodded.

"How many of our team are as passionate about this plant as you are?"

"The environment officers, Nick and Sally, are facing the same issues as we are. Jeremy has brought the fire teams up to the best they've ever been, but the equipment needs replacing. And the trainers need management support to ensure training is current."

Jack pursed his lips. "What were your plans to fix this?"

She stared at him. She hadn't expected him to ask for her opinion.

"Bridge, I know you wanted this job, and from what I've seen of your work, you would have had a plan in mind, if not written down. I'd like to hear it."

She ignored the pleasant tingle at being shown some respect. "Our team needs more cohesion," she began. "Jeremy, Nick, Sally, and I are all new since Dionysus bought the plant. We've seen how well things can run when they're done properly, but there are some, like Dirk, one of the safety officers, who are old school and don't like change. The thing is they have some amazing knowledge about the plant and if we can get through to them, they'll be an asset." She paused. "And finally you've got a couple who will do what they're told, they just need some direction."

"A team-building session?" Jack suggested.

She'd been considering that herself. "I've researched a few options. We could do a fun team exercise on one day and then a department brainstorm or action plan on the next day. Find somewhere to stay overnight to completely get away from it." She met his eyes as she said overnight and her cheeks heated at the intensity she saw in them. She looked away. "But that's probably stage two. We need to focus on those corrective actions, and now the line issues."

"Can we get contractors in to help?"

She'd been hoping he would ask. "Yes. It'll cost though."

"Send me the details and I'll do what I can. And while you're at it, send me the information about the team building."

Bridget got to her feet. "Sure thing."

"Thanks. I appreciate your help."

She smiled at him, a lightness in her chest. "No problem, boss."

As she walked back to her office she realized it was the first time anyone in management had thanked her for doing her job. It felt fantastic.

* * *

Jack's heartbeat sped up at Bridget's smile. She hadn't really smiled at him since he'd met her at the club. It was so warm, welcoming, and sent heat straight through him.

He was doing a much worse job than her at ignoring the attraction. In actual fact, he wasn't sure whether he hadn't already slipped from attractive stranger to never-going-to-go-there work colleague in her mind. He hated the thought it was a real possibility.

Her work ethic was admirable. She worked more hours than she had to, went beyond the call of duty, and had the best interests of the plant at heart. It made Jack respect her even more. To continue with that level of passion, despite the lack of management support, showed real dedication.

Which reminded him – he'd read through the fatigue management procedure and found Bridget was working too many hours. He wanted to give her the time off in lieu of all the extra work she did. It was the least he could do. He checked her hours on the security log and confirmed with Anthony that he could give her the time off. He caught up with her a couple of hours later.

"Bridget, can I have a word?" he asked.

"Sure." She turned from her computer.

He leaned against her desk, crossed his ankles, and tried to look as unthreatening as possible. He wasn't entirely sure how Bridget would take the order to have a couple of days off. Most people would jump at the chance, but Bridget wasn't most people.

"I've checked the hours you've been working," he began.

She shifted in her chair, sat straighter, bracing herself for defense.

"You've been working too many hours and, as I'm sure you're aware, fatigue can begin to creep in without you noticing."

She opened her mouth to say something but he held up his hand.

"You need to take two days off this month. You can choose which days."

She was already shaking her head. "Jack, I can't afford to right now. The work for the project has already been delayed for too long."

He'd prepared his counter argument. "You don't need to do everything, Bridget. Tell me what needs to be done on your days off, and I'll make sure it happens."

"There's too much to explain. It will be easier if I take time off after it's completed."

"Fatigue doesn't work like that. Do you want

to be so tired that you make a mistake?" He hated to say it, but he needed to convince her.

She reared back as if he'd hit her. "You think I'd put the plant at risk?"

He held up a conciliatory hand. "Not on purpose. You're too focused to think of some of the potential consequences." He continued before she could say anything else. "Let me know by Monday which days you'll take. It might be a good opportunity for you to do the dive training you've been talking about."

She glared at him but he simply smiled and walked out of the office. She was too busy taking care of everyone else. Someone had to take care of her.

* * *

It had long since grown dark by the time Bridget arrived home. She'd been so annoyed by Jack's insistence she take time off that she'd stayed past her normal working hours to get more of her project completed. At that time of the evening there was little chance of interruption.

He couldn't stop her from doing what needed to be done. The gall of him, to even suggest she might put the plant at risk, that she might make a mistake. She knew her limits and she was far from them.

"Bridget, is that you?" Tanya called from the back of the house.

She frowned. Tanya had barely been home since she'd met Hal, and Bridget hadn't expected her to be there.

"Yeah." She wandered down the hall to the kitchen. She hadn't eaten since lunch and her stomach was telling her it was way past time to be fed.

As she walked into the living area she found Tanya and Hal sitting side by side on the couch.

"You're later than usual," Tanya said.

"I had some work I needed to finish. It's easier to get it done when there's no one in the administration building."

"You're working too hard," Tanya admonished. "They don't deserve your loyalty."

Bridget glanced at Hal and back at Tanya. "They gave me a chance," she said and turned to rummage in the freezer. There had to be some sort of frozen meal in there.

She hated to remember the time when her world had crumbled around her, when her boyfriend had betrayed her and she'd lost all the credibility she'd worked so hard to gain. She was lucky Jeremy had convinced the safety manager at Dionysus that she was worth hiring.

She found a frozen lasagna and put it in the microwave to heat. It was the weekend, but she'd brought her laptop home to do a bit more work on the project. She could spend Saturday on it and then it was her turn to drive to her mother's for lunch on Sunday.

"You need to chill out. Why don't you come to the movies with Hal and me tomorrow?" Tanya suggested. "We're going to have lunch beforehand."

There was no way she was going to be a third wheel in their cozy party. She shook her head. "I've got some work to do."

"That's ridiculous, Bridge," Tanya stood up and walked into the kitchen. "If you don't take a break, I'll tell Jack. I'm sure there's something he can do."

Bridget groaned. It was not a good thing that her best friend knew her boss. "He's already told me I have to take two days off this month. Time in lieu."

"Good. When are you going to take them? We can have a girls' day."

Bridget shrugged. She should have kept her mouth shut. Now she'd have both Tanya and Jack hassling her. "I'm not sure. Jack suggested I look up diving courses."

The suggestion appealed to her. The idea

had been simmering in her mind since she'd first discussed it with Jack at the bar and she'd checked out prices only the other day. But she couldn't just take time off. Not with all the work that needed to be done.

Jack *had* said he would make sure it got done.

Could she rely on him to follow through on the promise? In the past the only person she could rely on at work was Jeremy. Should she take the chance?

Jack's comment about her being fatigued niggled at her. She didn't think she was, but she wasn't necessarily the best judge – she was too focused on what had to be done. She would hate to put the plant at risk.

Now might be the perfect opportunity to do the course.

"That's a great idea!" Tanya said.

Hal nodded. "Jack always raves about his dives."

Bridget took her meal out of the microwave and placed it on the table. She grabbed Tanya's tablet and searched for diving courses in Houston. She found a place that offered a three-day open water course and there was one coming up next weekend, starting on the Friday.

What did she have scheduled for Friday?

Quickly she fired up her laptop and opened the project schedule. It was contractor work. They needed someone to show them what to do and a number to call if they had any trouble. If she explained everything to Jack, or one of the chemical engineers, they could easily fill in.

She cross checked the diving course information and her chart. Could she actually do it? The price was within her budget, but was it a little bit decadent to spend so much on herself?

She shook her head. If she wasn't going to spend her money on herself, who else would she spend it on?

Acknowledging the little voice in the back of her head yelling, *Do it! Do it!* she clicked the "book now" button and signed up for the course.

Bridget sat back. It was a little terrifying now she'd booked it. She hoped Jack would give her the Friday off. She probably should have checked with him first. This was why she didn't do spontaneous very well. It always ended badly.

Knowing it would niggle at her over the whole weekend, she called his cell phone.

"Hi Bridget. Everything all right?" His voice warmed her body and made her smile. She was glad he couldn't see her.

"I've booked a diving course and realized I should have checked with you first. It's next Friday."

"That's great news! No problem on my end. Why don't you take the Monday off as well and make it a four-day weekend?"

She glanced over at Tanya. She always had Mondays off, and by the time Bridget had done the course she might need a day of pampering. She wasn't sure how physical it would be.

"All right. That would be great. I'll update the project plan this weekend to make sure we're on track and will give you the details on Monday."

"No. You're not going to work on the weekend. We'll sort it out next week." His voice was stern.

"Sure," she lied. "I'll see you then." She hung up.

"So when's the course?" Tanya asked.

"Next Friday. Do you want to do the girls' day the following Monday?"

Tanya's face lit up. "Absolutely! Let me organize everything. We should go shopping and then get a massage. It's time you had something more than high-vis in your wardrobe."

Bridget smothered a groan. She wasn't much of a shopper, and never had the time for hair and makeup. Her only weakness was painting her toenails, and she had a myriad of colors already. But Tanya was right. Most of the clothes in her wardrobe were at least two years old and it would be nice to have something new for a change.

"All right." Finishing her meal, she tidied up and grabbed her laptop from the table.

"I'll leave you love birds to it," she said. She wanted to give them some privacy and she wasn't comfortable sitting out there while they got all lovey-dovey on the sofa.

Besides, she had work to do.

Chapter 7

One of Bridget's favorite things about the weekend was being able to wake up without her alarm going off. She could sleep as late as she wanted to – a complete indulgence for her.

So when Tanya pounded on Bridget's bedroom door on Saturday morning, waking her up, Bridget swore. "What's the emergency?" she called, clearing her eyes of sleep as she reached for her cell phone to check the time. It was seven o'clock. *Way* too early for the weekend. Tanya was never out of bed this early. What had got into her?

"We're going on a road trip and you're coming with us."

Bridget frowned, trying to get her brain functioning. A road trip? "What happened to lunch and a movie?" She flung the covers back, knowing Tanya wouldn't give up until Bridget had at least shown her face. She got up and opened her bedroom door.

"We decided a road trip would be more fun. We're heading to Brenham – wine, food, and antiquing. What could be better?"

Brenham was one of Bridget's favorite places. She loved the atmosphere and the fact it was far enough from Houston and the plant for her to be able to relax. If anything happened, someone else would have to deal with it.

Down the hall she could hear someone making coffee. The smell wafted tantalizingly toward her. "Tanya, you don't want me tagging along. Besides, I've got work to do."

"No you don't. We called Jack and he said you shouldn't be working. He's going to come too, so you'll make sure he doesn't feel like the third wheel. Now, get ready. We leave in thirty minutes." Tanya whirled around and headed to the kitchen.

Bridget watched her go, her brain still processing what was going on. Tanya was awake and chirpy at seven o'clock on a Saturday *morning.* Hal must have some kind of secret potion. Then she focused on one point. Tanya had called Jack and he was coming too.

That should be enough to make her refuse, but the idea of spending a whole day with him away from the plant held significant appeal.

Which meant she couldn't possibly go.

But she'd think of a reason to give Tanya while she had a shower. She wasn't going to get back to sleep now.

As Bridget showered she thought about the last time she'd been in Brenham and the little winery they'd discovered with the most amazing wine she'd ever tasted. It also had a cute little café attached to it with the best apple pie.

Tanya wasn't playing fair. It was way too tempting.

As she turned off the shower she reminded herself she had work to do. If she was going to have a four-day weekend next weekend, she needed to get a few things sorted. She didn't have time to go gallivanting across the country, no matter how much the idea appealed.

She took her time deciding what to wear. It was a warm fall day, but everything in her wardrobe was old and tired. It was just as well she was going shopping with Tanya next week.

She'd been staring at her wardrobe for five minutes when she realized she'd made the decision to go with them. Why else would she be agonizing over what to wear?

With a sigh, she threw on a pair of black capri pants, some sandals and a blue top. She grabbed her purse and opened her bedroom door to find Hal and Tanya waiting for her with a travel mug.

"Here," Tanya said, handing her the coffee. "We're late picking up Jack."

"We should invite Trish and Sally," Bridget said, a little desperately. "They love Brenham." At least with a couple more friends, she wouldn't have to focus on Jack.

"Too late." Tanya bustled Bridget out of the house and into Hal's bright red four-door sedan.

Damn it. What had she got herself in to? She shouldn't be sitting in the back seat of Hal's car, sipping coffee and heading for a day out with the boss she was trying her hardest to pretend was just a colleague.

No other colleague made her body hum like he did.

Still if Tanya and Hal were going to stay together, it was inevitable they would socialize with each other outside of work. They needed to be able to be cordial and to work past the attraction. Today was a prime opportunity.

She'd never been so pleased her friend had

found someone.

She rolled her eyes. She was being ridiculous. She had her rules for a reason – a Lionel-sized reason – and so her attraction to Jack didn't matter.

She would be polite, friendly even, but she wouldn't respond to the feelings he evoked inside. She was an adult. She could ignore her baser instincts. Plus she wasn't going to let Jack scare her away from a chance to go to Brenham.

Hal pulled up in front of a house that had a seventies look and honked his horn. Jack was out of the front door before the noise faded. He wore black shorts and a striped shirt that clung to his chest, defining every muscle. It was a shame the usual high-vis work clothes did little to accentuate anyone's figure. Because Jack had a figure worth accentuating.

He gave a casual salute and climbed into the backseat next to her.

She had to stop staring.

"Morning," he said.

"Morning!" Tanya sing-songed back.

Bridget's mouth had gone dry so she merely nodded. She had to get a grip. This was her boss she was checking out. The whole day suddenly seemed like a really bad idea.

"So where are we going?" Jack asked as Hal pulled out of the driveway.

"Brenham." Tanya told him. "We can tour a couple of wineries, have brunch, check out some antique shops, and maybe do the tour of the ice-creamery."

"Sounds like a plan." He turned to Bridget. "I'm glad Tanya convinced you to come. It's too gorgeous a day to be inside."

He was right. The sky was clear and pale blue, the sun was warm, and the forecast was for the first cooler day since summer – which meant it might actually be pleasant.

"I didn't have much choice in the matter," Bridget said, wincing at the sarcasm in her tone. She sounded bitter and she wasn't. A day out in Brenham would normally be top of her list of things to do. She just didn't want to spend the day fighting her body's response to Jack.

"Don't be like that, Bridge," Tanya said. "You'll have a great time."

Bridget sighed. "I know."

"Plus you're under boss's orders not to work," Jack said with a smile.

She couldn't resist smiling back at him. It was too hard not to. "He does seem to be taking an inordinate amount of interest in the hours I put in."

"Just making sure my staff are looking after themselves," he replied.

It was nice. He noticed the hours she was working, *plus* he was taking on some of her work so she could have the time off she deserved. Not many people would do that.

But would others view it as favoritism? Was he checking the hours for the rest of his department, or was it just her? Her shoulders went stiff. This was one of the reasons why dating the boss was a bad idea. She was constantly second-guessing herself.

As they drove through the city, doing their best to avoid traffic snarls, they chatted about their favorite Brenham location. Their first stop when they arrived was to get food. After a brief argument they settled on a café that served breakfast. Bridget slid into a booth that had windows facing the street. The town was already buzzing with people – some striding purposefully to their destination, others just wandering, pointing out places of interest. Bridget breathed deeply, inhaling the coffee fragrance mixed with cooked bacon coming from the kitchen.

Jack slid in next to her. "Something smells good."

"Sure does." She wasn't referring to the food. Jack was sitting so close his leg brushed hers and his masculine aftershave teased her senses.

She resisted the urge to lean closer and sniff him. Shuffling a little further away she grabbed a menu. "I don't know what I want." She buried her face in it, hoping to get herself under control.

"It's a no-brainer," Hal declared. "The works every time."

"I'm going with pancakes," Tanya decided.

Everything on the menu sounded delicious, but Bridget couldn't go past the pancakes either. "Me too."

Jack agreed with his brother and after they'd ordered he turned to Bridget. "Which dive school are you going with?"

She named the school. "They do a three-day course, which suits me."

"Do you need any gear? My stuff arrived from Australia this week, so you can borrow it if you want, though the fins might be too big."

The idea of using his equipment was a little too intimate for Bridget. "It's all included in the price."

"Where will you dive?"

"I'm not sure. The website said there will be lake dives on Saturday and open water dives on Sunday." She hadn't considered lakes a source of diving, but when she'd researched it further, there were a few places around Texas.

"That'll be good. You won't have to worry about any swell for your first couple of dives. You can focus on the breathing and gauges."

"What's the most important thing to remember?" she asked, curious as to how difficult it would be.

Jack was quiet while he considered it. "Always keep an eye on your depth and the amount of oxygen you have."

That didn't sound so hard. Details were her specialty so she shouldn't have a problem.

"It's hard not to get caught up in what you're seeing – the whole new underwater cosmos – but you've got to be aware of your surroundings and your safety at all times."

Safety she could do. It was in her blood.

"Where shall we go next?" Tanya asked.

Bridget raised her eyebrows. There were two antique shops they had to visit every time they came to Brenham. Carly loved antiques and insisted Bridget tell her what they had in stock. Inevitably they ended up carting something home for her.

Tanya grinned at her. "OK, antiques first, then wine."

The men swapped a pained look and Bridget explained. "I can't come to Brenham without shopping for my sister, Carly. If she found out I came here today and didn't call her, there would be hell to pay." So she might be exaggerating a little. Carly never got upset over anything. She was the most level-headed person Bridget knew and had inherited none of the fiery temperament from her Salvadoran mother and Irish father. Bridget had no idea how she'd avoided it. Zita, Bridget and their mother were all known for their passionate natures.

"We'll be an hour, tops," Tanya promised. "You guys can stay here and have another coffee if you want."

"I'm game," Jack said. "There wasn't much that was considered antique in Australia."

They finished their meal and wandered down the street. Ahead of her, Tanya and Hal held hands and pointed out things in shop windows. Beside her, Jack walked at a comfortable pace. The temptation to take his hand was strong so Bridget stuck her hands into her pockets and nodded to Tanya and Hal. "They're so into each other, aren't they?"

"Yeah. It's nice. I've never known my brother to be so smitten."

"Tanya either. She usually flits from guy to guy but they don't catch her interest. I think I'm going to need to find a new roommate."

"Are you renting?" he asked.

Claire Boston

"Yeah. We've still got our place for six months." Their lease would run out about the time Hal and Tanya were talking about traveling. Bridget didn't think that was a coincidence.

They arrived at the first antiques shop and Jack held the door open for her. "Thanks." She cursed the flush that warmed her cheeks. She wasn't used to such old-fashioned gallantry, especially not working on the plant.

Getting out her cell phone, she video called her sister. "Guess where I am?"

There was a big sigh. "Where?" Carly had dark circles under her eyes and a defeated slump to her shoulders. Bridget stopped smiling.

"What's up, Carolina?" Bridget asked in Spanish.

"Nothing. Just work stuff."

Bridget frowned. If Carly didn't want to talk, she wouldn't, but Bridget would grill her on the drive to their mother's tomorrow. "I'm in Brenham, at your favorite antiques store."

"Now that's news to cheer me up," Carly said, her voice more animated. She forced a smile. "I'd love a jewelry box. What have they got in stock?" She indicated that Bridget should turn the phone around so she could have a look.

101

"Feast your eyes on these," Bridget said, and proceeded to take her sister for a tour around the shop.

"How about this?" Jack called, bringing over a beautiful, dark brown wooden box with intricate inlay. Bridget showed Carly.

"That's perfect!" she said. "Open it up."

Jack did as she asked and Carly said, "I'll take it." Then she asked, "Who are you?"

"Oh, that's my new boss, Jack." Bridget flushed and held up the phone to introduce them. "He's Tanya's boyfriend's brother." She made the other introductions.

"Nice to meet you," Jack said.

"Likewise."

Bridget turned the phone before they could start a conversation. Carly raised her eyebrows and mouthed "We'll talk later."

Bridget nodded.

By the time she was finished, Carly had bought the jewelry box and a gorgeous chaise lounge chair. Bridget didn't know anything about antiques so the names meant nothing to her. She handed her phone over to the shop assistant who knew them both well by now and Carly arranged delivery of the chair and payment.

"I'll pick you up at ten," she told her sister.

"Don't forget to bring my jewelry box."

Bridget hung up, taking the box from the shop assistant.

"I take it this is a regular occurrence," Jack said as they continued to the next antique shop.

"Tanya and I come out here a couple of times a year, but the assistant remembers us."

"I can see why."

"That lounge wasn't cheap," Hal commented.

"Carly's rich," Tanya explained. "Mega rich."

Bridget frowned. She didn't like people talking about her sister's wealth, because Carly hated it. She always said it was just luck that her software had taken off. She'd been in the right place at the right time. But she was selling herself short. She'd put hundreds of hours into her product, but Bridget didn't make a fuss because it made Carly uncomfortable.

"Lucky her," Jack said. There was no envy in his tone.

Bridget was pleased.

They went into the next antiques store and browsed. There was nothing Carly wanted but Bridget spotted a couple of mother-of-pearl hair clips that were gorgeous. She stood at the display cabinet, looking at them. They weren't too expensive, but really, when would she use them? She tied her hair up at work and she rarely went anywhere fancy. They were too pretty to be everyday wear.

"Found something you like?" Jack asked, walking up and standing too close.

She shifted a little away from him and shrugged. "Everything in here is lovely."

He glanced down at the cabinet and back to her. "Those clips would look pretty in your hair."

His tone was admiring and Bridget ruthlessly ignored the way her body reacted to it.

"I usually wear my hair back. I've got no use for them." She turned and walked away.

When they came out, Hal asked, "So do we get our wine tasting now?"

"Absolutely. We could all do with a drink," Tanya said. They piled into Hal's car and Tanya directed him to their favorite winery.

"That's a nice thing for you to do for your sister," Jack said. "Why doesn't she come out herself?"

"Carly's always working. She doesn't take time out for herself."

"Must run in the family," Jack said.

Bridget didn't say anything. Her dedication to work was due to her need to make sure everyone was safe. Carly's dedication was on a whole different level. She didn't know what motivated her sister to work so hard, especially now she was successful. They'd never discussed it. Too busy most of the time.

She'd have to talk to Carly about it tomorrow.

* * *

They arrived at the winery and Jack followed the others in, admiring the way Bridget's pants hugged her butt. Today was the first day he'd seen her completely relaxed since he'd started work. She'd had fun showing her sister the different antiques and her gaze had lingered on a couple of items, but her practical side had won out. What would it take to make her forget all practicality?

He smiled as the tour guide poured them each a taste of the first white wine.

"This one is quite tangy, and made from a blend of grapes. It goes well with chicken or seafood," the guide explained.

Jack lifted the glass. He was never sure what to do. He'd seen people swirl it and sniff it, but he just wanted to taste it. He copied the guide who swirled and sniffed, commenting on the fragrance. It smelled like wine to him.

Finally he tasted it. It was quite nice, fresh and tangy, but he was more of a beer person.

The guide took them through the different wines, three white and three red, plus a sparkling wine. Jack stood back while Tanya and Bridget discussed which one they wanted to buy. Bridget was animated, her cheeks flushed, and he suspected she might already be on her way to tipsy.

"We should get a case," Bridget declared. "We deserve it." She glanced at Jack and giggled.

He raised an eyebrow. He never would have picked Bridget as a giggler. Perhaps she was more than a little tipsy.

When they'd finally chosen and Hal had carried their wine to the car, they went to the café to have lunch. Both Tanya and Bridget ordered a glass of wine and Jack watched in fascination as Bridget became more and more relaxed.

"The Texans play tonight," Hal said. "First home game of the season. You want to watch?"

He hadn't seen a game since he'd arrived back in Houston and he'd forgotten when the season started. "Sure."

Bridget sat up straight. "Is that tonight? I lost track of dates." She turned to Tanya. "Pizza night?"

"Yeah. You guys want to come?"

"You follow the NFL?" Hal asked, his face a picture of disbelief.

Tanya looked down her nose at him. "You got a problem with that?"

He grinned. "Not at all. You're seriously my perfect woman." He leaned over and kissed her.

Jack turned to Bridget. "So how does a girl from El Salvador get caught up in football? I would have thought soccer was more your thing."

Bridget gestured to Tanya. "Blame her. In high school we had to watch every game. We couldn't go out to parties until the game had finished. She got me hooked."

Jack grinned. "You into any other sports?"

"Not really. I'll watch the occasional game of basketball if I have time, but generally it's the Texans or nothing." She turned to him. "What about you?"

"If it has a ball, I'll watch it," Jack admitted.

"Were you an athlete at school?"

"I dabbled in a few sports."

"What about college?"

"Never went." He took a sip of his beer, waiting for her reaction.

Her eyes widened. "But you're a manager. You must have qualifications."

He shook his head. "Learned on the job mostly. And took a few courses."

She frowned.

Jack knew what she was thinking. He had no formal qualifications and yet he'd been given the job over her. He waited for her judgment, for her to say he wasn't qualified to do the job.

"I guess that's the best way to learn," she said finally. "A lot of the theory doesn't make sense until you see the practical use. It was a real shock going to a plant straight out of college. We'd learned best practice in a best case scenario, and the real world isn't like that."

He sat back and blinked. She seemed to genuinely mean what she said.

"Theory's all well and good until you have to get the guys in the plant to do it," he said.

She grinned, her eyes scrunching up and her mouth wide. "Amen to that. Some of the guys don't like to be told what to do. Especially not by a girl."

"You don't seem to have any problems with them."

"It took me months to win them over," she said. "I had to earn their trust, show them I was listening to their concerns before they began to let me in. There're still a few who will do the opposite just to spite me. They think they know best because they've worked on the plant for twenty years."

That kind of attitude was dangerous. He was about to say so when she said, "I'm beginning to get through to them."

He wanted to ask more but didn't want to spoil the day talking about work. He'd follow it up next week. He'd ask the other managers what they thought the safety culture was like on site. But that was a thought for Monday.

The food was served and silence set in while they ate. His steak was cooked to perfection and tasted delicious. They were sitting outside on the veranda overlooking the vineyards. There was a children's playground to one side where children were playing while their parents enjoyed a quiet lunch.

Jack took a deep breath in. Life had been full on since he'd arrived back in Texas. He'd had very little time to get over his jet lag before starting work, and every weekend had been taken up either reviewing work or looking for a house.

He needed this, a relaxing getaway to forget about everything. Now his diving gear had arrived he'd find some dive spots, and his father had been hassling him to go out fishing. He'd have to make time.

"I ate too much," Bridget said, leaning back in her chair, closing her eyes, her hands on her stomach. "It was so good."

"Not up for dessert?" Jack asked.

Her eyes flashed open. "Wash your mouth out with soap," she said with a grin. "There's always room for dessert."

He met her gaze and her smile faded, desire darkening her eyes. Her tongue ran over her lips and Jack had to suppress a groan. He knew it. Their attraction was mutual. He just needed to figure out a way to get her to trust him, to take the risk.

"We should go for a walk," Tanya declared. "They do tours. We can have dessert when we get back."

Bridget turned her attention to her best friend. "Good idea."

"I'll pay," Hal said and left the table before anyone could protest.

"I'll be back in a minute," Jack said and followed his brother inside. He wanted to pay his share.

"I've got this, Jack," Hal said, handing over his credit card.

"I can't let you pay for me." His brother didn't earn as much and he was saving for his travel with Tanya.

"Sure you can." He took the receipt from the cashier.

Jack knew better than to argue with him. "I'll pay for dessert."

His brother nodded. "Come on, let's not leave the ladies waiting."

When they went outside, Bridget and Tanya were nowhere to be seen. Jack frowned as he scanned the area. Maybe they'd gone to the bathroom.

Then he heard the squeals.

Turning toward the playground he saw Tanya and Bridget on the swing set, competing for which one could swing higher. He nudged Hal and pointed.

He laughed. "She knows how to have fun."

Jack shook his head. Bridget kept surprising him today. He hadn't seen any playful side of her in the couple of weeks he'd known her. He liked it.

As he walked over, her laughter filled the air. It struck something inside him, made him yearn. He stood in front of the swing, but at a safe distance as she threw her head back and laughed.

He wanted her.

"Catch me!" Tanya cried and flung herself off the swing and into Hal's arms. Hal stumbled back a couple of steps but managed to break her fall.

Jack looked back at Bridget. Would she be as reckless?

He held his arms wide daring her.

Break the Rules

Her grin was fast, mischievous, and before he could blink, she launched herself off the seat toward him.

Chapter 8

Jack caught Bridget, her soft body hard against his. He took a couple of steps back to cushion the blow, his heel catching on something, and he fell flat on his back, Bridget on top of him, her head bumping into his. Pain shot through him.

"Ow." She tried to get up but his arms automatically tightened around her. Her body fitted perfectly against his; every curve pressed in to him and he didn't want to move. He ignored Tanya and Hal's laughter and looked into her blue eyes. They widened, and glanced at his lips. He lifted his head to kiss her, needing to taste her, and she pushed away harder. Disappointed, he let her go. She climbed to her feet and brushed herself off, her face flushed.

"Coordination's not your strong suit," she

said, looking everywhere but at him.

He stood up. "I tripped." He glanced around, picked up the rock he must have tripped on, and moved it into the garden bed.

"Any excuse," Hal said, his arm around Tanya. "Let's go for a walk."

"I've got to talk with my girl," Tanya said, moving away from Hal. "You keep your brother company."

Jack wanted to talk with Bridget but he knew when to take a step back. He followed his brother, wishing he could hear the conversation behind him.

* * *

Tanya tucked her arm into Bridget's. "What was that about?"

She shook her head. "I was stupid. I shouldn't have done it. I got – caught up, is all."

"I'm not talking about you jumping off the swing, I'm talking about you not kissing that man."

Bridget scowled. She could still feel Jack's warmth on her skin, his muscled body pressed against hers, and remembered their one night together. It was *not* going to happen again. "He's my boss."

"So what? He's sexy and his interested.

You're allowed to have fun."

"What happens when it stops being fun?" Bridget demanded. "When he's no longer interested? I still have to work with him. I can't keep it a secret at work. I'm too transparent." A work colleague had told her she could see her love for Lionel in her eyes every time she spoke to him. At the time Bridget hadn't cared, she'd been too in love to think of the repercussions, but now she knew better.

Not that she loved Jack. She barely knew him.

"And what if he's the one?" Tanya asked. "You can't push him away."

"I don't believe in soul mates," Bridget said. "There's not just one person for each of us." At least she hoped not. She wanted to see her mother happy again. To have someone she loved.

"Bridge, it doesn't have to be all or nothing. The attraction's obviously mutual. You can explore it outside of work hours."

She shook her head. She couldn't. She needed to be one hundred percent focused at work and Jack was already too much of a distraction. She needed to keep him in his work colleague pigeonhole. It would be easier for everyone that way. "Come on. It's time for dessert."

Break the Rules

* * *

Bridget tried to keep at a distance from Jack for the remainder of the day, but it wasn't easy. Her knee kept brushing against his as they ate dessert, as if it had a mind of its own. Then on the car trip home, it felt as though the back seat had shrunk – she was practically sitting on top of him.

Why did his presence need to be so strong?

When they finally arrived home, she jumped out of the car, glad to be free of him.

"What time does the game start?" Jack asked as he got out.

She wanted to curse. She'd forgotten Tanya had invited them to stay for the football game. Perhaps she could fake a headache and hide out in her room until they were gone.

But that would mean she'd miss the game. Jack wasn't worth missing a game for.

"We've got an hour or so," Tanya replied. "Time enough to order pizza."

Bridget couldn't eat another bite. The apple pie she'd had for dessert had taken up the remaining space in her stomach. All she wanted to do was take a shower, climb into her pajamas, and watch the game with Tanya. The pajama game night had been a tradition for them for as long as she could remember.

But it wasn't going to happen tonight.

She sighed as she dropped her purse off in her bedroom and then headed for the kitchen to offer the guys a drink.

"I'm going to take a shower and get into my jammies," Tanya said. She beckoned to Hal. "Wanna join me?"

Without a word, but with a big grin, he followed Tanya.

Great. Just great. Tanya was able to wear her pajamas. It wasn't fair. Besides Bridget didn't want to be left alone with Jack. He was too much of a temptation.

"Drink?" she offered, holding up a bottle of beer.

"Sure." He took it from her.

She stepped back quickly and looked in the fridge for something non-alcoholic. She'd drunk enough today. Pulling out a bottle of orange juice, she poured herself a glass.

Jack was still standing there, watching her.

"Have a seat," she offered, indicating the sofa.

She waited for him to sit, then she took a seat on the other sofa. She sipped her drink, not sure what to say to him.

"It was a fun day," Jack said, his voice loud in the silence.

She nodded. "Tanya has a knack for making things fun."

"I think it's the pair of you," he said mildly.

She didn't agree with him but she said nothing. Tanya had always drawn the fun out of her. When they'd first moved to Houston she remembered how quiet their house was. It had taken a year for her mother to come out of her grief shell enough to start bringing the music and fun back. By that stage, she and Tanya were firm friends and Tanya always led her into mischief.

She cast her mind around for something to say. "So what was the last NFL game you watched?"

"I don't remember. It was before I went to Australia."

"So what's the football like over there?"

"No padding, full contact, and you're only allowed to run a certain distance before you have to bounce the ball."

"Sounds weird."

"It took some getting used to, but the crowds are huge."

Silence fell again and then she heard Tanya giggling in the bathroom. She did not want to think about what they were doing in there.

Ugh.

She reached for the television remote. "Let's check if the pre-game show has started."

He nodded. She could almost feel his dare

to bring up the subject of their attraction. But she didn't do dares. She was happy to let things lie.

Finding the right channel, she focused her attention on the television. When Hal and Tanya finally came out of the bathroom, she was engrossed in the sports commentary on the Texans' chances this year.

"Have you ordered the pizza yet?" Tanya asked.

"No. We thought we'd wait for you," she said.

After a brief discussion about toppings, Tanya ordered a couple of pizzas. Then she came over to the sofa. "Scoot over, Bridge. You sit next to Jack."

Bridget scowled at her friend but Tanya waved her hand. "Go on."

Concealing her sigh, she moved so Hal and Tanya could sit on the couch together. She tucked her feet up next to her and leaned on the armrest. She couldn't get any further away from Jack, but his heat pulsed out toward her. This was ridiculous.

Luckily the game started, and it was on-the-edge-of-your-seat brilliant. The lead swapped multiple times and came right down to the last seconds. The Texans had possession and as the seconds ticked down they kicked a field goal.

Bridget leapt to her feet as the ball sailed through the air toward the goal posts. She held her breath and then shrieked when the ball made it over the crossbar. "Yes." She hugged Tanya next to her, gave a celebratory booty shake, and in her excitement, turned and hugged Jack.

Bad idea.

His arms swept around her, pulling her close and before she could think, his lips met hers. Instant heat. Desire shot straight through her as her body recognized his lips. She clung on to him, pulling him closer, matching his passion with her own. To hell with what was right. She wanted him. She slipped her tongue between his lips and he groaned.

"Get a room, you two."

The voice spiked through her consciousness and reason flooded back to her. Holy hell! She shoved him away, stepping back, breathing heavily. What had she done?

She met Jack's eyes. He was waiting for her reaction. What the hell was she supposed to do now?

She cleared her throat. "Good game."

She grabbed her glass from the coffee table and retreated to the kitchen. Behind her Tanya said, "Hal! You shouldn't have interrupted them."

Bridget was glad he had. Her attraction to Jack would lead nowhere.

She placed her glass on the sink and turned. She flinched. Jack was right behind her. She held up a hand. "Don't." She needed some space.

"Bridget you can't keep ignoring this thing between us." He kept his voice low so the others couldn't hear him.

Wanna bet? "Jack, we're work colleagues. You're my boss. What will HR say if they find out we're involved?" Her stomach twisted itself into knots just thinking about it.

"It's none of their damn business."

"Of course it is. All it'll take is one person saying I'm getting preferential treatment because I'm sleeping with you and it will open up a whole can of worms."

She hoped outlining the consequences would get through to him. Her rational side was clinging on to control by its nails. All she wanted to do was throw herself back into his arms – to hell with the consequences.

"So we don't tell them. Don't tell anyone. At work we continue as we have been, and we see each other outside of work."

Her body went cold. She'd heard that before.

"No." Her tone was ice. She shook her head. "I won't pretend." She would not be fooled again. She moved to walk past him but he put his hand out to stop her.

"Why not?" His voice lowered. "What happened to you?" There was compassion in his voice.

She could have ignored him if he'd been demanding. She sighed. Maybe if she told him the whole story, if he knew about the Lionel affair, he'd stop pushing, he'd understand.

Behind Jack, Tanya took Hal's hand and led him to her bedroom. She held up crossed fingers.

Bridget closed her eyes briefly. "Have a seat."

He sat next to her on the sofa, his knees brushing hers. She shifted further away.

Where to begin?

She'd never told another guy about what had happened, hadn't had anyone remotely serious since. She took a deep breath. "A couple of years ago, I was involved with a guy called Lionel. We met at work – a different company from Dionysus – and hit it off. He was my boss."

Jack was silent, waiting for her to continue.

"I didn't think much of it at first. All I knew was I liked him and he liked me, but after our first date he said we needed to keep it between ourselves. That people at work might talk." She huffed out a breath. "It made the whole relationship much more exciting, almost illicit."

"Was he married?"

She shook her head. "I would never date a married man."

"I thought that might be why he wanted to keep it secret."

"No. But he was watching out for himself." She sighed. "We used to talk work all the time. He'd ask me for my opinions and I'd give him all of my ideas. It never bothered me that he took credit for them. He said they'd have a better chance of getting the go-ahead if the suggestions came from him, and the safety of the site was the most important thing." She'd been so caught up in the adventure of it.

"Sounds like a schmuck. So what happened?"

Bridget hesitated. This was the hardest part. "One of the projects I suggested was approved. While I was waiting for Lionel one day, I flicked through the project file and noticed he'd taken a short-cut, used inferior quality materials to save some money. I asked him why and he made some excuse about management reducing the funds. I didn't question it." Her gut had been uneasy, but she'd trusted Lionel, she'd thought she was in love with him.

She closed her eyes, her voice soft. "Then there was an incident. Three people injured, one had third degree burns on ten percent of his body. They traced the root cause back to the inferior quality materials." She sighed. "I should have said something. I should have insisted he replace the items."

"Did Lionel get fired?"

Bridget laughed. "Of course not. He came clean." The sarcasm was clear in her voice. "He admitted the project was all my idea, that we were having an affair and he'd let me run the whole project. He'd been too caught up in our relationship to check what I was doing. He'd trusted me."

Jack's mouth dropped open. "How could they believe him?"

"I'd raised a couple of purchase requests for him. I didn't think anything of it at the time. He wanted the project completed quickly and if he'd raised the requisition he would have had to wait for his supervisor to approve it. If I did it, he could approve it and have the goods straight away."

"The requisitions were for the inferior materials?"

She nodded.

"Son of a bitch."

His anger was a balm. "It was my own fault. I ignored my instincts."

"The hell it's your fault. The man used you and didn't have the balls to admit when he was wrong." Jack's eyes flashed fire and his voice was raised. He took a breath to calm himself. "What happened to you?"

"There was an investigation. I was basically told I could quit or they would fire me. I quit."

"They had no right to do that."

"It turned out the company had a "no relationship" policy. Lionel and I were never supposed to be in a relationship." It was another reason why Lionel had wanted to keep it a secret.

"How hard was it for you to find a job after?"

Her smile was grim. "If you ask anyone in the industry about the Lionel affair, they'll be able to tell you all about it. I was lucky Jeremy had worked with us, knew what Lionel was like, and convinced the manager at Dionysus to take a chance on me."

"The man has good sense."

Jeremy had been betrayed by Lionel as well.

"What happened to the men who were injured?" Jack asked.

"They recovered. The one who was burned

the worst has scars, but he's alive. He couldn't go back to working on the plant so he took my place as safety advisor. I hear he's dedicated."

"And Lionel?"

"He's still there. I occasionally run into him at safety workshops." She'd worked through the betrayal and her anger, and was trying to be civil to him.

She wasn't working too hard at it.

Jack placed his hand on her thigh. "I understand why you don't want to be in a work relationship," he said. "But it doesn't mean I have to like it. I would never do that to you, you know that, right?"

Sadness swept through her and she placed her hand over his to soften the blow. "No, I don't. We don't know each other well enough, Jack. I thought I knew Lionel ... I can't – no, I *won't* go through that again."

He frowned briefly before he sighed. "I'm not going to change your mind, am I?"

She seriously wanted him to, but she couldn't ignore the Lionel factor. "No."

"How about friends?"

"I'd like that."

He leaned forward. "Just one last kiss," he murmured.

"Just one," she agreed.

The kiss was soft, sweet, and oh so

luscious. Bridget didn't want it to end. She felt it right down to her toes.

When they eventually parted, Jack cleared his throat and got to his feet. "I'd better go."

She nodded. If she spoke, she'd ask him to stay.

He grabbed Hal's car keys from the table. "Tell Hal to give me a call if he needs to be picked up tomorrow."

"Sure." She followed him to the front door. "Drive safely."

It was an inane thing to say but they both knew what she meant. She closed the door before he drove away. She couldn't watch him do that. She went into her bedroom and flopped on to the bed.

She'd done the right thing. She was sure of it.

She just wished she didn't feel so awful.

Chapter 9

"So spill," Carly said as she got into the car the next morning.

Bridget handed her the jewelry box, hoping to distract her.

It worked for a couple of minutes as her sister oohed and aahed over it and then turned back to Bridget. "Why were you out with your boss yesterday?"

She focused on the traffic. "He's Tanya's boyfriend's brother. Tanya thought it would be good to do something together."

"Didn't you say that guy you met a couple of weeks ago was named Jack?"

Carly never forgot details. Damn it.

"Same guy."

Carly turned to face her. "The guy you told Mama about is your new boss?"

"Yeah. What a coincidence, right?"

"Oh, *chiquita*. I'm sorry. What are you going to do?"

"Nothing. Last night I told him about Lionel. We're going to be friends."

"If you told him about Lionel he must mean something to you."

"It doesn't matter, Carolina. I'm not risking myself that way." Bridget had made her decision. She didn't need anyone making her doubt it now.

"What's Jack like?" Carly wasn't going to let it drop.

"He's nice. He listens to my suggestions at work and got the financial approval for those issues I was telling you about."

That distracted her sister. "Really? You've been trying to get that approved for months."

"I know. He went into the management meeting, outlined the issues, and Kevin told him to call the CFO. I don't know what he did but he's got a magic touch."

Bad choice of words.

"Or he's male," Carly said.

Bridget didn't answer. She could be right.

"Are you sure ignoring your attraction is for the best? He's got great taste in antiques." She ran her hand over the box.

Bridget laughed. "It is. I need to be focused at work. No one would trust me if they knew I was dating my boss."

"Maybe you could get a new job."

Bridget scowled at her and then returned her gaze to the road. "I'm not leaving my job because of a guy. Dionysus gave me a chance when no one else would. I owe them."

"They've been working you to the bone and ignoring your advice for the last six months. You don't owe them anything. I'm sure no one remembers the Lionel affair any more."

Bridget shook her head. She wasn't leaving her job for a man ever again. She would go on her own terms when she was good and ready. Changing the subject, she asked, "What was wrong with you yesterday? You shouldn't have been working on a Saturday."

Carly sighed. "You know how it is. No rest for the wicked."

"You're hardly wicked. Besides, you're the CEO. Shouldn't you have minions to do the grunt work for you?"

"Not this stuff." She sounded really tired.

Bridget glanced at her. "What is it?"

"Just business. Did you hear they might have found Jacinta and Mario's mother?"

She knew her sister was deliberately changing the subject, but she let her. "Zita mentioned something about Wisconsin."

"No, she's in Mississippi."

Bridget sat back as Carly told her the details. She would have to get to the bottom of Carly's worries another time.

* * *

Lunch at Carmen's was as loud as ever. She had six foster children at the moment and the three new girls were fitting in well. A couple of them were helping with lunch, the youngest, Mario, was setting the table and two of the pregnant teenagers were sitting on the couch, resting.

The aroma of chili drifted through the house as Bridget and Carly walked in.

"*Hola, Mamá*," Bridget said, giving her mother a hug.

"*Mi niñita*." She hugged Bridget tightly. "How are things with your Jack?"

"There isn't anything, Mama. It didn't work out."

Her mother tutted. "That's sad."

"It sure is, Mama." Bridget scurried into the kitchen before her mother could ask anything else.

"So what happened with Jack?" Zita asked, kissing her cheek.

"Turns out he's my new boss," she said.

"Oh." Zita knew all about the Lionel affair. "No chance then?"

Bridget shook her head.

"That's a shame."

Wasn't it just? Not wanting to dwell on Jack she asked, "So what's new here?"

"I think we've found Mario and Jacinta's mother," Zita said. "She's in Mississippi, not Wisconsin. Immigration are confirming and then I'll take them home."

"Yeah, Carly was telling me. That's fantastic."

"It is. We've already been sent details of the next foster kids we'll get."

It was a never-ending revolving door. More and more children were fleeing Central America unaccompanied. Those who were allowed to stay needed someone to live with and the farm had plenty of beds. Their mother had designed it with that in mind.

"How's Alejandra? The baby must be almost due."

"It is. We're in countdown mode now. Her bag is packed for the hospital and Mama's covered all the necessities with her. She's going to be fine."

Alejandra was fifteen and had been involved with a gang member in El Salvador. She didn't want her baby becoming part of a gang so she'd fled the country.

Bridget was worried for the girl. Fifteen was

so young to be having a baby, but she knew her mother and the rest of the girls at Casa Flanagan would help her. She would be able to finish her education and make something of her life. Alejandra already spoke about wanting to be a teacher.

"So what's new with you?" Zita asked.

"I'm going to learn to scuba dive next week."

Zita's mouth dropped open. "Get out!"

Bridget grinned at her. "Yeah. Jack's given me a couple of days off in lieu and I decided to finally learn to scuba dive."

"Sounds awesome. You'll have to tell me all about it."

Feeling comfortable and at home, Bridget proceeded to do just that.

* * *

The Monday management meeting was Jack's least favorite part of the week. It lasted several hours and all they did was talk without any decisions being made.

"How are the audit actions coming along?" Kevin asked Jack. Now he understood the urgency of the matter, Kevin wanted full updates each meeting.

"It's moving quickly now we have the funds," Jack said. "I've hired a couple of contractors to help complete the actions due to the delay in approval."

Kevin scowled. "How much is that costing us?"

"It's coming from my budget," Jack assured him.

"Bridget obviously didn't budget correctly. I should have guessed she wasn't capable."

Jack reined in his temper. "Her budget was based on the assumption it wouldn't take three months to get approval. If the authorizers had signed it off immediately we wouldn't have this problem." He wasn't going to let Bridget take the blame.

"She didn't communicate the urgency."

Oh, he was pretty sure she had. He'd witnessed her passion first-hand. She wouldn't have pulled her punches for the management team. They just hadn't listened. But there was no point in making a big deal of it now. What was done was done.

Besides, he had another issue to raise. "It's come to my attention that the technicians don't check their email regularly. Email is one of the only ways we can communicate with the guys who are on night shift. My team has had to work extra hours to speak with them in person, in order to ensure they have the information they need."

The production manager straightened in his

chair. "Most of the guys are computer illiterate. They wouldn't know how to use email even if they tried."

Jack glanced at him. "Email is an essential part of our communication strategy. If they don't know how to use it, isn't it your responsibility to ensure your team has the skills they need?"

"They work with tools and machinery, not computers. They're so rarely near one," he argued.

"Then I suggest you come up with a better communication strategy so my team doesn't have to work extra hours. They work long enough as it is." So, he wasn't making any friends in today's meeting. It didn't matter. Jack wasn't here to make friends, he was here to make sure the plant's safety was sufficient and his team wasn't overworked.

By the time the meeting was over Jack had made sure the management team understood the status quo wasn't good enough anymore and he expected their full support. Since safety was theoretically the company's number one priority, it wasn't hard to get them to agree. Whether they actually followed through remained to be seen.

Kevin stopped him on the way out of the meeting and congratulated him on his progress. "It's nice to see you in charge."

"Thanks." Jack continued to his office. The praise only depressed him further. He wasn't doing anything differently from Bridget. He slumped into his chair.

Bridget ducked her head around the door. "Hey, boss, I've developed the new safety topics and sent you a link to check them." She smiled and then frowned. She stepped into the office. "You all right?"

The sight of Bridget made it all worse, not better. It was the job keeping them from exploring what they could have together. "Rough meeting. I'm not popular with production or maintenance at the moment."

"Told them how it is?"

"Yeah."

"Well, you should get a better response. Kevin is raving about you."

He frowned. "I'm not telling them anything that you didn't."

"But you're male, it makes it easier to take. Men expect other men to be forceful. Old school men don't like it in their women, and Kevin is one of the old boys."

Jack didn't argue with her.

"Need a hand with anything?" she asked.

"No, I've got it covered. Let me know by Thursday what needs to be done while you're away."

"Will do." She smiled at him and it did lift his spirits. "It'll get easier."

"I hope so."

He wasn't just referring to the job. Seeing Bridget today after their talk on the weekend was difficult. He could see her point of view, he could even understand it, but it didn't make it easier. If he ever met this Lionel he wasn't sure what he'd do. The jackass had ruined his chance with Bridget.

Jack shook his head. He had to stop obsessing and accept that he and Bridget were colleagues and hopefully friends. That's all it could be at the moment.

But he wasn't ruling out the future.

* * *

Sunday evening Bridget practically floated through her front door. Her dive course had been *amazing*. She'd wanted to stay underwater for longer, but her instructor – and the level of oxygen in her tank – made her head to the surface.

Jack had been right. It was like exploring another world. She couldn't wait to go again. The dive shop ran regular dives each weekend if the weather was good. She'd already signed up for next Saturday.

Walking into the living area she found Tanya reading.

"Oh good. You're home." She shut her book. "Hal's invited us around for dinner. Are you up for it?"

Bridget only hesitated for a moment. "Sure. I'll take a shower before we go."

The idea of seeing Jack outside of work set her heartbeat racing faster than normal. It was something she was going to have to deal with. At work she kept her contact with him to a minimum, which wasn't too difficult. She was busy with her projects and he had his own work. It was only the occasional meeting or update where she had to see him. At those times she ignored her body's reaction to him, said what she needed to say, and left. It wasn't getting easier, but at least it was manageable.

Tonight she wanted to see him. She wanted to talk to him about her dive. He'd understand the elation, she was sure of it.

It didn't take her long to get ready and she drove them both over to Hal's place.

The living room was comfortable with big, blue cushy sofas. Hal directed them to sit while he got them drinks.

Jack walked in looking incredible in a pair of red board shorts and a black T-shirt. He was delectable. Bridget looked away before she did something stupid. She was still on her high from the dive and was likely to make impulsive decisions, like asking him to show her his room.

Not a good idea.

"How did your course go?" Jack asked after greeting them both. "Are you certified?"

Certifiable was more like it. Bridget gripped the sofa arm. "Yeah. I passed."

"Did you enjoy it?" He sat down next to her.

It was too close in her current mood, but she didn't care. "You were right. It's a whole other world down there," she said. "And being able to stay down, breathe through the respirator, and experience it without any hurry was such an incredible feeling." She couldn't describe it.

"It's freedom," he said.

"Yes!" She placed a hand on his thigh. He understood exactly. Down there, under all of that water, there was no world on the surface, no responsibilities, no plant. There was just the ocean, the animals, and your dive buddy. All there was to do was enjoy the dive.

"So when are you going again?"

"Next Saturday. The dive shop runs regular dives. The weather's going to be perfect and they're going out to one of the shipwrecks in the Gulf."

"Mind if I tag along? It's been a while since I've been diving."

"Sure." Bridget didn't hesitate. She wanted to experience a dive with him. He knew what to do and he'd love it as much as she did.

Bridget turned to include Tanya in their conversation, only to find she wasn't there. Sometime during her conversation with Jack, Tanya must have left and she didn't notice.

Suddenly she realized Jack had covered her hand on his leg and was stroking the back of it. Sensation shot up her arm and through her body. She glanced at him, not moving her hand.

"Sorry, I can't help myself," he said.

Today was too good a day for anger, for responsibility. Today she wanted him to touch her. Today she wanted to experience life. Today she wanted him.

"I had an idea," Jack said.

She waited for him to continue.

"We can't date at work – that's a given."

She nodded.

"But what about the weekend? There's two whole days when work doesn't interfere – as long as neither one of us is on call. It seems a shame to waste them." His eyes were cautious, his tone light.

It was *so* tempting. "What would the

conditions be?"

"The work week ends when we both finish work on Friday. It starts when we arrive at work Monday. If we're on call, that's considered a work weekend."

Bridget considered it. The issues with being involved at work were: the distraction, the gossip, and the potential for blame. But if it was just an occasional weekend thing then it could be classed more as a fling than a relationship. They wouldn't be distracted because there would be no work involved, no one need to know because they wouldn't be seen, and she couldn't be blamed for something that happened outside of work hours.

Who was she kidding? She wanted him and today she didn't care about the consequences.

"Deal."

They dove at each other.

Chapter 10

Jack dragged Bridget on to his lap and she straddled him. Her lips met his and she sighed in pleasure. This was a damn good idea. She shouldn't have waited so long. She slipped her tongue into his mouth, tasting, teasing.

Jack moaned, caressing her breasts, rubbing his thumb over her nipple. She arched against him as heat rushed straight to her core. His fingers slipped under her shirt and brushed her hot skin.

She tore her mouth away from his and said, "Bedroom. Now." If they didn't move, things were going to get indecent.

She followed him willingly down the hall, not registering whatever it was that Hal said to them as he passed. She didn't care. All that mattered was Jack.

He almost carried her into his room,

slamming the door behind them and pressing her up against it.

"Better," she breathed before he claimed her mouth again.

Her hands slid under his shirt and he stepped away, stripping it off, before he was back, his body hard against hers. It wasn't enough. She was wearing too many clothes. She yanked off her top and he unsnapped her bra, finding her breast with his mouth.

Bridget gasped. "Yes." Her body sung in a way it never had before.

Her hands found his hair again and pulled him up so she could taste his mouth. She ached, her whole body pulsing with need. He unbuttoned her shorts, sliding them and her panties off. She stepped out of them as he stepped back.

"You're a goddess," he said, running his hands over her breasts, down to the heat between her legs.

Sparks flew through her. She felt like a goddess. "I want you."

He stripped off his pants. His naked body was sexy as hell. She reached for him, pressing her body against his. "Bed," she said, pushing him toward it and stalking after him. She shoved him onto the bed and climbed on top of him, straddling him. She captured his mouth, needing him. She didn't want to wait. "Condoms?"

He gestured to the bedside table.

She grabbed what she needed and then sat back. Her hand wrapped around his shaft and his hips jerked. Power surged through her. She sheathed him with rubber and then sheathed him with her body, every nerve ending in her body tingling.

Bridget paused, her head back, eyes closed as she savored the sensation. Then she opened her eyes, met his, and grinned. "Ready to ride?"

* * *

Bridget slid off Jack and collapsed on the bed next to him. Every cell in her body was warm and satiated.

She hadn't expected the passion to equal their first night together. She'd only wanted to scratch an itch but it was so much more than that. His body was divine, hard and firm, needing to be touched. Her lust had taken control.

Glancing at Jack, he didn't seem to mind.

She smiled as he cleaned up and then slid back on to the bed with her. He pulled her close and kissed her.

"I like this new deal," he said.

She laughed. "Me too."

"Should I apologize to Hal for missing dinner?"

"We missed dinner?"

He laughed, such a warm and happy sound that it made her heart sing. "Yeah, about the time I was dragging you into my lair."

So that's what he'd said. "In that case, we probably should. I think he'll understand."

"I'm *sure* he will," Jack agreed. "But he can wait a little longer."

He took her hand and kissed her knuckles. Her rapid heartbeat slowed to a flutter as his other hand lazily drew circles on her hips. This man made her whole body respond. She wanted him again.

"So since our new deal doesn't end until tomorrow morning, you could stay the night," Jack said, moving from kissing her knuckles to kissing her breasts. "I'll brave Hal's wrath and get us something to eat, and then we can hide out here for the rest of the evening."

It was far too tempting. Their deal was supposed to be casual, temporary, just for fun.

Bridget sat up, keeping her voice light. "That would hardly be polite," she said. "Hal went to all the trouble to cook for us." She climbed off the bed and began to dress.

She couldn't get more involved with Jack.

This was just sex. She felt his eyes on her, but she didn't look at him while she hooked her bra and slipped her shirt over her head. Finally she heard him move behind her.

"I hope his lasagna is worth it," Jack said.

Bridget breathed out a sigh of relief as she turned to him, buttoning her shorts. He pulled his T-shirt on and took her hand. Her hand fit perfectly in his.

"Let's go face the music," he said.

* * *

As they entered the kitchen, both Hal and Tanya grinned at them. Bridget's face heated.

"Any dinner left?" Jack asked, pulling out a chair at the table for her.

"We saved you some." Hal indicated the tray in the oven.

As Jack dished them up some food, Tanya gave Bridget the thumbs up, grinning widely. Not wanting to discuss it in front of the others, Bridget turned away and hoped the blush wasn't showing. There was nothing to be embarrassed about. It wasn't as if Hal and Tanya hadn't been doing the same thing over the last few weeks.

Jack placed a plate in front of her. "Wine?" he asked, holding up a bottle they'd bought at the winery last weekend.

"Sure."

This was OK. He was being casual, friendly. There was none of the intensity she'd felt in his bedroom. There couldn't be any intensity, not if this weekend thing was going to work. It had to be casual.

Bridget tasted the lasagna. "This is good," she told Hal.

"Glad you like it."

They fell into easy conversation.

When it was time to go home, Tanya came with her, so they could get an early start on their girls' day.

Bridget stood at the door to her truck and turned to Jack. "Were there any problems on Friday? Do you need anything for tomorrow?"

He shook his head. "No work talk, remember," he said as he pulled her close. "Just you and me."

The idea was so tantalizing. Just forget about work.

He bent his head, lowering his mouth toward hers. "I'll see you Friday night?"

She frowned. He'd see her at work on Tuesday. Then she realized what he was doing. "That would be great."

"What was the name of the dive company? I'll book a tour on Saturday."

She told him and finally he kissed her. It was

a slow kiss, long and luscious, drawing the heat to her core slowly. The fire of earlier was replaced with a long burn, like a log fire on a cold night. Comfort and warmth.

Breaking the kiss, Bridget looked at Jack, not able to read his expression in the darkness of night. Did he feel it too?

She hoped not. She had to get her emotions under control and treat this how it should be treated. As a fling.

She slid into the car, and lowered her window. "Until Friday."

She backed out of the driveway and drove off.

* * *

"I'm thinking about asking Hal to marry me," Tanya said as soon as they were on the road.

Bridget's jaw dropped and she glanced at her friend to check if she was kidding.

She wasn't.

"Wow. That's … quick."

"I know, it is, right? But I've never been so happy. He gets me. And it's not about the sex, which is fantastic. Some evenings we just sit on the couch and watch television, and others we talk into the early morning. I can talk to him about anything."

It sounded nice. A companion and a lover.

There was a tiny part of Bridget that was sad. She would miss being Tanya's best friend and confidant. "So what's your hesitation?"

"It's only been three weeks. What if we're still in the love bird stage?"

"My parents married a week after they met," Bridget said. She adored the story of how it was love at first sight for them. "Can you imagine having kids with him, buying a house, growing old together?"

"Yeah." Tanya's voice was soft, dreamy. "We both want two kids."

If they'd already had that conversation then perhaps Hal felt the same way about Tanya. Bridget smiled. "Then maybe that's your answer."

"We should look for rings tomorrow," Tanya said. "Do guys get engagement rings if the girl asks?"

Bridget shrugged. "I don't know. I don't see why not."

"I should have checked his size." She was fretting, Bridget could hear it in her voice.

"There's no rush, Tanya. You've got the rest of your lives together."

"You're right. It doesn't matter, we can get it resized."

Bridget smothered a grin. Tanya heard what she wanted sometimes. She pulled into the driveway.

"What have you got planned for us for tomorrow?" Bridget asked.

"Shopping in the morning, followed by a casual lunch at Eat, Drink, Read, and then facials and massages in the afternoon."

"Sounds great." Well, the facial and massage definitely did. The shopping she'd endure. Bridget unlocked the door to the house and turned on the light.

"Oh, and ring shopping," Tanya added.

"Of course," Bridget agreed. "I'll see you in the morning."

As she lay in bed she wondered what it would be like to find the one you wanted to spend your life with, and fell asleep thinking of Jack.

* * *

At eight o'clock the next morning, Tanya banged on her door. "Time to get up."

Bridget groaned. The only thing to get Tanya to rise early was shopping or a road trip. Just her luck.

"I'm getting up," she called.

Tanya was already dressed and ready to go when Bridget came out. She handed Bridget a slice of toast and a coffee. "I never asked you how it was with Jack last night," she said. "I didn't believe Hal when he said Jack had dragged you to his bedroom."

Bridget's body warmed as she remembered it.

"So how was it?"

She took a sip of her coffee. "Fine."

"Fine?" Tanya sounded disappointed. "I would have thought with a package like that, Jack would have rocked your world."

Though she didn't want to go into detail she couldn't prevent the smile from crossing her face. "Actually I think I rocked his world."

"You go, girl!" Tanya hollered. "I'm so glad you two got it together. He's so nice."

Bridget hummed an agreement, hoping it would be enough for Tanya. It was Monday, which meant Jack was off limits in that way.

"When are you seeing him next?"

"Friday night."

Tanya frowned. "That's ages away."

"We work together, remember?"

"Yeah. What made you change your mind?"

"It's a weekend thing. During the week we're colleagues and at the weekend we date."

Tanya stared at her. "How's that going to work? You can't separate it that way."

"Sure we can." Bridget was still trying to convince herself. "It's called compartmentalizing."

"Bridge …"

She got to her feet, swallowing the last of her breakfast. "I'll take a shower and we can go." She left before Tanya could lecture her further.

She had enough doubts as it was.

* * *

Their day started with shopping. Bridget bought herself a few tops, a cute dress, and on a whim, some sexy lingerie. Tanya dashed in and out of jewelers before finally choosing an engagement ring for Hal.

After an amazing facial and a full-body massage that made Bridget's bones melt, they headed home.

Bridget dumped her purchases on her bed and walked into the kitchen. "What do you want to do for dinner?"

Tanya turned from the fridge where she was getting a drink and screwed up her face. "I was hoping to see Hal tonight."

Of course she was. She had the ring burning a hole in her pocket. "Good luck!"

Tanya beamed at her. "Thanks, Bridge. You're the best for understanding." She gave her a hug and then left the room. "I'm going to get ready."

Bridget poured herself a glass of wine and

sat on the couch. Things were changing rapidly. If Hal accepted Tanya's proposal – and Bridget hoped he would – they'd probably want to move in together as soon as possible. But Bridget couldn't afford the rent on her own. She might actually have to find a new roommate. Then again, Tanya wasn't likely to move in with Hal while Jack was still living there.

She sighed. There was no point worrying about it until she had to.

She sipped her wine. Tomorrow she was back at the plant. She wasn't sure how much work would be waiting for her, and she couldn't help fretting about Jack. They had slept together again. It shouldn't be a big deal. She'd acted on her attraction and she was happy with the results. Bridget shook her head. Way to analyze things.

But she'd been high on the dive experience, she'd not been thinking rationally. Had she made the best decision? Could she keep her work relationship with Jack separate from her other relationship?

They'd not agreed to keep it secret – just separate. Part of her wanted no one to know, but the other part reminded her she'd kept her relationship with Lionel secret too, and that had led to disaster.

Tanya walked into the room. "How do I look?"

Bridget turned. Tanya was wearing the new blue dress she'd bought that fit her curves perfectly. "Gorgeous."

"Are you sure?" Tanya plucked at the dress.

Her friend was nervous. Bridget couldn't remember a time when Tanya was nervous about anything.

She stood up and walked over to her. "Hal's going to swallow his tongue when he sees you," she assured her friend.

Tanya gave her a small smile. "I'm so sure I want to spend the rest of my life with him, but my nerves are humming."

"It's a big deal, honey. But you'll be fine." She hugged her.

"You're right." Tanya huffed out a breath. "I'll see you tomorrow."

Bridget stood where she was until Tanya shut the front door. What was she going to do now? She hadn't brought any work home with her and there was no game on television.

She walked in to the kitchen and checked the fridge for something to eat, then closed it again. Nothing appealed.

She could get some take-out but there was only herself to order for. It felt a little bit pathetic today. She should be thrilled for

Tanya. She should be happy her friend had found the man she wanted to spend the rest of her life with. Instead she felt lonely.

It was tempting to call Jack, ask him to come over, but it was a week night. She wasn't breaking their deal on the first day. Besides, that would mean it was more than just casual.

And it couldn't be anything more than that.

There was always one person who could cheer her up. She picked up the phone and dialed. "Hey, Zita. What's up?"

* * *

An hour later, after she hung up from talking to her little sister, her phone beeped.

Checking it, she grinned. There was a photo of Tanya and Hal, with smiles as wide as a rainbow, both holding out their hands to show off their engagement rings. The message read, *Great minds think alike*.

Not wanting to interrupt their celebration, she texted, *CONGRATULATIONS!!!* and put down her phone.

It was official. Her best friend was getting married.

Bridget tucked her legs up under her on the sofa and crossed her arms. It was fantastic news. Really, it was.

Half an hour later she was still sitting there

contemplating what it all meant when someone knocked on the door. Getting to her feet, she checked the peephole. She frowned, opening the door.

Jack shuffled on the spot, a little uncertain. "Hi. I guess you've heard the news. I wanted to give Tanya and Hal a little privacy." He shrugged. "I know it's a work night, but you weren't at work today … I can go to my mother's if you'd prefer."

She knew what he was suggesting. She didn't hesitate. "Come in."

Chapter 11

They took separate cars to work the next morning. Jack left first and Bridget tidied the kitchen before she followed him.

She'd convinced herself they hadn't broken the rules of their deal. Her work week started today. And she couldn't regret last night. They'd gone straight to bed, made love slowly, exploring each other's bodies, and then had slept curled up together.

She hadn't had a man sleep over since Lionel but there was no time to be awkward about it in the morning. At that early hour, she was on auto-pilot; taking a shower, grabbing a bite to eat and making some lunch.

If her morning routine had been broken up by a brief dalliance in the shower, she wasn't complaining. But now she needed to get back into work mode.

She greeted the security guard at the gatehouse, reviewed the incidents on site since she'd last been at work, and when she deemed it time, she ducked her head into Jack's office and said, "Morning, boss. What's new?"

His grin was quick before he answered, "Production has implemented a new communication strategy. Any messages for nightshift are to go through the shift supervisor. He'll make sure they're passed on."

"That's great." It would take a little bit of time to see if it worked, but she'd be optimistic.

"Take a seat and I'll update you with the progress we made on your project."

Bridget took the seat he offered, her knee brushing his. Heat zapped between them. She had to get herself under control. Focusing on the paperwork in front of her, she shifted her seat slightly further away from him, ignoring his small smile, and got to work.

* * *

The week at work was the best that Jack had had. The awkwardness between he and Bridget had disappeared and was replaced by a lovely anticipation for the weekend. They shared the occasional secret smile, but were able to work together without any fuss. Bridget focused on the job and got it done.

He'd never met anyone more dedicated and more efficient. The project she was implementing was right on schedule and a few people had commented it was a relief that the issue was finally being addressed. It made him question yet again why she hadn't been given his job.

At the end of the day he stopped by Bridget's office. "I'll pick you up at seven?"

She nodded. "Tanya's staying at Hal's," she said in a low voice.

He grinned. "Is that an invitation?"

She looked up at him through her eyelashes. "Yes."

Desire swept straight to his groin. It was just as well he'd left talking to her about this until the end of the day. He checked the hall but there were too many people still about. "I'll see you then."

He left before he did something silly, like give himself away. As he walked out of the administration building, his name was called. Turning back he saw the production manager waving to him.

"We've got a problem."

Jack swallowed his annoyance and walked back. "What is it?"

"We've got an unplanned shutdown and need a safety person to help with the risk assessment."

Something like that was going to take at least an hour, maybe longer depending on the situation. Most of his team had already left and he wasn't going to call them back. "I'll do it. Where are we meeting?"

"Room three."

"I'll be there in five."

He stuck his head into Bridget's office. "I need to take a raincheck."

"What's happened?"

"I've got to help with a risk assessment for an unplanned shutdown."

"I can do it if you want."

"No. I need to sit in on one of these anyway. There's no point both of us staying."

"Do you still want to come over when you're done?"

"If it's not too late."

She smiled, brightening up his spirits. "Any time."

He wanted to kiss her, but he couldn't, not here. "I'll call."

* * *

It was seven o'clock before Jack was able to leave work. There was still a chance he and

Claire Boston

Bridget could go out to dinner, but he was exhausted. He'd spent the last two hours insisting they do a proper risk assessment and that the likelihood and consequences were higher than the others wanted them to be. It was all just an exercise in avoiding paperwork.

The unit shutdown was a high risk operation which meant more safety processes than production wanted. Well, that was too bad. They had the processes for a reason and no one could justify why they should skip them.

When they'd finished the meeting, he'd printed out the details agreed upon, and emailed a copy to Kevin so he was kept in the loop. Jack couldn't understand why these people didn't understand the risks they were taking. There were plenty of examples of major incidents at oil refineries where not following procedures was reported as one of the causes. Perhaps he needed to print a couple of those reports out, show them to the people in charge. Maybe that would highlight the risks to them. Just because they'd done it that way in the past and not had an incident didn't make it safe, it made them lucky.

He pulled out his cell and dialed Bridget's number. "We've finished." He couldn't hide the tiredness in his voice.

"Why don't I order take-out? You can pick it

up on your way here."

He could have kissed her. "That would be great."

"There's a fantastic Chinese restaurant around the corner." She gave him the address. "Do you want anything in particular?"

"Just you," he said.

She was silent for a moment. "I'll see you when you get here."

Jack wasn't sure what to make of her silence, but he'd figure it out when he got there. Right now he needed to leave before something else came up.

* * *

Bridget opened the door before Jack could knock. She'd been waiting for him. He held up the bag of take-out food. "The hunter-gatherer has arrived."

She smiled, took the bag from him and kissed him. His day got a hundred times better.

"Come in. Do you want a shower before we eat?"

The idea was tempting, but he hadn't stopped at home to pick up a change of clothes. "Let's eat first."

He followed her into the kitchen.

"Sit down. I'll get the plates."

162

More than happy to do what he was told, Jack sat and took the plate she handed him.

"How did the assessment go?" Bridget asked.

He wanted to talk to her about it, ask for her thoughts about how to change the lackadaisical culture on site, but he had promised their weekends wouldn't involve work. "I'll tell you about it on Monday."

She frowned at him.

"No work," he reminded her.

Handing him a serving spoon she nodded. "All right."

They dished up the food and began to eat.

"What do you think about Tanya and Hal's engagement?" Jack asked. He'd only been mildly surprised when they'd returned home flashing their rings.

"They fit together, and they seem happy."

He agreed. "Tanya's making noises about moving in."

Bridget's eyebrows raised. "That I didn't know."

"She hasn't said it in so many words, but she's spent the last few nights helping me search for a place of my own."

"That's being subtle for Tanya."

He laughed. "I thought so too." As he ate, he wondered whether he should bring up the idea he'd been playing with. He was about eighty percent sure Bridget would freak out and he didn't want that. But it would solve a few problems if he took Tanya's room and Tanya moved in with Hal.

Perhaps she'd come up with the same idea on her own.

Not wanting to spoil the evening, he kept his mouth shut. "So what time do we leave for the dive in the morning?"

* * *

Bridget woke early the next morning, before her alarm went off. They needed to get down to the docks in order to make their tour, but they had to stop by Hal's so Jack could get his things.

Light from outside filtered through her blinds, lighting the room so she could see Jack as he slept. She sighed softly and carefully got out of bed so as not to wake him. He could sleep for another ten minutes. She'd turn on the coffee maker and take a shower. They didn't have time for shenanigans this morning.

Closing her eyes she let the warm water flow over her. What should she do about Jack? The most important question was probably how did she feel about him?

She was attracted to him. That was a given.

She liked him. He was intelligent, thoughtful, and he made her laugh. If he wasn't her boss, she'd happily start a relationship with him.

But that was the whole issue. He *was* her boss. There was no skirting around that gigantic fact.

So the way she saw it she had three choices: forget her second rule, ignore her past, and have a relationship. The idea sent chills through her. That wasn't going to work.

She could continue how they were – weekend lovers – and keep work and her personal life separate. But she'd already acknowledged it was getting harder and harder to do.

Or she could find another job. The thought made her anger stir. She shouldn't have to do that. She didn't want to do it. No one else would hire her. Plus if she did, she'd end up resenting Jack, she was sure of it.

So really, she had no idea what to do.

The bathroom door opened. "I didn't hear you get up," Jack said.

"I thought I'd give you a few more minutes to sleep," Bridget answered, pushing aside her worries for now. "Do you want to get in?"

He slid across the shower curtain, already naked. "I was hoping you'd ask."

His smile and his naked body sent a thrill

through her. She kissed him quickly, and then slid past, out of the shower. "I'll make breakfast. We don't want to be late."

She grabbed her towel and ducked out of the room before he could convince her to stay.

* * *

It was fresh and sunny on the docks where the dive boat was moored. Half a dozen people lingered on the jetty and Bridget introduced Jack to the dive master.

He checked Jack's qualifications carefully before admitting them on to the boat. "When was your last dive?" he asked after the boat had set off.

"A couple of months ago on Ningaloo Reef," Jack told him.

"I've heard that's a great spot. I've not been there myself."

"It's worth the trip."

"I've got it on my bucket list."

While the two men chatted about dives they'd done, Bridget spoke with one of the other divers. The boat ride lasted just over an hour before they dropped anchor and began to suit up.

Nerves played around Bridget's stomach as she put on her wetsuit, checked her equipment and ran through the checklist in her mind.

"How're you feeling?" Jack asked her.

"Excited. Nervous." But she felt better to be buddied with Jack. He was far more experienced than she was, and while she was sure she remembered everything she'd been taught, if something did go wrong, he'd be able to fix it.

"Those nerves will settle once you hit the water," he promised as they ran through the buddy checklist. The dive master had already taken them through the safety briefing before they arrived at the spot, and he now pointed out the areas he'd referred to. They were diving on an old wreck.

"You ready?" Jack asked.

Bridget nodded. They lined up behind the other divers and at their turn, Bridget put the mouthpiece in her mouth and jumped in.

Immediately on entering the water, the weight of her tank lightened. The water was cold for a moment before her body grew used to it and it settled into a pleasant temperature. She followed Jack a few yards from the boat, out of the way of the other divers, and gave him the OK signal. Then, facing each other, they descended.

The first breath after submerging always gave her a thrill. The idea of breathing underwater was truly foreign, but exhilarating. The ambient noise disappeared, replaced by the bubble of the water and the rasp of her breathing.

Bridget slowed her inhalations and exhalations, allowing herself to relax. About ten yards away on her right, two other divers were making their way down, and she saw her first fish. Then the wreck came into view and there were fish everywhere. They swam lazily back and forth, darting into the shelter of the wreck when they got too close. The metal wreck of the ship was now alive, covered in seaweed, in sponges and in coral.

Jack tapped her hand and pointed. To the left and below them was an eel, sticking its head out of its home, having a look around. Bridget wished she had an underwater camera to capture the moment but she wouldn't truly be able to do the scene any justice. Something like this had to be experienced. A photo couldn't record the cool of the water surrounding her, the rasp and bubble as she breathed in and out, the gentle pull of the current.

She followed Jack around the wreck, stopping to explore further when something caught her eye. It truly was another world.

After about half an hour, Bridget motioned to

Jack. Her oxygen was getting low. It was time for them to head back to the surface. Slowly they swam up, pausing for their safety stop before resurfacing not far from the boat.

Bridget took her mouthpiece out. "That was incredible."

Jack nodded. "That eel has made itself a comfortable home."

They swam the remaining few yards to the boat and were helped on board. Bridget breathed out a sigh of relief as she took off the tank and felt about a million times lighter.

"Lunch is ready," the dive master said. "Before you eat, you might want to swap out your tank ready for your next dive."

"You're really comfortable under there," Jack said over lunch. "I've dived with people who have been diving for years who weren't so relaxed."

She smiled. "It's easy. I was told the more relaxed I am the less oxygen I'll use, and I want to stay down for as long as possible."

"That's great. Some people never truly relax. They're too busy checking gauges, or looking for sharks."

Sharks. Why had that never crossed her mind?

"I shouldn't have mentioned the S word, should I?"

She shook her head. "What's the likelihood of seeing a shark?"

The dive master heard her. "We see one every two or three outings," he said. "Haven't had any attack though. They generally mind their own business."

OK. So the likelihood was pretty low. The consequences might be high though. She'd do a bit of research about shark attacks when she returned home, but right now Bridget wasn't going to let it bother her. She wasn't worried enough to stay on the boat and miss her next dive.

* * *

They had one more dive before returning to shore. On the ride home, Jack pulled Bridget into his arms and she sat with her back to his chest, secure and warm. She sighed.

"What do you want to do tomorrow?" he asked quietly.

"Carly's picking me up. We go to Mama's for lunch every other week."

She was almost tempted to invite him, see her Mama's reaction to her bringing a boy home. But she needed the space from him, the time to think more.

"What about tonight?"

She hadn't thought that far ahead. She had

no desire to go out – her body had that lovely fatigue from spending a day swimming. But she did want to spend it with Jack.

She yawned. "Maybe there's a game on. We could order pizza."

"Sounds good to me." His breath was warm against her ear and sent shivery loveliness through her.

This was only supposed to be a casual relationship, a bit of fun, but she was drawn to him. She *wanted* to spend more time with him.

But she had to keep reminding herself – it would never work.

Chapter 12

Jack woke Sunday morning and stretched luxuriously. Last night had been really great. On their way back from the harbor, they'd picked up pizza and then watched the football game. It was casual and fun. Then they'd gone to bed and there'd been steamy fun. He turned and gathered Bridget into his arms. She snuggled into him.

"What time is it?"

He reached over and grabbed his phone. "Nine."

"Ugh. We'd better get up. Carly will be here in an hour." She brushed a kiss against his cheek and then rolled out of bed. She slipped on her robe and his disappointment was swift as the fabric covered her naked body.

He got to his feet, grabbing some shorts. "Shower?" There still might be time for a little bit of action before Carly arrived.

"Yeah, let me put the coffee on first."

Jack headed for the shower and turned on the spray. His muscles were a little sore from their day of diving yesterday. It had been a couple of months since his last dive and there were certain parts of his body that didn't get much work normally.

Bridget entered the bathroom. "Coffee's on."

He opened the curtain as she stripped off her robe and his body immediately reacted.

Her grin was slow and wicked. "No time for that now, big boy. My sister is always on time and I need to tidy the house before she arrives."

He gathered her into his arms. "I can help. That should give us plenty of time." He kissed her, slightly smug when she responded with a moan.

"Maybe if we're quick."

* * *

They were quick, coming together in an explosion of passion and lust. When they were finished, they were definitely running a little late. They both threw on some clothes and Bridget towel-dried her hair while Jack made them both coffee.

Bridget grabbed her drink and checked the

time. "She'll be here in fifteen minutes."

Jack was looking forward to meeting Bridget's older sister. She'd seemed nice when he'd spoken to her on the phone in Brenham, but now Bridget was a little agitated.

"What else needs to be tidied?"

"It's fine." She checked her watch. "You almost finished your coffee?"

The realization hit him hard. She didn't want him to meet Carly. She wanted him gone. It was why she was checking the time yet again in a three-minute period. He tried to keep his voice casual. "Yeah." He drained his cup and went to wash it.

"I'll do that. You've got a lot of houses to visit today."

Confused, he grabbed his bag from her bedroom and gave her a kiss at the door. Was she embarrassed of him? Did she want to keep their relationship a secret from her family as well? Jack didn't know what to make of it. Yesterday their relationship seemed perfect and Bridget was relaxed and normal, and now suddenly she was uptight and closed off.

Was she worried what her sister would say about her dating her boss? Did Carly know about Lionel? That could explain why Bridget was in such a rush to get him out of her house. But it didn't stop the hurt.

He backed out of her driveway and gave a wave. Maybe the weekend thing suited her fine, and anything more – like him meeting her family – was too much of a commitment. He pushed aside his disappointment. He wasn't going to worry. He'd ask her about it if it happened again.

Jack made a quick stop at Hal's place to grab the list of houses he'd shortlisted. If Bridget was acting so weird about him meeting Carly, there was no way she'd agree with his idea to move in with her. He needed to find somewhere else to stay. The situation at Hal's was getting uncomfortable, but luckily Tanya and Hal had gone away for the weekend to celebrate their engagement.

Hopefully he'd find somewhere else to live today.

* * *

By the end of the day Jack had had enough. The house hunting had been a complete waste of time. Nothing grabbed him and he couldn't block out the voice in his head that kept asking, would Bridget like it as well?

He did *not* want to explore why he was thinking those things. He'd known her less than a month, why would she care about the house he bought?

But if they did make it work, he wanted something she would like as well.

Jack was sitting on the back deck, sipping a beer when Hal and Tanya arrived home from their weekend away.

"Jack?" Hal called.

"Out back." He stood and wandered inside to make sure his brother had heard. He'd made the mistake of not checking once before and had gone into the kitchen ten minutes later to catch Hal and Tanya in a compromising position.

Both Hal and Tanya had huge grins on their faces and they were holding hands. What now?

"We're married," they said in unison.

Jack's mouth dropped open. They had to be kidding. Tanya flashed her hand at him and there were two rings now on her left hand.

"We were staying in this cute little bed and breakfast and the owner was a wedding officiant. I said to Hal, why wait? We could get married right away and avoid all the fuss and expense of a wedding. I got the license last week after we got engaged and the owner had nothing else booked."

"Congratulations." Jack forced himself forward and hugged Tanya, giving her a kiss on the cheek. "Welcome to the family." He had no idea why they were in such a rush, why they couldn't wait. He turned to his brother and slapped him on the back. "Have you told Mom and Dad?"

"Not yet. We're going to do that now."

Jack knew his father wouldn't care, but he wasn't sure how his mother was going to react. Her youngest son getting married without her knowing was likely to upset her. But neither Hal nor Tanya would have considered that.

"I'll talk to her when you do and ask to move in with her." Jack wasn't sticking around now they were married.

Tanya grabbed his hand. "Don't feel like you have to move out because of this."

He smiled. "It's no problem. You two deserve to have the house to yourself." Besides he was pretty sure her concern was only a token.

She beamed at him.

"Have you told Bridget you're moving out?" Jack asked. "Is she going to be able to afford to live on her own?"

The surprise and then guilt that crossed her face told him Tanya hadn't even considered her best friend. He managed to stop himself from frowning. Tanya was a genuinely nice person, but she didn't think much further past what she wanted.

"I'll keep paying the rent until the lease agreement is up," she said.

"What about water and other utilities?"

She hesitated. "But I won't be living there."

And yet the consumption would stay about the same, and Tanya knew it.

"I'll go start packing." Jack was annoyed and he didn't want to ruin their good mood by saying something he shouldn't.

Moving in with Bridget would be the perfect solution now Tanya had left her in a lurch, but he hated the thought she might feel forced into accepting it.

He wanted her to *want* to spend time with him as much as he wanted to spend time with her.

* * *

Bridget's cell rang as she was saying goodbye to Carly. She answered the phone as she waved her sister off.

"Bridge, it's me. I've got amazing news."

She smiled at Tanya's excited tone and unlocked the front door to the house. What was it this time? "Well tell me."

"Hal and I got married."

Her steps faltered and she sunk down on her bed. "You got married?" she repeated, hoping her ears were playing tricks on her.

"Yeah." She giggled. "There wasn't any point in waiting, or having a big fancy wedding. We'll have a party and invite everyone in a couple of weeks, but weddings are so hard to organize and we didn't want to wait."

Bridget shook her head. She knew Tanya was impulsive. This should not surprise her in the least.

But it did.

And it also worried her. How was she going to afford this place on her own? They were already living in a house that was more expensive than Bridget would have liked because Tanya had fallen in love with it and had insisted on taking this one. Her budget wouldn't stretch to paying all of the rent and all of the bills.

"Don't you need a marriage license?"

"I got one last week." She grinned. "I'll still pay my share of the rent," Tanya said. "I don't want to leave you out of pocket. But you'll be fine. You always manage."

Bridget tamped down her anger. This was her best friend's day – a time for celebration not accusations. Tanya had always been like this – spontaneous and short-sighted. "I'd better advertise for a roommate tomorrow," she said. "Congratulations, Mrs. Gibbs."

Tanya squealed and Bridget winced, holding the phone away from her ear. "Thanks so much! I knew you'd understand."

Bridget shook her head. "When are you going to move in?"

"I don't know. Probably not until next weekend. I need to pack my things."

Jack was going to love living with the love birds. Unless he had somewhere else to go. "What's Jack going to do?"

"He's going to move in with his mom."

Of course. That made sense.

Tanya gasped. "He could move in with you instead," she said. "He could have my room and you could split the bills."

"No." Bridget's response was instantaneous. She didn't need the complication.

"Why not? It makes perfect sense," Tanya said. "You're seeing each other and you need someone to help pay the bills."

Bridget frowned. Tanya was never this practical. Not unless it suited her own needs. And this did, perfectly. She shook her head. "No, Tanya. Don't even mention it to him. We've only *just* started dating."

"Come on, Bridge. It's a great solution."

She didn't care. "Promise me, Tanya. Promise you won't say anything to him."

Her friend gave a deep sigh. "All right. I'd

better go, we need to tell our parents. I'll talk to you later."

Bridget hung up and then wandered into the kitchen. She needed to crunch some numbers. When she was finished she sat back with a sigh. Even with Tanya paying half the rent, the rest of the bills were too much for her on her own. She was still paying off the loan on her truck and doing the diving lessons had wiped out most of her savings.

There was no way around it, she was going to have to find another roommate. She couldn't remember anyone at work mentioning they needed a place to stay. Opening up an internet browser, she searched for a forum where people were looking for a roommate. Though she didn't want to invite a stranger to live with her.

Carly would always give her a loan but Bridget wasn't going to ask her. Too many people took advantage of Carly that way. Just because she had money, didn't mean she should have to bail everyone out when they had problems. Bridget would solve this on her own.

Tanya's suggestion flicked through her thoughts. She sighed. Jack moving in made the most sense. And even worse, the idea appealed to her.

She enjoyed being with Jack, whether it was talking about safety at work, or chatting about the Texans' chance this year. She could picture sharing the house with him. But Bridget was far more practical than Tanya. She didn't leap into adventures without thinking them through. She considered everything.

But it *was* practical. Tanya was moving in with Hal, Jack was moving out, and Bridget needed a new roommate. It was win-win any way she looked at it.

But what would people at work say when they found out? And they would find out, she was sure of it. If she and Jack were sharing a house, it wouldn't be a weekend-only affair any more.

That made the whole deal too complicated.

* * *

Jack looked up at the knock on his bedroom door.

"Got a minute?" Hal asked, poking his head around.

"Sure." He was almost finished packing because he hadn't unpacked much of his stuff in the first place. Staying with Hal was always only meant to be a temporary thing. He could move in with his mother tomorrow.

"Tanya feels kind of bad about you moving

out and about leaving Bridget without a roommate."

Jack didn't care about himself, but he was annoyed about her lack of consideration for Bridget. "I'll be fine. Mom's already clearing a room."

"But that still leaves Bridget," Hal said. "We thought it would make sense for you to trade places with Tanya."

Jack grinned. "I'm not marrying you, bro."

Hal laughed. "No. You move in with Bridget. Take Tanya's room. You can share the bills."

The idea held a lot of appeal, but he was reluctant to suggest it. Bridget would feel trapped.

Had Tanya considered that? Had she considered her friend might not be ready to take the next step? Or had she only wanted to assuage her own guilt? Jack was pretty sure it was the latter.

"I'm not sure Bridget would go for it."

"You should ask her at least," Hal insisted. "She might be stressed about how she's going to pay the bills. It would give her another option to consider. She might not want to ask you herself."

So now he was going to be the bad guy if he didn't make the suggestion.

Feeling manipulated himself, he sighed. "I'll

talk to her tomorrow."

* * *

Jack waited until almost everyone had gone home the next day before he approached Bridget. The less people around to hear the argument, the better.

"Got a minute?" he asked as he walked into her office.

"Sure. I wanted to thank you for the work you did while I was away and over the last week. The project's still on schedule."

He'd made sure of it. The last thing he wanted was for Bridget to come back from her days off to find the project at the same stage as when she'd left. He wouldn't be able to convince her to take any more time off if that had happened.

"Don't mention it," he said. He shut the door behind him and she frowned. "I know you want to keep work and our private life separate," he began, "but I need to run something by you."

Bridget looked to the closed door and sighed. "All right."

"Now Hal and Tanya are married, I was planning to move to my mom's place, but Hal suggested you need a roommate."

Bridget's eyes narrowed to slits. "*Hal* said that, did he?"

184

Jack recognized barely concealed anger when he saw it. "He did. He said Tanya felt guilty about the whole situation and he thought this would be a good solution."

"When did he suggest this?"

"After Tanya told you about their wedding."

Bridget hissed. She got to her feet and paced to the window and back again. "I told her not to say anything. She promised me she wouldn't say anything to you."

"Tanya already made the suggestion to you?" he guessed.

She nodded once, her whole posture stiff and angry.

"You told her not to say anything so she got Hal to say it instead." That was pure manipulation. Surely Tanya would have realized how upset the suggestion made Bridget, but she'd had to appease her guilt.

"It is a practical solution ..." He held up a hand as Bridget whirled around, her eyes full of hurt. "I'm just saying. It doesn't mean it's the right solution." He'd known Bridget wasn't going to be enthusiastic with the idea, but she didn't need to be quite this upset.

She collapsed into her chair. "It's not you, it's –" She waved her hand around the office, "– this."

He understood, or at least tried to tell

himself he did. She'd lost her job, credibility, and boyfriend all at once. But she needed to move on. What would it take for Bridget to stop worrying about them being colleagues and embrace what they had together?

"It could be a temporary measure," he said. "I move in, help pay the bills until you find someone else to share with, or until the lease runs out. Then you can find somewhere smaller."

"What do we say to people at work?"

"We tell them about Tanya and Hal, explain their impulsiveness and say we're doing each other a favor. I'll take Tanya's bedroom."

"We stick to our weekend thing?"

He didn't want to have to keep a distance from Bridget if he was living with her, but right now he'd agree to anything to make her happy. "If that's what you want."

She looked away, but not before he saw the confusion in her eyes. Lionel had really done a number on her.

"Why don't you think about it?" Jack brushed a hand down her arm before opening the door and letting himself out, hoping she would let her practical side win.

* * *

When Jack left her office, Bridget slumped

down in her chair and put her head on the table. She could kill Tanya. If her best friend walked through the door she'd have to plead temporary insanity when accused of the murder.

She'd told her not to tell Jack, had made her promise. She hadn't considered Tanya would be sneaky enough to work around the promise by getting Hal to do her dirty work.

Now Bridget had to make a decision. Jack was waiting for it.

And hadn't he been so rational and pleasant about the whole thing?

He didn't understand what it was like – the looks, the comments, the insinuations. It would happen if he moved in with her, whether they were sleeping together or not. There were always people ready to spread rumors and believe the juiciest gossip. Was she willing to put up with that for the sake of practicality?

The worm of insecurity that she normally kept locked down, wriggled its way into her thoughts. Once the rumors started, how long would it be before someone began questioning her commitment and her projects?

The second she made a mistake, if not sooner.

But maybe people knew her better here than they had in her last job. Maybe people would ignore the rumors and give her the benefit of the doubt. She just didn't know.

Bridget visualized the spreadsheet she'd made up last night. She could manage on her own for the rest of the month. The bills had been paid and nothing was due. This morning she'd asked a few people at work if they knew of anyone looking for a place to stay. She'd explained about Tanya and received some pity but no one knew of anyone.

Bridget closed her eyes. What would it be like living with Jack, even if they did have separate rooms?

It would be difficult if they were continuing their weekend deal. She was honest enough to know having Jack around every evening would be like having chocolate within arm's reach that you weren't allowed to eat. The thought of having him there every night was appealing as hell.

Which was another reason to say no.

She sighed. She had to make a decision. It wasn't fair to get Jack to move to his mother's and then move again to her place if she agreed to his suggestion.

Jeremy stuck his head around the door. He opened his mouth to say something and then he frowned. "You all right, Bridge?"

He'd be the perfect person to ask. She took

a deep breath. "No, I've got a bit of a problem." She told him about Tanya moving out and how Jack needed to find somewhere else to stay. "I thought of suggesting Jack take Tanya's old room, but I'm worried about what people might say."

Jeremy pulled out the other chair and took a seat. "The Lionel affair."

"Yep. What do you think? Is it a bad idea?"

Jeremy rubbed his chin. "It's been a couple of years. Everyone here knows how capable and dedicated you are. It might not matter. Particularly when it's just a favor and you're not sleeping with Jack."

Bridget didn't address that comment. He didn't need to know. "You don't think people will talk?"

"People will always talk, Bridge. Not many people will listen to them though. You're tough enough to ignore the few."

Was she? She wasn't entirely sure.

"You'll be fine," said Jeremy. "Listen, I wanted to talk to you about next week's training session. I've got a thing I've got to go to. Could you run the training without me?"

Bridget hadn't run any of the emergency response training sessions by herself before, but she had all the qualifications now. "Sure. Is everything all right?"

"Yeah. I'll be at the team-building session on Tuesday."

She'd forgotten that was next week. Jack had arranged it while she was away. She might have to put in some extra time on the project this week to make up for those days.

"Thanks. I'll see you tomorrow." Jeremy left and Bridget swiveled her chair around to face her desk.

If Jeremy didn't think it would be a problem, and he knew how bad the Lionel affair had been, perhaps it would be all right. She'd consider it some more tonight, maybe give Carly a call. Carly always knew what to do.

Chapter 13

When Bridget got home, the house seemed quieter than usual. She walked through to the kitchen, and as she passed Tanya's room she stopped and stared.

It was empty.

Tanya had used her day off to move out.

In the bathroom they shared, Tanya had cleared out her shelves of beauty products, leaving just Bridget's things: a toothbrush, toothpaste, and can of mousse. In the living room, the cushions and paintings Tanya had bought were gone, as were the stools from the breakfast bar.

Her phone rang and seeing it was Tanya she answered it.

"Hey Bridget. I moved out today."

"So I see."

"Oh, are you home already? I didn't think

you would be. I just took a few things. Hal's place needs a woman's touch."

"I'm surprised you didn't take a sofa and half the kitchen table." They'd bought them together.

Tanya laughed. "Don't be silly. Hal's got those things. You can pay me my share of the sofa and table when you have it."

Bridget let out a long, slow breath. It was another expense.

"Is there anything else you need to take?" she asked.

"Not as yet. I didn't want to leave you without any dishes so if you tell me when you buy yourself a set, I'll come and pick mine up."

Of course. Tanya had brought a lot of things with her when they'd moved out together because she'd had a big twenty-first birthday party and people had given her things for her house. Which meant on top of finding someone to share the bills, Bridget would need to buy dishes and silverware. Anger and frustration simmered in her stomach.

"Why don't you give your key to Jack?" Bridget suggested. "He can give it to me in the morning." Right now she didn't want to see her friend.

"Oh, is he moving in? I knew you'd ask him once you stopped worrying." Tanya sounded delighted.

That was the last straw. Her anger bubbled out. "I haven't made a decision yet," she said. "But how dare you go behind my back that way? I trusted you, Tanya. You promised me you wouldn't say anything to him about it."

"I didn't. Hal did." Tanya defended herself.

"Don't pretend you didn't ask Hal to say something. I know you did. That's as bad as telling Jack yourself."

"Bridge, don't be mad," Tanya wheedled. "I know how much you care for him. It's the perfect solution."

"For you," Bridget said. "Did you even consider my feelings while you were convincing Hal to talk to Jack? Or did you only think about how much easier it would be for you?"

Tanya was silent.

"That's what I thought." Bridget hung up before she said something that would truly end their friendship. Right now she wasn't sure whether that might be the best for both of them.

With a sigh she placed her phone on the table. The living room was rather bare now without all of Tanya's finishing touches. Bridget had never bothered with knick-knacks because Tanya had enough for the both of them. But now the house was soulless.

She opened the kitchen cupboards and wrote down what she needed to buy. It would have to wait until her next pay day, and then she would have to choose the most important things.

Did Jack have any of this stuff?

She shook her head. She hadn't made a decision about that. With that in mind, she called Carly.

"What's wrong? We only spoke yesterday," Carly said as she answered.

Bridget sighed. "Tanya got married and moved out."

"What?" The disbelief in Carly's voice made Bridget laugh.

"She and Hal went away for the weekend to celebrate their engagement and eloped. She's moved her things in to Hal's place today and I've arrived home to a half-empty house."

"That was quick," Carly said.

"Yeah. She always charges ahead when she's got a plan," Bridget said.

"So what do you need from me?" Carly asked. "Do you need some furniture? I can transfer some money into your account."

"No," Bridget said firmly. "I'm after some advice is all."

"That doesn't come cheap," Carly joked. "Hit

me."

Bridget explained about the Jack solution. She didn't need to voice her concerns about the Lionel affair because Carly already knew all about that.

"Is he worth the potential heartache?"

The question made Bridget stop. Not once had she wondered whether Jack was worth it, whether what they had started between them might actually be really good. She wasn't certain she trusted her judgment about men.

She did enjoy spending time with him when she wasn't worrying about what other people might think. Even at work they had a good rapport.

"Birdy?"

Bridget smiled at the childhood nickname. "I'm still here. I don't know. I've been too busy worried about the work consequences to think about it." But perhaps that was the key to her decision.

"Mama once said Papa had three traits that made her know instantly that he was the one for her," Carly said.

"What were they?"

"He made her laugh, he had a kind heart, and he made her blood heat."

Bridget smiled. She had some memories from when her father was still alive, of the music and laughter that filled the house.

"He does make me laugh," she admitted.

"Is he kind?"

He'd given her those days off, he'd noticed her hard work, and she'd seen him working with others on site to help them. "Yes."

"So that leaves the third point, which I don't need to know about." Carly laughed.

There was no question he made her blood heat and her heart pound.

Should she allow herself to explore what they had between them? Should she ignore all of the rumors when they came her way? Was she strong enough for that?

"Thanks, Carly. You've given me some things to consider."

"Anytime, little sister."

Bridget hung up and sat on the sofa with her knees pulled up underneath her while she thought things through.

Finally she picked up her phone and entered a number. "Jack, can you come over so we can talk?"

* * *

Jack knocked on Bridget's door. There was a little bundle of nerves in his stomach that fidgeted while he waited. He wasn't sure what to make of Bridget's request to talk. She sounded so serious.

Was she going to break up with him?

He hoped not. He enjoyed spending time with her and the weekend deal was better than nothing.

The door opened and she stood there in a bright red dress which showed off her curves. Her toenails were painted red today. She looked sensational.

"Thanks for coming." She gestured him inside and took him into the living room.

As he walked past Tanya's room he noticed its emptiness. "Tanya doesn't waste much time when she decides on something."

"No, she doesn't." Her tone was aggravated. "Do you want a drink?"

Jack risked stepping closer, touching her hand. "I just want to know what's bothering you." He had a fairly good idea but he wanted it out in the open.

"Have a seat." She pointed to the sofa but remained standing after he sat. She hugged herself, opened her mouth to speak, and then closed it again.

"Bridge, just say what you need to say," he said gently, his nerves still swishing inside him.

"This has happened so fast," she said. "When we met and I didn't know you were my boss, I was so excited. I'd met someone who seemed like such a decent guy and he liked me back."

"I felt the same way." And every day the feeling grew.

Bridget perched herself on the arm of the sofa opposite. "I was so gutted when Anthony introduced you, when I realized you were my boss, that we couldn't explore what was between us."

Jack didn't speak, didn't want to interrupt her.

"But Tanya and Hal kept pushing us together and I couldn't ignore the attraction. The weekend deal was a reasonable alternative." She stood up again, pacing. "But the idea of you moving in ... that's on a whole different playing field. There will be speculation at work, gossip will spread, and whether it's fair or not it will affect me more than it will affect you."

He didn't deny it.

"So I need to know two things if you're going to move in here."

The first spark of hope fired in Jack's chest.

"That you will stick to whatever reason we give management about the move and you will defend it when necessary."

He nodded. "Of course."

She stopped pacing. "And I need to know whether you think what we have is worth it, that this isn't just a fling for you." She stared him straight in the eye, defiant with a hint of vulnerability.

Jack was across to her in two steps, his arms around her. "Bridget, you are most definitely worth it. I hate that this is an issue, that neither of us are in the position to find another job, that you've been treated so badly in the past. I want to explore what we have and see where it leads."

Her eyes were uncertain.

He kissed her gently. "Bridget, no matter what decision you make, I will respect it and stand up for you."

"We'd need to have separate bedrooms," she said. "I'm not sure whether we'll use them both, but in case we have visitors, or we need a break from each other, we need our separate spaces."

He nodded, the hope flaring into flames.

"It will be just until the lease runs out here. Then we can reassess and make a decision about where to go from there."

"Absolutely." He'd agree to anything.

Bridget let out a deep breath. "All right. Do you want to move in?"

"I thought you'd never ask." He hugged her

tightly and kissed her again. "I'll do right by you, Bridget. Don't worry."

She nodded, but he could tell she wasn't entirely convinced. He'd show her he meant it. Somehow.

* * *

Jack moved in the next day. He went to Anthony, gave him his change of address and explained about Tanya and Hal. He didn't mention he and Bridget were in a relationship and Anthony didn't ask. The situation between Tanya and Hal was clear enough. No one thought it was strange he didn't want to live with newlyweds.

He left work an hour early to retrieve some of his things out of storage: his bed, a chest of drawers, and his bedside tables. He hadn't had a chance to ask Bridget what else Tanya had taken, but he'd ask her tonight.

When Dionysus had said they were paying for the relocation, he hadn't bothered selling anything, he'd just packed up his whole house and shipped it to the US.

Hal met him at the storage company, helped him load up the trailer he'd hired, and then followed him back to Bridget's to unload.

"I appreciate you moving out," Hal said when they were finished and drinking a beer in the kitchen.

Jack shrugged. "I appreciate you letting me stay."

"Are you and Bridget ..." Hal searched for the word, "cool with the situation?"

"We'll make it work." He'd be much happier if Bridget had asked him because she wanted him to live with her, not because she had little other choice.

"Tanya feels really bad about it," said Hal.

Jack raised an eyebrow.

"Bridget was pretty unhappy with her."

"Then she should learn not to manipulate people."

Hal frowned and then sat back. "She just wants Bridget to have what she has."

Jack let it lie. "When's the party?" Jack's mother had been upset to learn her youngest son was married and had insisted they have a celebration.

"Soon. We're going over to Mom's tomorrow to arrange the details."

"What about Dad?"

"He was more concerned about whether we knew each other well enough." Hal got to his feet. "I'm going to head home. Tanya will be there soon and I want to have dinner ready for her."

Jack smiled and stood to walk his brother to

the door. He was pleased for him, even if the speed with which it had happened was unbelievable.

When Hal left, Jack looked around the house. Making dinner was a good idea. With that in mind he got to work.

* * *

Bridget's day had been full-on. The contractors had been on site to implement the crucial part of her project and when she went to check on them an hour after they arrived, she discovered they were waiting for a permit.

She'd had to do the permit herself, and then was told that production didn't have anyone spare to supervise them, so she'd had to do that as well. Afterward she'd written out the permits for the remaining days, double checked her work requests had been converted into work orders, and confirmed with the shift supervisor he would have people on the job for the next couple of days. Reluctantly he agreed.

By the time the contractors had finished what they could that day, Bridget was running so far behind it wasn't funny.

She took a few minutes to accompany them to the gatehouse and make sure there were no issues and then started on the work she should have been doing all day.

It was seven o'clock before she was able to leave. As she did, her phone rang.

"You're working late." Jack's voice held a hint of a reprimand.

That was something she hadn't considered when asking him to move in. He would know exactly how much she was working. "Yeah, I'm leaving now. Can I tell you about it when I get home?"

"Sure. Dinner will be ready."

She hung up, a warm glow in her stomach. It was nice having someone to go home to, someone who was cooking for her. She and Tanya had largely made their own meals because Bridget was never sure when she would finish work.

The drive was less busy than usual and it wasn't long before she was walking through her front door, the scent of garlic bread in the air. She dumped her purse on her bed and went through to the kitchen. Jack waved at her, his eyes wide, pointing to the phone he held in his hand.

"Mrs. Flanagan, I assure you, Bridget is fine. In fact she's just walked in the door." There was a pause. "Yes, I'll hand it over."

Bridget frowned. Jack looked panicked. She took the phone. "*Hola, Mamá. Qué pasa?*"

Her mother chuckled, low and mischievous. Her response was in rapid, strongly-accented English. "Who was that man? Why is he answering? Should I call the police?"

Bridget laughed. "Mama, what did you do?" On occasion her mother had fun playing the stereotypical hysterical Hispanic woman, and seeing how people reacted.

"How anxious is he?"

Jack was watching her, concern on his face. "Anxious enough. What did you say?"

"I merely asked if he was holding you hostage."

Bridget groaned, but couldn't prevent the smile from crossing her face.

"So who is he?"

"He's my new boss, Mama. Tanya got married on the weekend and moved out. Jack needed a place to stay, and I needed a roommate."

"Is that wise?"

Bridget sighed. "I don't know."

"You must bring him to the next family lunch," Carmen insisted. "I want to meet him, make sure he doesn't take advantage of you."

Bridget winced. There was no getting around it. If she didn't bring Jack to the lunch, her mother was likely to appear on her doorstep demanding an introduction. But when

Carmen realized Jack wasn't *just* Bridget's boss, she'd be worried.

"Sure, Mama. I'll see you then. Love you." She hung up.

Jack handed her a glass of wine. "I'm sorry. I didn't think before I answered the phone."

Bridget shook her head. "She was just playing with you. She didn't mean it."

Jack frowned. "So she wasn't about to call the police on me for holding you hostage?"

Bridget laughed. "No. She was having fun."

"That's a relief." He chuckled. "She sure had me fooled. I can't wait to meet her."

She took a sip of the wine. "She's invited you to the next family lunch." She waited for his reaction.

"That's great. Maybe you can tell me what I need to do to win her over."

Bridget smiled. She had thought the idea of meeting her mother would have freaked him out. "I've got a couple of tips."

Jack went over to the stove. "Hungry?"

"Starved," she said as she took a seat at the table. "Did you get your things in all right?"

"Yeah, it wasn't hard. I do have some more stuff I can take out of storage if we need it. I wasn't sure what Tanya had taken."

"Most of the kitchen things are hers and we went halves on the sofas and table. I might sell both, give her her share and then buy something cheap."

"Well I've got sofas and a kitchen table in storage. Why don't we check them out on the weekend and you can see if they suit?"

"Sounds good." She didn't have the extra cash to spend right now.

Jack dished up the fettuccine carbonara with garlic bread on the side, and topped up her wine glass.

"This looks fantastic." And smelled even better.

"It's my go-to dish," Jack admitted. "It's not hard to make." He took the seat next to her. "Are we allowed to talk about why you were so late?"

They had their no-work talk deal for the weekends, but this was mid-week. Their agreement was going to have to change, plus Bridget wanted to talk to someone about it.

"A few issues with the contractors," she said and explained what had happened.

Jack frowned. "Is it sorted for the rest of the week?"

She nodded. "I've spoken to the production superintendent. He's going to make sure it all goes smoothly."

"You didn't need to stay late though."

"We've got the team-building sessions next

week," she told him. "That eats into my time to complete this project."

He sighed. "You're right. I would have liked to postpone it until afterward but we need more cohesion as a team."

She agreed. "So what are we going to do?"

He grinned at her. "It's a secret, but it will be fun."

She finished off her pasta and sat back with a sigh. "You can cook in future."

"No way. I'm into equal opportunity. We'll share." He paused. "But there's one thing I want to ask."

"Go ahead."

"Are these plates Tanya's?" He grimaced at the pink floral decoration and purple border.

Bridget laughed. "They're hideous, aren't they?" she said. "Tanya's aunt gave them to her and we never got around to replacing them."

"Hallelujah. Do you want me to get my kitchen things out of storage on the weekend?"

"As long as they're not as bad as this."

"Definitely not."

She got to her feet and cleared the table, stacking the dishwasher. "I need a shower," she said. She hesitated for only a moment. "Do you want to join me?"

He grinned. "Absolutely."

* * *

Bridget was a little edgy for the next few days. Every time someone called her she flinched, and then relaxed when the question was about work.

She and Jack continued driving to work separately. Neither of them knew when they might have to work late, and while they had decided not to keep the fact they were living together a secret if someone asked, they didn't want to provoke the question by arriving in the same car.

Bridget was surprised at how easily they fell into a rhythm. Whoever arrived home first would cook dinner, and often they were both happy to sit on the couch and watch television in the evening. They had a couple of favorite shows in common, but if Jack was watching something she wasn't interested in, she'd curl up next to him and read a book. More often than not, they shared a bed and fell asleep, content and sated.

On the weekend, they loaded Tanya's remaining things into Bridget's truck and delivered them to Hal's place. Tanya was working so she wasn't there. They hadn't spoken since Bridget had hung up on her, but she'd have to call her soon. There was no point staying mad at her. Her heart had been in the right place.

Afterward, they drove to Jack's storage shed. It was packed full of boxes and furniture, but everything was clearly labeled.

"The kitchen things are over there." Jack pointed to a stack of boxes on the left side of the unit.

Over several trips they transported the sofas and kitchen table, as well as several boxes of kitchen items. Jack had good taste in furniture. The couches were gray and soft enough to really get comfortable, without being too soft to sit straight. The dining table was rectangular, made from pine with six matching chairs. His dishes were plain white. It would be wonderful to eat off something that didn't make her feel ill.

Bridget lifted the last box onto the kitchen cabinet and opened it. Face up in front of her was a framed photo. Jack grinned at the camera while a gorgeous brunette kissed his cheek.

Chapter 14

Bridget's chest constricted and she took a sharp intake of breath. The flash of jealousy was fast and unwanted. She stared at the woman. Who was she?

It was only natural that Jack had had other girlfriends before her. Just because he knew about Lionel, didn't mean he had to tell her about his ex-girlfriends.

Swallowing down her jealousy she held up the frame. "Where do you want to put this?"

He glanced over and his eyes widened. He took the frame from her. "I didn't realize I'd packed it," he said, putting it face down on the counter. "I dated Melanie for a couple of years in Australia. When I told her I was going back to Texas we broke up. She didn't want to move and I didn't want to stay. Neither of us loved the other enough to change where we were living."

The green-eyed monster quietened in Bridget's head. "Do you keep in touch?"

"We're friends on social media," he said. "We've both moved on." He turned her toward him. "Do you want me to get rid of the photo?"

She shook her head. She wasn't quite that insecure. Melanie was part of his past and their relationship had ended amicably. Not like her relationship with Lionel. She and Tanya had made a bonfire in the backyard to burn all her photos of Lionel and everything he'd given her over their relationship. It had been incredibly cathartic.

"Keep it," she said. "Though if you want to display it, it can go in your room."

He smiled. "I'll put it in my drawer. Melanie was a good friend, we had fun together. But I didn't feel for her what I feel for you."

His words sent a stream of delight through her, followed closely by concern. Why was this moving so fast?

He kissed her, drawing her closer, sending a lovely shimmering warmth through her body, and she pushed aside her concerns.

"Well, that's all right then," Bridget said when she got her breath back.

"Want to go to the movies tomorrow?" Jack asked, changing the subject and throwing her off balance.

"Sure. What do you want to see?"

"I don't care. We could go to dinner afterward."

It sounded like fun. The last time she'd gone to the movies, she'd chosen what had been advertised as a romance, but the hero had died. She and Tanya had gone through a pack of tissues and come out with red eyes and tear-stained cheeks.

"The latest Avengers movie is out," she told Jack. "We could see that."

He grinned. "I knew you were my perfect woman." He hugged her and turned back to unpacking his box.

Bridget stood there. She wasn't sure she wanted to be anyone's perfect woman. It sounded like too many expectations to her.

With a small sigh, she continued to unpack.

* * *

Jack made sure he kept their Sunday date as casual and fun as he could. Things were moving fast and he didn't want to overwhelm Bridget.

But it was difficult. There were so many things about her that made him smile, and he didn't want to hide his feelings. He enjoyed living with her, liked how they were both so easygoing, and was pleased she was beginning to relax at work again.

As they lined up to get their movie tickets he asked, "Do you want anything to eat?"

"Whoppers," she said instantly. "It's not a movie without Whoppers."

He ordered the candy and the tickets and then put a hand over hers when she tried to pay. "It's my treat today."

"All right. I'll pay next time."

Bridget picked up her box of Whoppers and they moved away from the concession stand.

"Hey, Jack. Fancy seeing you here."

They both turned at Ken's voice. Bridget dropped Jack's hand like it burned.

Ken noticed Bridget and his eyes widened. "Hi Bridget."

He glanced between the two of them and Jack wanted to swear. Just when the day was going so well.

"We're going to the new Avengers movie. What are you seeing?"

Ken indicated his two children next to him. "We're watching a cartoon."

There were questions and speculation in Ken's eyes, but Jack wasn't going to give him a chance to voice it. "We'd better get in there before it starts. See you tomorrow."

With a gentle nudge to Bridget, they walked

away.

She let out a deep breath. "Damn it."

He couldn't agree more.

"Should we have explained?" she asked.

"Explained what? That we're dating? It's none of his damn business." Jack couldn't help the annoyance in his voice.

"No, about the Tanya and Hal thing. Ken's a gossip."

"So we'll straighten out anything he says on Monday." They walked into the dim theater. "Try not to let it worry you."

She opened her mouth and then shook her head.

Finding seats, he took hold of her hand. It stiffened for a moment and then relaxed. "Forget about it and enjoy the movie."

She gave him a small smile and turned her attention to the screen.

She *would* worry about it. Perhaps he should duck out and find Ken to explain the situation. But then it might seem worse somehow. He didn't know how to solve this problem.

* * *

It took until the firefighting training on Monday afternoon for someone to ask Bridget about the rumor. She was surprised it had taken that long. The slightly guilty expression on Ken's face when she'd run into him in the hall earlier told her he'd already gossiped about what he seen at the cinema the day before. She'd been tense all day, waiting for the insinuations, and it was almost a relief when the first one came.

"Bridge, I hear you went to the movies with your boss," one of the operation technicians said.

She couldn't prevent the instinctive tensing of her muscles. But she'd debated so many options of how she was going to answer any questions and had decided to be mostly honest. "And did you hear we're living together too?"

The guy's eyes almost popped out of his head.

She laughed. "Relax. My best friend and roommate ran off and got married to Jack's brother. Jack had been living at his brother's house, I needed a new roommate, so we figured it made sense in the short term." She shrugged, trying for casual and unconcerned, but her shoulders were stiff. "We both wanted to watch the same movie, so we went together."

"Your best friend and his brother? Small world."

"Isn't it?" she agreed. "I'm lucky he's helping me out because I'd be in a real bind otherwise." She clapped her hands together. "Shall we get to work?"

The guys grabbed the equipment they needed for the fire-fighting exercise and Bridget breathed a sigh of relief. That's all she had to do. Admit to parts and make it seem like no big deal. Most wouldn't be interested enough after that to question it.

She hoped.

* * *

After training, she headed for the breakroom to get a drink.

"Bridge, I hear Tanya eloped," Trish said.

"Yeah. Tanya's always been the spontaneous type. She only met Hal when we went out dancing a few weeks ago."

"I wish I'd been able to go with you, but I had a family thing. So who is he? What's he like?" She filled her mug with hot water as she asked.

"Turns out he's Jack's brother."

"Wow. So is it true he's living with you?"

"Temporarily," Bridget said. "We were both left hanging when Hal and Tanya wanted to move in together."

"You're lucky you already knew him."

Bridget shrugged. "It's kind of awkward, him being my boss and all, but it was the practical solution."

"He's a bit of a hottie," Trish said. "It could be worse."

Bridget smiled. "I suppose so."

It wasn't so bad. There were no sly remarks, no insinuations – yet. She wasn't naive enough to think they wouldn't come, but she'd take it one day at a time.

* * *

"You almost ready?" Jack called as he put his overnight bag for the team-building session by the front door.

"Yes," Bridget said coming out of her bedroom. "You want to car-pool?"

Jack raised an eyebrow. "You sure?" It was bound to raise questions and she'd been so adamant about secrecy.

"Pretty much everyone knows you're living with me," she said.

Jack frowned. "You think Ken said something?"

She snorted. "I *know* Ken said something. Several people asked me about it yesterday. Didn't anyone ask you?"

"No." He hadn't noticed any speculative looks either, but he'd been in the manager's meeting all afternoon. Perhaps news was slow to travel to upper management. "Are you all right about it?" She was awfully calm.

She nodded. "I told them about Hal and Tanya. They think we're doing each other a favor. I didn't say anything about our relationship. Like you said, it's none of their business."

"Tell me if anyone gives you a hard time."

She kissed his cheek. "I can fight my own battles."

A little ray of hope shone through him. Maybe she was coming to realize it wasn't so bad, that people wouldn't question her motives. Then they could admit they were in a relationship.

Jack followed her into the kitchen where she was making up two travel mugs of coffee. "Is one of those for me?"

"If you behave."

He stood behind her and wrapped his arms around her waist. "What if I'm really bad?" he whispered in her ear.

She turned, pressing further against him. "I'm hoping you will be."

Her kiss was possessive, hot, and heat seared through him. He gripped her butt and lifted her up onto the kitchen cabinet, opening her legs so he could move between them. Her hands dug into his hair and pulled, sending lust straight to his groin. He had to have her. He unbuttoned her shorts, and slid down the zipper.

"Jack," she said, her voice breathless. "Do we have time for this?"

"Yes." He'd damn well make time for it. He tugged on the shorts and she lifted her butt so he could slide them off. He moved his hand between her legs as she fumbled with his pants. She was so wet. He teased her clitoris and slid a finger into her.

She groaned and flung her head back. "Jack, please."

He wanted to make her come. He wanted to drive her crazy until she was begging for him. Moving his fingers, he set up a rhythm. Her breath came in gasps as he used one hand to free himself of his pants. She clenched and he knew she was near. He captured her mouth and kissed her as her orgasm rocked through her.

"Jack!"

As her waves began to settle, he lifted her up and thrust into her.

"Yes."

She was so incredibly wet. He moved inside her, feeling her muscles begin to clench again. "Come for me again, sweetheart."

She opened her eyes, looked directly at him and grinned. "Make me."

His heart flipped over in his chest and he was lost. This beautiful, sensual woman was all he ever wanted, or would ever need. "Challenge accepted."

This time, when she came, he did too.

* * *

After Jack was sure his legs would support him, he turned away and cleaned up, pulling up his pants.

Bridget sat on the benchtop, her hands behind her, her head tilted back, looking incredibly sexy and satisfied.

"If you stay like that, we may never make the team-building session," he said.

"It'd be worth it."

His practical Bridget was considering playing hooky. He grinned, smugness squeezing his chest. He tucked his hand behind her head and drew it up so he could kiss her. "I'll finish the coffee."

She huffed out a breath. "All right." She shuffled off the cabinet, picked up her shorts, and walked out of the kitchen, her bottom peeking out from under her shirt.

He felt himself stir again and turned his attention to the coffee maker. As tempting as it was to stay here, he could hardly miss his own team-building session.

But what was he going to do about her? About the way he felt? He didn't want to hide their relationship anymore. He wanted to proclaim it to everyone who was willing to listen.

He loved Bridget Flanagan.

He fastened the lids on to the mugs and carried them down the hallway. Bridget came out of her room, now fully dressed.

He handed her one of the mugs. "Ready to go?"

She nodded, taking a sip. "Do you want to take my car or yours?"

"We'll take mine."

He grabbed both of their tote bags in one hand and carried them to the car while Bridget locked up. It was only a short distance to the location of their team-building session but the Houston traffic always ensured it took twice as long as expected. He'd forgotten that about the city, but luckily Bridget had convinced him to leave early. Though their dalliance had them a little behind schedule.

Not that he was complaining.

* * *

When they arrived at the complex, Jeremy and

Ken were the only ones who had got there before them.

Jack left Bridget with them while he went to find the facilitator and see to the sleeping arrangements. By the time he returned, the rest of his team had arrived. He introduced the facilitator.

"First task today is a scavenger hunt," the facilitator said. "Clues are made up of general knowledge as well as some questions specific to your roles. This isn't a race and you'll have to work together in order to solve many of the puzzles."

Jack hoped starting off with a little bit of fun would engender some team spirit and enthusiasm. Dirk and Trish, two of the safety advisors, looked like they'd missed their morning coffee.

He split the teams so there were people from each section in each one.

They worked methodically through the puzzles. Jack stepped back to see who would take the lead in his team. He wasn't surprised when Jeremy took charge. He let him go, occasionally offering suggestions and making sure everyone had their say.

Dirk wasn't at all interested in taking part. "This is a waste of time," he complained. "It's got nothing to do with safety."

Jack smiled at him. "This allows us to bond as a team. I think we could all do with a break from the plant and a bit of fun."

Dirk grunted. At the next puzzle he went off on his own, refusing to listen to the advice of the others in the team who thought the clue was somewhere else.

Jack made a mental note. Dirk was not a team player and wasn't willing to consider that others might be right. He'd have to talk to him about it when they got back to work.

The scavenger hunt finished at midday and they gathered in the dining room for lunch and to swap stories.

Jack took Bridget aside. "How did your team go?"

"Fantastically. Ken was a little too enthusiastic and I had to ask him to give some of the others a chance to offer suggestions, but when they realized they'd be listened to, they all took part."

"Great. We'll split into different groups this afternoon for the next exercise."

He joined one of the tables while Bridget joined the other. It was for the best they didn't fraternize too much now that people knew they were living together.

Chapter 15

Bridget took a seat between Jeremy and Ken.

"What was that about?" Ken asked, motioning to where she and Jack had been speaking.

"Jack wanted to know how our team went."

"Oh, I thought he might be asking what's for dinner tomorrow night." Ken laughed, thinking himself the funniest guy on the planet.

Bridget froze. Curious questions she could handle, but not an insinuation that she couldn't separate her home life from her work life. From there it was a slippery slope to being charged incompetent.

She glared at Ken. "This is a team-building exercise, and as Jack's second-in-command it's my duty to report how you went."

"Why would he ask Bridget about dinner?" one of the trainers asked.

Bridget closed her eyes briefly. Somebody wasn't up to date with the latest gossip.

"They're living together," Ken explained, with a grin.

Bridget suppressed her growing temper. If she let it go it might be misconstrued. She took a deep breath and explained the situation. Maybe she should have recorded it so she could just play it back without having to repeat herself over and over.

"That's gotta suck, living with your boss," the trainer said.

She shrugged. "Better than going broke."

"Isn't your sister, Carolina Flanagan?" Ken didn't know when to give up.

"Yes."

"Wouldn't she help you out?"

"Sure, but I'm not one to go running to my family at the first hint of trouble. I can sort it out on my own, which I did with Jack."

Jeremy nodded. "I can understand that. My parents would throw it in my face," he said. "This steak is pretty good."

Relieved with the change of topic, Bridget took a bite of hers. "It is."

She didn't know what Ken's game was. Was he just stirring and didn't know how much was too much, or had he seen them holding hands at the cinema and wanted to prove their relationship was something more?

Either way, Bridget didn't like it.

* * *

The next exercise after lunch was a brain teaser, followed by an obstacle course.

Ken was struggling to crawl under wire that was stretched at about knee height above the ground. Bridget crawled next to him, shouting words of encouragement. He was dripping sweat by the time he finished but he let out a holler and pumped his arms in the air. Bridget high-fived him and then checked the rest of the team were ready to move on.

She was missing someone. "Where's Dirk?"

"He went on ahead," Sally said. "Got tired of waiting."

Dirk was the only guy in the department who'd ever given her any real trouble when she was acting safety manager. He'd thought he deserved the job, not her. Bridget scowled and scanned the course ahead of them. Dirk was swinging on a bar over a pit of mud. The next obstacle after that was a huge wooden wall that she doubted he would make over on his own. They'd probably catch up with him there.

Sure enough, after they had all cleared the mud pit, Dirk was sitting with his back against the wall waiting for them.

"Need a hand?" Bridget asked him.

He grunted and nodded. She made him wait until last, because she was sure he would continue on ahead of them, but afterward Sally kept him with the group by chatting to him.

* * *

By the end of the day, almost everyone was in cheerful spirits and telling Jack how much they'd enjoyed themselves. Bridget was pleased with the way he'd been accepted in to the department. It didn't matter that he was in charge, that he was their boss, if the team didn't like him it would be that much more difficult to get things done.

She headed off to the room she was sharing with Sally and Trish.

"Bridget, can I have a word?" Jack called.

"Gotta go," she said to the other women. "I'll see you there."

Walking over to Jack she couldn't help admiring the way his shirt clung to his muscles.

"Was Dirk giving you trouble?" he asked.

She smiled. "No more than usual. He doesn't like taking instructions from me."

Jack frowned.

"He was pretty annoyed when I got the

acting safety manager job, instead of him," Bridget explained. "He's been at the plant longer and had more experience, but he's impatient and doesn't like working with people."

"So he has no idea how to lead."

She nodded. "It's his way or not at all."

"I'll speak with him when we get back to work," Jack said. "Now what was Ken talking about over lunch? I only caught a bit."

Bridget sighed. "He was trying to be funny, making jokes about us living together. I'm not sure it was meant maliciously."

"Are you all right?" His voice was low and he reached out and touched her arm.

Bridget stepped away and checked to make sure no one had seen. "I'm fine, Jack. I'll handle him."

He was quiet a moment before he said, "OK."

She gave him a half smile and headed for her room, wishing their relationship didn't have to be so complicated.

* * *

Inside, Trish lounged on one of the beds, and in the adjoining bathroom the shower was running.

Bridget took out the clothes she wanted to

wear to dinner and sat down on her bed. "Today was fun," she said, hoping for some casual conversation.

"Yeah. We should do things like this more often," Trish agreed. "It's nice to get away from the plant every now and then."

"Have you got many suggestions for our planning session tomorrow?"

"A few. It always comes down to money."

It did.

"Bridget, can I ask you something personal?" Trish asked.

Bridget tensed and forced herself to relax. "Sure. As long as I don't have to answer it," she joked.

"It's about you and Jack. You mentioned living with him was just a convenience thing. I wanted to check that was true. I didn't want to step on your toes if I ask Jack out for a drink."

Bridget was glad she was sitting down. Her face heated and her skin prickled, as she tried to figure out a response. She had not expected that *at* all. "I can't say I'd recommend getting involved with your boss." She was such a hypocrite.

"I met Lionel once at a safety conference. He seemed like a self-absorbed jerk to me."

Bridget wasn't surprised Trish knew about the Lionel affair, or about her assessment of

Lionel. She didn't know why she hadn't seen Lionel for the jerk he was.

"So you're fine with me asking Jack out?"

No, of course she wasn't, but she couldn't say that. "You can ask."

"Great. He's damn fine when he's out of his high-vis gear."

Bridget didn't comment.

Sally came out of the bathroom, her hair damp, and wearing a green and white checked summer dress. "I feel so much better."

"My turn," Trish said and grabbed her clothes, disappearing into the bathroom.

Sally waited until the door closed and then said, "So, how awkward is it living with your boss?"

Bridget reminded herself it was natural for their living arrangements to be a hot topic of conversation. She hoped by next week there'd be some other piece of gossip worth talking about.

"It's OK. We tend to stick to our own space." She had to remember to tell Jack about that.

"I like him. I can't imagine he'd be difficult to live with."

"He's pretty easygoing." Bridget wished Trish would get out of the shower so she could escape.

Sally put the clothes she had been wearing in her tote bag. "I can't believe Tanya just moved out. It's so inconsiderate. You must have been freaking out."

"A bit. I guess love affects your judgment."

"I guess so." Sally turned around. "What's planned for tonight?"

"I'm not sure. Jack arranged it all."

"I hope it's not karaoke or something."

"Me too."

Finally Trish came out of the bathroom and Bridget was able to escape. She hated lying to everyone, hated telling half-truths, but what else could she do?

* * *

Jack hadn't arranged any activities for after dinner. He wanted to see what everyone would do – who was happy to spend an evening chatting with their colleagues and who wanted to be left alone.

On purpose he positioned himself on the opposite side of the room from Bridget. The temptation to touch her was too much in this casual environment, and he didn't want to make matters worse by forgetting they were only supposed to be colleagues here.

He talked to Jeremy about the emergency response team, discussed the upcoming competition that allowed them to test their skills against other teams in the area, and listened to Jeremy's plans to improve them even further. Jeremy reminded him a little of Bridget in his passion for his job. Jack suspected he could let Jeremy have free rein and not have to worry about what he was going to do.

When Jeremy left to get another drink, Trish sat down next to him. "Great day today," she said. "Thanks for thinking of it."

"No problem. It's been beneficial to us all."

Someone turned on the radio and music piped into the room, not too loud for them to have to shout. Jack tapped his foot in time.

"Great song, isn't it?" Trish said.

"Yeah."

"I think Adahy Woods is playing at Whitewash on the weekend. Do you want to go?"

It took Jack a second to register what Trish had said, and then a second more to realize she was asking him out on a date.

Hell.

"Ah, no ... thanks for the offer though."

Trish pouted, but didn't seem too put out. "Don't date team members?"

His gaze found Bridget without meaning to. "Something like that." He looked back to Trish and her expression had turned knowing.

Shit! He had to be more careful.

"Lucky girl," Trish said as she stood. "But be careful, she's been burned before."

Before Jack could figure out how to deny it, Trish was over talking with Sally. He had no idea whether Trish was a gossip, whether she was spreading rumors right now as he watched her. Bridget wasn't going to be happy, but a small part of him hoped it would all come out, that they'd stop having to keep it a secret. Bridget would soon discover she wasn't treated any differently because she was in a relationship with him.

He sighed. She needed more time and he had to respect that. Scanning the room, Jack saw Dirk sitting by himself reading a book. He needed to do something to get him involved. Dirk was part of the team and he had to start acting like it. Jack wasn't sure how he'd get through to him, but he had to try.

* * *

The next morning, fueled by coffee and croissants, Jack stood in front of his team. They were in a large meeting room that had a wall of windows on one side, overlooking the garden. Jack planned to move things outdoors after lunch for a change of scenery.

"It's budget time and we need to decide what projects to include for next year," he began. "You all have ideas you want to see implemented, so we need to work out which are the most beneficial to the plant. I also want to hear your suggestions for improvements that won't necessarily cost a lot of money. This is going to be part business plan and part budget plan."

Around him people nodded. He was pleased to see most had brought notes with them. "We'll start with the environmental section." Jack had neglected them a bit since he'd arrived because safety had been such a high priority.

"Do the rest of us have to stay and listen to this?" Dirk complained. "What they do doesn't affect us."

Jack kept his expression pleasant. "Of course it does. Environmental projects might have a safety effect and vice versa. Plus the more people thinking about a problem, the more options we can discuss."

Dirk scowled, crossing his arms and leaning back in his chair.

Jack was going to have to take Dirk aside and talk to him after this. He wasn't being part of the team. He gestured for Sally to begin the discussion.

* * *

By the time they broke for lunch, Jack's head was spinning and he figured everyone needed a break. He was grateful Jeremy had offered to take notes, because he wouldn't have been able to keep up himself. His team was not short of ideas and most of them were good ones, but there was one common theme that ran through the session. They'd been asking for the same things for years and kept getting knocked back because of budget considerations. Jack asked them to review their projects and check if they could be broken down into smaller stages. If they only had to ask for money for one stage at a time, they might have a better chance of approval.

The problem was, Jack's department wasn't directly involved in making money for the business. They were a support team and while if something in safety or the environment went wrong it could cost the company millions, no one outside of the department thought there was a big risk. He was going to have to get his figures together, find examples of where things had gone wrong and use all of his powers of persuasion when it came time for the budget meeting with management.

They ate lunch outside on the veranda, everyone more than pleased to get out of the room. In the middle of the garden there were two picnic tables, shaded by a couple of trees. Jack decided moving out there might work to keep the ideas fresh and people awake.

They carried their things to the tables and finished their discussions about training. They were considering an online training program to allow shift workers to keep their skills up to date without having to sit down with a trainer, which would also enable them to do their training on night shift when the workload was lighter.

"It might be modular," Bridget said. "We could buy one module, whichever would have the best return on investment, and then get the other modules in future years."

"I'll look into it," one of the trainers said.

Jack was impressed by the way Bridget had taken part in the session so far. She had so many ideas and sensible suggestions to improve the plant. He was looking forward to hearing what she had to say about safety.

He wrapped up the training discussions and turned to his safety staff. "I've been a little alarmed at the level of safety around the plant," he began. "We're in real danger of someone getting badly injured. The project for encasing the relief valves in the crude unit is well underway and I appreciate all the support you've given Bridget."

"The auditors don't know what they're talking about," Dirk grumbled. "They think they know about safety but they don't know shit about what will work on this plant."

Jack couldn't let Dirk's comment go unanswered. "You don't think the issues they highlighted in their audit report are a problem?"

"They've always been there and nothing's happened."

This was the kind of attitude Jack was trying to change on the rest of the site, he didn't need someone in his own department with it as well. "We've been lucky so far. Bridget developed the action plan from the department's suggestions, and its implementation will go a long way in improving the safety on the plant."

Dirk grunted. "You're just saying that because you want to get in her pants," he mumbled.

Bridget gasped and then it was so silent Jack could have heard a pin drop. His staff exchanged glances, waiting for his reaction.

Dirk crossed his arms. "I'd be careful, Jack. She almost killed three guys at her previous job because she was sleeping with her boss."

Chapter 16

Jack clenched his fists. Across from him Bridget flinched, her mouth dropping open, and then fire appeared in her eyes, telling him she was about to explode.

"That's enough," he said, struggling to maintain a calm tone. "By suggesting the project is a waste of time, you're not only insulting Bridget's and my integrity, but also the rest of the team's. Go inside, and I'll talk with you in a minute." He wasn't going to dignify Dirk's disgusting comment with a reply.

Dirk glared at him and then looked around the table. He swore and stomped inside.

Jack let out a breath and slowly unclenched his fist. "I want to set a few things straight," he said, making eye contact with each of his team members. "I moved in with Bridget because her roommate married my brother. I needed to find new accommodation and she needed someone to help pay the rent. It was a practical solution." He paused, glancing at Bridget who was watching him carefully, waiting for what he was going to say next. "If any of you have concerns this arrangement will affect the way either Bridget or I behave at work, you need to raise it with HR or with me." His team members had expressions of shock and interest. All of them met his gaze. "But if anyone insults either Bridget or myself the way Dirk just did, there will be disciplinary action. Am I clear?"

Everyone nodded.

"We'll take a fifteen-minute break." Jack waited until they all stood and moved away.

Bridget made a beeline for her room and both Sally and Trish followed her. He didn't have time to go after her himself like he wanted. He needed to control his anger and deal with Dirk. He really did not need this now. Dirk's reaction was exactly the thing Bridget had feared. Would she use this as a reason to break up?

Taking another breath, he went to face the jackass.

* * *

Bridget moved as fast as she could without

running, heading to the privacy of her room. Part of her wanted to rage and part of her wanted to sob. She'd never got along with Dirk, but for him to say those things in front of the whole department was just plain wrong.

She burst into the room and slammed the door behind her. She paced, clenching and unclenching her hands. She really wanted to hit something.

Preferably Dirk.

Was he the only one thinking those things, or were the others too polite to say it out loud? Was she ever going to escape the stigma of the Lionel affair? Did everyone secretly believe she was to blame?

The door behind her opened and she whirled around to find Sally and Trish.

Trish gave her a sympathetic smile. "How are you holding up?"

Bridget took a couple of breaths, trying to calm herself enough so she could speak. She focused on business first. "Does everyone believe my project is a waste of time?"

"Of course not," Sally said. "Dirk's a bitter man who can't handle being told no."

"It's a nightmare working with him," Trish added. "I hope Jack can get rid of him."

Feeling a little better, Bridget stopped pacing. She turned to Trish. "We discussed the corrective actions as a group. You all had suggestions of your own." She was sure of it.

"Yeah, and you listened to them. That action list was developed by the whole department."

The relief was soothing. Dirk had made her doubt herself. Bridget took a breath. "What about what he said about me and Jack?"

Sally and Trish exchanged a look.

"There's always going to be talk," Sally said. "You know what people are like."

"And it's no one's business," Trish added. "You're both adults. I'm pretty sure you can keep work and your private life separate."

Bridget stared at Trish. "You think there's something going on between us?" Had they been so obvious or was it only because of the house situation?

"I saw the way Jack looked at you when I asked him out." Trish shrugged. "I figured even if you're not involved, he's interested."

Damn him! Bridget sat down on the bed and put her hands in her head.

"Hey, Bridge, there are worse things than having a single, sexy man interested in you."

"He's my boss."

"Once bitten, twice shy," Sally said to Trish. "You know what happened."

Everyone knew. That was part of the problem.

"Bridge, we know how dedicated you are," said Trish. "We've heard you take on Kevin. There's no way you'll let anyone come before the safety of the plant."

Trish's confidence in her was comforting.

"Why don't we go out there before Jack gets back?" Sally suggested. "You can ask the others what they think. They'll tell it to you straight."

She was right. If anyone disagreed with her they'd let her know. Bridget got to her feet. "Let's go."

Outside the others were hovering in a group talking. Jack and Dirk hadn't returned. When Bridget approached, they stopped talking and faced her.

"All right," she said, taking a deep breath. "Who agrees with Dirk? If any of you think I'm incompetent or that living with the boss will skew my judgment, you need to speak up."

Jeremy was the first to respond. "We know Dirk was talking bullshit, Bridge."

She smiled at him. He'd always been on her side.

Ken stepped forward. "I was just messing around earlier. I didn't mean it."

"You've always got our backs," one of the trainers said.

"I've never seen anyone stand up to Kevin

the way you do," Sally said. "We've been able to achieve a lot for the environment this year because of you."

Bridget breathed out a sigh of relief. "If you have any concerns, you'll let me know?"

They nodded. She glanced at her watch and then at the door where Dirk and Jack had gone. She wasn't sure how long they would be.

"Shall we get back to work?"

* * *

Jack took a moment outside of the room to calm himself further before walking in. Dirk was sitting slumped in one of the chairs.

He looked up as Jack walked in and scowled. "It's not like I didn't say what everyone's thinking."

"Your comment was completely unacceptable and Bridget would be perfectly within her rights to raise a harassment case against you."

Dirk paled.

"What's your problem with Bridget?"

"She's got everyone fooled. The incident at her last job proved her incompetence but Jeremy was so blinded by her that he convinced Dionysus to hire her. To give her the job that was meant to be mine." His words were bitter. "Then she besotted your predecessor so much she was asked to be acting manager when he got sick."

"So you think you deserve to have my job?"

Dirk nodded, glaring at him.

Jack kept his tone even. "In the five weeks I've been here, I haven't seen a single example of your ability to lead," he said. "During the exercises yesterday you didn't listen to others, you went off on your own and seemed incapable of working as part of a team. I would suggest that's more likely the reason you didn't get the job you wanted."

Dirk flung his chair back and got to his feet. "Nobody's going to listen to me anyway. Not if it means disagreeing with you or Bridget. I could go to HR."

"That's a good idea," Jack said. "I'll arrange a meeting with them tomorrow. I'll send you the details." He stood. "It's time for us to rejoin the others."

He took immense satisfaction at the shock that crossed Dirk's face as he walked out of the room.

* * *

The rest of the afternoon went without a hitch. Jack was pleased that Bridget seemed OK. Whatever had happened while he was talking to Dirk had calmed her, and she took part in as much of the discussion as she had before Dirk's interruption.

Dirk returned to the group and sat silently, scowling the whole time. There wasn't much Jack could do about that but he would document exactly what had happened when he got home and present it to HR in the morning. He did not want someone so toxic in his department and this was the first step in getting rid of him.

When they were finished, Jack promised his team he'd collate all their ideas and they'd meet again next week to whittle the projects down to something he could present to the management team. While the team collected their things and said their goodbyes, he packed up. Bridget was talking with Trish and Sally and they both hugged her before they left.

Jack waited until everyone was gone before he approached Bridget. "How are you feeling?"

She ran a hand through her hair. "Exhausted. I want to go home and soak in the bath."

He shut the image out of his mind. She did look tired. As they walked to his car he asked, "What happened while I was speaking with

Dirk?"

"Sally and Trish talked to me. Trish is convinced we're involved, but she doesn't care. Neither does Sally." Bridget shrugged. "I spoke with the rest of the team, asked them straight out if they had a problem and they don't. I think it's just Dirk."

"I'm sure it is."

"Did he tell you what his problem was?"

Jack hesitated. "I can't tell you that, Bridge. But I can tell you I made it clear his behavior was unacceptable."

"Thanks. I appreciate you sending him away. I was going to blow my top."

He smiled. "I know." Jack unlocked the car and put their bags in the trunk, before sliding into the driver's seat. Pulling into the traffic, he said, "You came up with some great ideas today, both for safety and the other sections."

"I've been involved in everything for the last six months," she reminded him.

"The team respects you a lot."

"I listen is all," she said. "Sometimes all they need is someone to listen to them."

Jack nodded. They all had limitations as to what they could do, whether they were time, money, or approvals, but to have someone listen to your concerns helped.

"Were you pleased with the outcomes?"

Bridget asked.

"Yes. I got to know the team better and we've got a lot of great ideas to work toward."

They were silent for the rest of the drive. Jack carried their bags inside and once the door was closed, he gathered Bridget into his arms.

"I've been wanting to do this for hours." He held her for a long moment, needing to touch her, to offer her comfort.

She hugged him back. "What was that for?"

"For not being able to go to you after Dirk said those things."

"You did the right thing," she said. "Work has to come first."

Bridget was right. She came first in everything to him, but while he was her boss, he had to be the manager and not the lover. Perhaps they couldn't work on the same team and be involved. Perhaps it was a distraction for them both.

But he wasn't willing to let her go.

She stepped back. "I'm going to take a bath. I need to soak my muscles and relax. Some of the exercise we did yesterday is creeping up on me."

He wanted to ask if the bath was big enough for two, but he suspected she needed some space. "Do you want anything to eat?"

She shook her head. "I'll make some toast when I get out if I'm hungry. We ate a lot today."

He let her go. She wouldn't like it if he tried to crowd her, she wasn't one who needed pampering or molly-coddling.

No matter how much he wanted to.

* * *

Jack's cell rang as he sat down on the couch with a beer and a sandwich.

"Jackson, did your move go well?" his mother asked.

"Hi Mom. Yeah, I got a few of my things out of storage because Tanya took her stuff to Hal's."

"How are things with your new roommate? Is it working out all right?"

Jack hadn't told his mother about his relationship with Bridget. He hadn't wanted to jinx it. "Fine, Mom. Bridget's easy to live with."

"It was so good of you to move in with her to help her out."

"It came as a surprise to both of us when Hal and Tanya got married so suddenly."

His mother murmured in agreement. "That's what I'm calling about. I haven't received your RSVP for the party."

"What party?"

Claire Boston

"Hal and Tanya's of course. This Saturday. Don't tell me your brother didn't pass on your invitation."

"I haven't seen Hal since I moved out." Jack wasn't surprised. Hal had been so caught up in Tanya that he'd barely seen him even when they were living together.

She tutted. "Well, you must come. It's six o'clock at my house. Bring a date if you like."

"How many have been invited?" Bridget hadn't mentioned anything about the party. Didn't she know about it either?

"About a hundred. Tanya sure does know some people." It was said in a half affectionate, half exasperated tone.

"Do you need any help setting up?"

"That would be wonderful. Your father is going to come over a little early to help with tables and such. Perhaps you could come at three and help him. I've hired caterers but I need to decorate the garden."

"Sure thing. I'll be there."

He'd talk to Bridget when she got out of the bath. He didn't want to interrupt her or upset her. She'd been angry with Tanya, and they'd had words, but surely Tanya would invite her best friend to the party? Though with what little he knew about his new sister-in-law, he wasn't so certain.

Break the Rules

* * *

The water was almost cold when Bridget got out of the tub. She'd had a long soak while she'd reflected on the day. The team-building session had been well worth it. Getting away from the plant and having some time to bond had been good all around. And the fact they'd been able to brainstorm and plan their projects for next year uninterrupted was also a boon. The only blip in the entire two days had been Dirk's outburst. All her doubts and insecurities had flooded in, though Sally and Trish had done a lot to relieve her anxiety. After she'd spoken with the team she'd settled for a 'screw Dirk' attitude. The most important thing was to have the respect of her department. As long as they believed she was capable and competent, it didn't matter what others said.

Or at least that's what she tried to convince herself. That nasty little worm kept squirming and whispering doubts in her mind. Could she survive another Lionel affair? Could she ignore the insinuations? Would her career be over if there was another incident? She squeezed her eyes shut and ignored the voice.

After drying herself, Bridget slipped on a pair of pajamas and padded barefoot out to the kitchen. Jack was sitting on the couch watching television.

"I'm making some toast," she said. "Do you want some?"

"No, thanks. I had a sandwich. Did you have a nice soak?"

"Yeah. It was just what I needed." She made peanut butter and jelly toast and brought it with her to the couch, where she sat down next to Jack. "What are you watching?"

"It's some renovation show," Jack said, reaching for the remote and turning it off.

"You don't need to turn it off on my account."

"It wasn't very interesting," he said. "My mom called earlier."

"How is she?"

Jack hadn't told his parents about their relationship and Bridget was fine with that. They hadn't really defined it properly themselves.

"Great. She wanted to know if I was going to Hal and Tanya's wedding party on Saturday."

She stopped chewing and swallowed. "This Saturday?"

He nodded. She hadn't spoken to Tanya since she'd hung up on her, but Bridget had figured it was Tanya being Tanya – too caught up in her newlywed excitement to call.

"I take it you didn't know about it either."

She shook her head and acknowledged the stab of hurt from being so easily cast aside.

Jack took her hand. "Do you want to be my date?"

Did she want to turn up when Tanya hadn't invited her? Hell no. She obviously wasn't wanted there. "No, I don't think so."

She caught the flicker of hurt as he withdrew his hand and she hurried to clarify. "I would love to be your date, but I'm not going to my best friend's party when she didn't invite me. Tanya might cause a scene." She shrugged. "I'd hate to ruin her day."

"It's probably a mistake," Jack said. "Hal was supposed to give me my invite but I haven't seen him. Mom was the one who invited me."

It may easily have been an oversight for Hal, but Bridget knew it wasn't for Tanya. Bridget had always been the first person Tanya turned to to share exciting news, or to help plan things. Should she make the first move toward reconciliation? Did she want to stay friends with Tanya?

Yeah, she did. As impulsive as Tanya could be at times, Bridget still loved her. Tanya had brought sparkle into Bridget's life when she'd needed it and had been doing so ever since. "I'll give her a call." She picked up her phone and dialed. It went straight to voice mail. "Hey, Tanya. It's Bridget. I'm calling to find out how wedded bliss is. Talk to you later." She kept it light and friendly. The ball was in Tanya's court now.

She finished her toast and placed the plate on the coffee table. The urge to cuddle up to Jack was strong so she gave into it, smiling as his arm came around her.

"I'm sure she'll call you soon," Jack said.

"Mmm." If Tanya didn't call by Friday, she'd drop by. It didn't matter whether she was invited to the party, what mattered was she made an effort to get their friendship back together. And if it didn't work, there wasn't a lot she could do about it. Her heart was heavy at the thought.

Her phone rang. Tanya. She grinned.

"Oh, Bridget. I'm so glad you called. I thought you were going to stay mad at me forever," Tanya gushed.

Bridget blinked. So it was her fault they hadn't spoken. She shook her head, bemused. "Of course not."

"Great! You have to come to our wedding party on Saturday. You and Jack, of course. I need you to be my maid of honor."

"Tanya, you're already married. You don't need a maid of honor."

"I know, but it's kind of going to be like a wedding. There are going to be flowers and cake and everyone's going to be there. Oh and speeches of course. You have to give a speech."

Sometimes it was hard to keep up with her best friend. "You want me to give a speech?"

"Yes. We're doing hair and makeup at three and you need to wear something fancy, a cocktail dress or something."

She had nothing in her wardrobe that was suitable and now she had all of two days to find something. She sighed. "Anything else?"

"Lots. You and Jack should come over for dinner tomorrow night. Are you free?"

She checked with Jack. "Tomorrow's fine."

"Great. See you at six."

Bridget hung up and stared at her phone.

"Sounds like Tanya's being Tanya," said Jack.

She nodded. "Yeah, she was waiting for me to call."

"Well it's good you did then. That means you can be my date."

She smiled and snuggled back into him. "All right. I'd like that."

Chapter 17

Jack arrived at his mother's place at the designated time on Saturday afternoon.

"Jackson! Thanks for coming to help." His mother hugged him.

"Any time, Mom."

He followed her out to her large backyard where a white tent had already been set up at the rear. Its sides were open to let the small amount of breeze pass through. His father was already at work, setting up tables underneath. Jack was pleased his parents had remained civil with each other after they split up. It made things so much easier, and allowed family celebrations like this to happen without potential issues.

"You help your father set up the tables and chairs and I'll continue hanging the lanterns."

"Where's Hal?" He knew Tanya was having

her hair done with Bridget but his brother should be helping out.

"He'll be here shortly, I'm sure."

Jack wasn't as certain, knowing how bad Hal was at keeping time, but he didn't say anything. He just went to help his father.

* * *

When they had set up the tables and chairs, they stopped for a drink. Hal hadn't turned up yet.

"So have you met Tanya?" Jack asked his father.

"Sure. Hal brought her over when they got engaged. She seems like a nice girl, though how they'll organize anything between them I have no idea. They're both as bad as each other." Eric's smile was affectionate, but his eyes were worried.

"They'll manage." Though they'd rushed into marriage, Jack thought their enthusiasm would make anything work.

"You're living with Tanya's roommate?"

Jack nodded. "Bridget. You'll meet her tonight."

"That was real nice of you, but if it doesn't work out, you've always got a place to stay with me."

Jack clapped a hand over his father's back.

"Thanks, Dad. Bridget and I are just fine."

Hal arrived then, coming out through the bi-fold doors and looking around at what had been done. He spotted Jack and his father. "If you two have stopped slacking off, there's work to do."

Jack swapped a grin with his father. "Tell us what you need."

* * *

Bridget wasn't very good at sitting still and doing nothing, so being at the hairdressers having her hair and makeup done was her idea of torture, but at least she was off her feet.

Tanya had picked her up at nine so they could find her something suitable to wear. Tanya's younger sister had come along, and between the two of them Bridget was dragged into what felt like every dress shop in Houston.

Finally they had all agreed on a deep red satin dress with spaghetti straps that showed a hint of cleavage and a split that revealed a lot of leg. Tanya had insisted she buy a pair of matching heels which were far higher than Bridget was comfortable with. She kept reminding herself this was Tanya's day, and if it truly had been a wedding, then she wouldn't have had a choice in what she wore at all.

They'd eaten a late lunch at Eat, Drink, Read and then walked down the street to the salon where Tanya worked to get their hair and makeup done. Tanya's sister went into the chair first and Bridget made small talk with Tanya. She was already exhausted and the evening hadn't even begun.

"We should straighten your hair," Tanya said.

Bridget groaned. She hadn't straightened her hair since the time in high school when it had gone so badly she'd had to have it cut into a short bob to remove all the burnt bits. It had been Tanya's idea then as well.

"Can't we just put it up?"

Tanya laughed. "With all your curls we'd have more pins than hair."

The hairdresser nodded. "It will have to be straightened if we're going to do anything with it."

Bridget sighed. At least the chances of her hair burning should be less with a professional.

When it was Bridget's turn she did her best not to fidget. "Who's coming tonight?" she asked Tanya, hoping some conversation would distract her.

"Oh, everyone. All Hal's family and my family, of course. Some friends from work, and

Sally and Trish of course."

Bridget's stomach clenched. "From my work?"

"Yep." Tanya nodded.

Bridget huffed out a breath. Sally and Trish might not care about their relationship but still her gut clenched. After the fuss Dirk made, she was reluctant to confirm Trish's suspicions. Was she ready for further gossip?

Tanya was watching her. "What's wrong?"

"No one at work knows about me and Jack. They think he moved in to help me out."

"Are you still worried about that? No one cares, Bridge. You can date whoever you want."

For Tanya the whole Lionel affair was so far in the past it was ancient history, but for Bridget it was still too raw. She couldn't forget everything she'd gone through. And she couldn't forget Dirk's accusations during the week.

"I need to call Jack."

"Not until your hair is finished," Tanya ordered.

Bridget waited impatiently for her hair to be straightened and some kind of product to be added and then got to her feet.

"Don't go outside. The less humidity you expose your hair to, the better."

It was getting near closing time and the other side of the salon was empty so Bridget crossed the floor and called Jack.

"How are things?" he said as he answered.

"Hair's done, makeup is next," she said quickly. "Listen, Jack, Tanya's invited Sally and Trish tonight."

"From work?"

"Yeah. I can't be your date."

"Why not?"

She hissed out a breath. "Because they will be there."

"There's nothing to say roommates can't accompany each other to the same event, is there?" He was being rational.

She didn't like it. "But I'm meeting you there."

"And I'm taking you home." His tone brought all kinds of ideas springing to Bridget's mind.

She pushed them away. "They're work colleagues."

"And you said Trish thinks there's something between us anyway. They're not going to care."

"They could mention it to someone."

"They could say something whether we dance together or not. Bridget, I can't just turn off the way I feel about you, and that's going to be reflected in the way I look at you, and the way I behave around you. At work I'm doing my best to remain professional, but this isn't work. This is family, a celebration between your best friend and my brother. Don't deny me a dance because you're afraid of what some people might think."

There was a plea in his voice. She wanted to say yes, she wanted to dance with him as well. But there was still the little voice in her head that whispered a warning.

"Can we play it by ear?"

He was silent for a moment. "Sure."

"Bridget, you need to have your makeup done," Tanya called.

"I've got to go. I'll see you tonight." She hung up, feeling as if she was being the bad guy in their relationship.

* * *

It was six thirty and Bridget still hadn't arrived. Jack wasn't overly concerned because Tanya wasn't here either, he just wanted to see her and sort things out. He'd already greeted Trish and Sally who had arrived together, and had spent some time catching up with cousins, uncles, and aunts. He wanted to be able to introduce Bridget to everyone, the way Hal was about to do with Tanya.

"Jack, have you seen Hal? Tanya wants to

make her entrance with him."

His heart lightened at Bridget's voice and he turned, then stared, his mouth open. It was Bridget, yet somehow it wasn't. Her hair fell straight to her shoulders without the fun bounce it usually had, and her mouth was painted a glossy fire engine red. His groin tightened as he panned down, taking in the dress with its hint of cleavage and the split which started at the top of her thigh and ran all the way down to the matching red stilettos. She looked like a seductress. He couldn't talk, he could barely breathe. The woman standing in front of him was way out of his league.

"Jack?" She waved her hand in front of his face and he blinked. "Are you all right?"

"You look incredible."

She blushed and smoothed out the dress. "Thanks. It's a bit fancier than I'm used to but Tanya insisted."

He'd have to remember to thank Tanya later.

"Do you know where Hal is?" she repeated.

"He was over by the bar talking to my uncle," Jack said, taking her hand and searching for the closest nook he could drag her to. Spying the garden shed, he moved in that direction.

Bridget shook him loose. "Where are you going? The bar's over there."

"You don't want to make a scene, so I was trying to find somewhere private I could get you out of that dress."

Her eyes went dark, her lips smirked into a little grin. "Don't you like it?"

"I like it very much."

She glanced around, spotted Trish and Sally and her grin disappeared. "I've got to make an entrance with Tanya. I'll talk to you later."

Jack gritted his teeth. Every step forward with Bridget seemed to bring a step backward as well. He wasn't getting anywhere. Watching her walk away he noticed she captured more than one person's attention.

"Wow, Bridget looks amazing," Sally said from nearby.

"She won't have a problem finding someone to take her home," Trish replied, giving Jack a look.

He ignored them. He couldn't be expected to hide his emotions. Bridget *did* look amazing. He wanted to be able to declare to everyone that *he* was the one taking her home, that she was his, that he loved her.

Patience.

If Dirk hadn't made a fuss that week she might have been fine to be his date at the party.

His father tapped the microphone and

announced, "Ladies and gentlemen. Let me introduce to you, Mr. and Mrs. Gibbs."

He pointed to the veranda where Hal and Tanya were standing – Hal dressed in a black tuxedo and Tanya in a white lacy dress. They walked down the red carpet, smiling as everyone applauded. Behind them was Tanya's sister, then Bridget and the two groomsmen. Bridget kept a smile fixed on her face but Jack could tell she wasn't comfortable. Her steps were small and cautious, her balance not the best on the lumpy carpet and on those killer heels. She grabbed hold of the groomsman next to her and a rush of jealousy flooded Jack as the guy said something to make her laugh.

He was being ridiculous. Bridget wasn't interested in the groomsman. He waited until she was finished in the receiving line and then he crossed to her and held out his arm. "May I?"

She grabbed his arm, putting some weight on it as she adjusted her footing. "Please."

He grinned at her and helped her across the lawn to a spot under a tree.

"Thank you. Tanya insisted on these heels."

"You're as tall as me in those things."

She grimaced. "I feel like I'm on stilts. The sooner I can get them off, the better."

"Maybe I can help," he said, still thinking of the garden shed.

"Who have we got here?"

Jack grinned and kissed his grandmother on the cheek. "Grandma, this is Bridget Flanagan. She's Tanya's best friend."

"Ah. The girl you're living with." The older woman looked Bridget up and down. "I don't know how you walk in those shoes."

"I'm still trying to figure it out myself, ma'am," Bridget said, with a smile.

The older woman laughed.

"Bridget this is my grandmother, Mary Sue." He was a little wary about introducing them. His grandmother had a tendency toward bluntness and could offend people. Bridget was skittish enough tonight as it was.

"Pleased to meet you."

"All this," she waved her hand at Hal and Tanya, "must have come as a surprise to you. I'm glad Jack was able to help you out."

"That's Tanya for you. When she knows what she wants, she's determined."

His grandmother hummed.

Recognizing the gleam in her eye and realizing she was in a prying mood, which could end badly, he asked, "Can I get you a drink, Grandma?" He held out an arm to lead her away.

"A gin and tonic would be mighty fine," Mary Sue said, ignoring his arm. "What would you like, dear?" she asked Bridget.

"A lemonade, please. I won't be able to walk if I get any alcohol into me."

He sighed as his grandmother winked at him. He should have known she wouldn't fall for his attempt to distract her. He rushed to get the drinks.

When he arrived back they were laughing together.

"I'll have to remember that if Jack ever gives me any kind of trouble," Bridget said, as she took the drink he handed her.

"You haven't been giving away family secrets, have you, Grandma?" Jack asked, giving the older woman her gin and tonic.

"Nothing of any value." She glanced over his shoulder. "There's your uncle, Neville. I must go and talk with him." She patted his arm and walked away.

"What were you two talking about?"

"This and that."

Bridget smiled as she took a sip of her drink, and her lips on the glass reminded Jack of what he'd been about to do before the arrival of the newlyweds.

Bridget's eyes widened and she took a step back, holding up her free hand. "Don't." It was said with a laugh. "I know what that look means. I'm under orders to mingle, as I'm sure you are too. Plus I don't have any more of this lipstick on me and I have to give a speech later. I don't want to look like I've been ravished."

He took her hand and kissed the back of it. "I'll make it worth your while."

"I'm sure you will." She kept her hand in his.

"I hope I'm not interrupting."

Jack turned to his mother, letting go of Bridget's hand. "Mom, this is Tanya's best friend, Bridget. Bridget, my mother, Anna."

"I'm thrilled to meet you," his mother said, giving Bridget a hug. "You look absolutely gorgeous."

"Thank you. The place looks beautiful."

"Jackson and his father did most of the work," Anna said. "Now I want to grab you and run through the program for this evening. You're giving a speech, aren't you?"

Bridget nodded.

"Great. I'm going to steal her for a little while," she said to her son. "Why don't you go catch up with your cousins?"

Before Jack could argue, they had both walked off.

He was going to have to wait a little longer to get her alone.

* * *

After Anna had gone through the details of the night, Bridget returned outside to resume mingling.

She caught up with Tanya's immediate family before she was cornered by Trish and Sally.

"You look amazing, Bridge!" Sally said.

Bridget forced a smile to her face. She felt like a fraud. She just wasn't the slinky dress, high heels, and daring makeup kind of girl. "Tanya will use any excuse to get me into a dress."

"And every guy here is thankful for it," Trish told her.

She rolled her eyes.

"Jack can't keep his eyes off you," Trish assured her, nodding to where Jack was standing talking to Tanya's mother.

Bridget tensed, debating what she should say.

Trish reached out and put a hand on her arm. "Relax, Bridge. Your secret is safe with us. We won't tell anyone, if you don't want."

Was there any point in continuing to deny it? Bridget was torn – she wanted to be open about her relationship with Jack, but still there was her past. "Please don't. I never meant … If people knew, what with Lionel." She hated the uncertainty and the quiver in her voice.

"We understand," Sally said.

"No one's going to hear it from us," Trish told her. "And one day I hope the truth comes out about the bastard, Lionel."

Bridget's stomach was in rollercoaster mode and she put a hand there to calm it. Could she trust them to keep quiet? Maybe she should relax.

Jack's father tapped a microphone. "Ladies and gentlemen, if you'd like to find your seats, dinner is about to be served."

"I'd better go," Bridget said.

The 'bridal' table was at the back of the tent. One of the groomsmen pulled out her chair for her. Bridget thanked him and glanced over at Jack who was sitting at Hal's family table. He winked at her and she smiled. She hated that every time she considered telling anyone her stomach tied itself into knots. But surely she was safe here. The only people from work had promised to keep the secret.

So maybe she could have that dance with Jack. And maybe after the speeches they could sneak away to the garden shed. Her blood heated just thinking about it.

To her right, Tanya and Hal got to their feet.

"We want to thank everyone for coming today to help us celebrate our marriage,"

Tanya said. "It's been a whirlwind romance, and we're pleased y'all were able to make it."

"There are going to be a few speeches tonight," Hal continued. "Just like the award ceremonies, everyone has a strict time limit and music will play if they go on for too long."

People chuckled.

"So sit back and enjoy the night." They raised their glasses and everyone cheered.

The food was delicious, and between the courses people made their speeches. Both Tanya's and Hal's fathers said a few words, as well as one of the groomsmen, and then it was Bridget's turn. She had a glass of champagne in front of her and she took a small sip. She didn't want to overdo it.

She stood carefully, brushed a hand over her dress and swallowed. Her eyes roved the crowd and she found Jack. Seeing his smile, she relaxed. "I met Tanya on my first day of school in the United States. I'd just moved from El Salvador, spoke only a little English, and was terrified about going to this foreign school. After my mother left, I stood in the playground, not knowing what to do or where to go, and this beautiful blonde girl came up to me and said, 'My name's Tanya. Let's be friends.'" Bridget paused as some people in the crowd "awwed". She smiled at the memory, so clear in her head. Tanya had seemed like an angel to her at the time.

"And so it was. We became best friends on that first day and we've been friends ever since. Once Tanya puts her mind to something you better not get in her way, because she has such determination." Bridget looked down at Tanya, the years of friendship warming her heart. "The day after she met Hal she said to me, 'He's the one' and I knew if Tanya had her heart set on him, he didn't stand a chance."

People laughed.

"But it turns out, he was as besotted by her as she was by him, and you won't find two better suited people." Bridget picked up her glass. "So I'd like to make a toast. To Tanya and Hal."

The crowd echoed her words as they raised their glasses.

* * *

When the final plates were cleared and the DJ started playing, Bridget got to her feet to find Jack. Tanya stopped her.

"Thank you, Bridge," she said. "I was selfish leaving to move in with Hal and forcing you to move in with Jack. I'm sorry for the way I behaved. I was only thinking about myself." She was absolutely sincere in her apology.

Bridget could never hold a grudge against Tanya. She hugged her. "No harm so far," she said with a smile.

"You're not having difficulties at work?"

"There was one guy who made a fuss, but most believe it's just a convenience thing."

"But it's not, right?"

Bridget looked over at Jack who was laughing with his grandmother and her heart gave a little twist. "No, it's not."

* * *

At Mary Sue's insistence, Jack had the first dance with her. She bopped around the dance floor to the latest pop tune, waving her hands and having a great time. Jack wasn't the greatest dancer but he managed to keep up with his grandmother and not embarrass himself completely.

Then the music slowed so the happy couple could have their first dance. Jack stood back off the dance floor next to his grandmother as Hal and Tanya danced together. One by one, other couples joined them. Someone tapped him on the shoulder and he turned to see Bridget.

Her hands were clenched together. "May I have this dance?"

Her smile hit him straight in the chest.

"Absolutely."

She took his hand and led him on to the dance floor, before wrapping her arms around his shoulders. He placed his hands around her waist and they swayed together.

"So you decided it was OK for us to be seen together?"

She nodded. "I'm doing my best. The girls from work don't care and they promised not to say anything."

It was definitely a step in the right direction and Jack was going to take it. He didn't want to spoil the evening by pushing for anything more. He pulled her closer to him, enjoying the way she fit with his body. This is what he wanted – to be able to hold her close, and declare in public that she was his and he was hers.

Jack ran his hand down her back, enjoying the soft warmth of her skin under his hands. "You gave a lovely speech."

"Tanya may have her flaws, but she is my best friend."

"I understand your dedication to her now. The first friendly face in a strange country."

Bridget nodded. "She was so different with her blonde hair and pale skin – and so enthusiastic I couldn't help but be drawn along." She smiled. "We've had our differences of opinion at times, but we'll always be friends."

It was nice she had someone like that, though he wasn't convinced Tanya deserved Bridget's dedication, especially not after the way she moved out. But he didn't want to go into that now.

"So what do I need to know about tomorrow?" He was finally going to the family lunch at Bridget's mother's insistence.

Bridget groaned. "With everything else that's been happening, I'd forgotten about it. Mama is going to give you the third degree when she realizes you're not just my roommate. She knows about the Lionel affair and she'll be worried about me. Don't take it personally."

Jack's stomach clenched. He wasn't expecting that. "Would it be better to keep our relationship secret?" He felt like a wimp suggesting it.

She shook her head. "Mama always knows. Carly will run interference if necessary."

"We're picking Carly up tomorrow?"

"Yeah. It's my turn to drive. Don't worry, it'll be fine."

Bridget didn't appear to be the least bit concerned about facing her mother, but he was a bundle of nerves. Is this how Bridget felt when faced with telling the people at work that

they were in a relationship?
   If so, he'd be more empathetic in future.

Chapter 18

Jack's skin was humming with nerves by the time they picked Carly up the next morning. He had little idea what to expect from the day but he'd imagined all manner of horrific encounters. Meeting his girlfriend's family had never been a big issue before.

Carly soothed some of those nerves with her casual greeting as she climbed into the backseat. She was significantly shorter than Bridget, but had the same brown hair, though hers was straight. She wore a tailored peach-colored skirt and a white shirt, looking more like she was going to a board meeting than lunch at her mother's house. Was he underdressed in his black jeans and blue shirt?

"So Jack, how are you enjoying your new job?" Carly asked.

"It's got its challenges," he said. "Bridget has been a great help. She knows the plant like the back of her hand."

"She sure does."

He wasn't sure what to make of that comment. Was Carly annoyed her sister hadn't got the job? "What do you do?" he asked.

"I own a software company."

That's right, he remembered Tanya mentioning it.

"How do you think Mama's going to behave today?" Bridget asked.

Carly laughed. "That depends on how scared Jack looks."

The nerves shifted from Jack's skin to his stomach.

"Does she know you're dating?"

That was a good question. He glanced at Bridget.

"Not yet."

"She'll figure it out fairly quickly. Then she'll want Jack's life story."

He took a deep breath. He could deal with that. He was serious about Bridget and had no secrets. He was sure he could convince Carmen he wasn't out to take advantage of her daughter.

Bridget pulled in to the property. A huge two-story house dominated the drive and was surrounded by lush tropical plants. To one side there appeared to be some smaller cottages and an orchard.

"What does your mother do?" Jack asked. They had never talked much about her family. He wasn't sure whether her mother still worked.

"She's a foster mother," Bridget said. She opened the car door to get out, fending off two dogs; one brown Labrador cross, the other with hints of German Shepherd.

"*Mis niñitas!*" came the cry from the house.

Jack slowly got out of the car as a petite older woman, who looked very much like Carly, came out to meet them. She flung her arms around Bridget and then Carly.

"Mama, this is Jack. Jack, my mother, Carmen."

He'd learned basic Spanish in high school. "*Buenos dias, Senora* Flanagan," he said. "*Cómo estás?*"

Her response in rapid-fire Spanish went completely over his head. "Ah …" He looked at Bridget for help.

"She said she is well and welcomes you to her house." She turned to her mother. "It's best if we speak English with Jack."

Her mother nodded. "If you wish," she said

with a strong accent. "Come in."

Jack followed the women through the house to the kitchen out back. A rich tomato aroma filled the air and he sniffed with appreciation. Three girls stood at a long wooden bench, chopping vegetables. One had strawberry blonde hair and lightly tanned skin, and was in her mid-twenties. The other two were younger, perhaps mid-teens, and were obviously of Hispanic descent.

"Zita, this is Jack," Bridget said.

The strawberry blonde looked up and grinned. "*Hola!*" She left the bench and came to hug him. "Welcome."

Jack blinked back his surprise as he hugged her back. Zita was Bridget's younger sister, but he was expecting her to look like Carly and Bridget.

The other two girls kept their eyes down on what they were doing.

"This is Teresa, and Elena," Zita introduced them.

"Howdy," he said.

Both girls' eyes widened and they looked at each other and giggled. They must be the foster kids Bridget mentioned.

"How was the party last night?" Zita asked her sister.

"Lovely. Tanya and Hal are really happy."

"Do you think it will last?"

Jack glanced at Zita. The question wasn't malicious, merely curious. He was interested in Bridget's answer.

She was quiet for a moment. "Yes, I think it will. It may have happened quickly but when Tanya makes up her mind, she sticks with it."

Jack was pleased. He loved his brother and would hate for him to be hurt.

Carmen harrumphed. "She is the reason you had no roommate and that you had to ask your *jefe* to move in with you."

Jack didn't know what a *jefe* was and he wasn't sure what to say.

Carly rolled her eyes. "Mama, let's talk about this after lunch."

Carmen frowned but nodded.

Bridget led Jack into the dining room while Carmen called out something in Spanish. A moment later four more teenaged girls came into the room, all chatting to each other. Zita made the introductions and when everyone had started serving themselves and talking he leaned over and asked Bridget quietly, "How many children does your mother foster?"

"It varies. At the moment she has six. Zita helps her out."

He wanted to ask more questions, but it seemed rude to ask in front of the girls. He wasn't sure how sensitive they were about the situation. The conversation around the table proceeded in Spanish. Carmen clapped her hands together. "We have a guest. This is a good chance for you to practice your English, girls. No Spanish for the rest of the day."

A couple of the girls grimaced, but dutifully began speaking in halting English as they talked about a television show. Jack stayed silent, content to listen. He sympathized with the girls struggling to express their opinions in a language that was foreign to them. He wouldn't be even half that articulate if he'd had to remember much more of his high-school Spanish.

"So Jack, you're the new safety manager at Dionysus," Carmen said.

Immediately alert, he nodded. "Yes, ma'am."

"Are you enjoying it?"

"It's certainly a challenge," he said. "Bridget had a lot to contend with when she was in the role and she's been a real asset to me since I started."

"She's not just a pretty face."

He wasn't touching that comment.

"You were living with your brother?" Carmen asked. "That's why you needed somewhere else to stay?"

"That's right. Hal and I met Tanya and

Bridget when we were out one night recently."

Immediately Carmen's expression turned speculative. "You're that Jack?" She raised her eyebrows at her daughter.

Bridget winced and nodded. What had she told her mother?

"That's interesting," said Carmen.

Jack stayed silent and was relieved when the meal was over. He helped carry the dishes to the kitchen and offered to clean up.

"No, you are our guest," Carmen said shooing him out of the kitchen. "Bridget can show you the garden."

He followed Bridget out of the back door and stopped, staring at the food oasis. Everywhere he looked there were fruit trees, or vegetable patches filled with ripening produce. "Wow."

Bridget grinned at him. "Mama loves to garden."

"I'll say."

She led him down the steps. "When we lived in El Salvador we went through periods when food was scarce. This is her way of ensuring it never happens again."

"I can understand that. You said she misses it a lot."

Bridget nodded. "She misses her family and the country, but I'm not sure she will ever go back, even if it is safe. My father died there."

"How did he die?"

"Mama never gave us the details. He went to work one day and never came home."

"I'm so sorry." He wrapped his arms around her and held her tightly. When he let go she gave him a small smile.

"It is what it is."

He changed the subject. "So you mentioned me to your mother after we first met?"

"Yeah. I told her I'd met a nice man. I'm fairly certain she's connected the dots and knows we're not just colleagues."

"I'd say so. Should I expect a grilling?"

Bridget smiled. "Probably."

He'd have to allay Carmen's concerns. He could do that. They walked down the path toward a greenhouse. "Your mom has a lot of foster kids. Do Hispanic families struggle with moving to the US?"

Bridget frowned. "The girls are all refugees. They've come to the States without their families."

Jack took a step back. "But they're so young. Why would they do that?"

"The situation in many parts of Central America – Guatemala, El Salvador, and Honduras – is not good. Gangs rule the streets and if you don't join them you can be killed. Many of the girls who flee have been raped or were going to be forced into marriage. They figure it is better to take their chances with the people smugglers and the US."

Jack had been out of touch with what was going on in the US while he was living in Australia and had no idea things were so bad.

"The detention centers are often full," Bridget continued. "Mama takes girls while authorities are searching for family they may already have here, or girls who have been granted refugee status and have nowhere else to go. She and Zita teach them English, home school them until their education is at a level where they can go to school here, and support them until they are ready to move out."

They walked along the path until they came to the little cottages Jack had noticed on the drive in.

"Some of the older foster kids live here," Bridget explained. "They've graduated high school and are studying at college or doing an apprenticeship. It gives them a little bit of independence, but Mama is still close by if they need a hand."

Jack shook his head. "What an incredible thing to do," he said. "Though it must be difficult. It sounds like those girls have been traumatized."

She nodded. "Both Mama and Zita have had training in counseling."

"Who pays for it all? Do they get help from the government?"

"No. Carly pays for it all. She bought this whole property and set up a not-for-profit organization."

That software company of hers was obviously doing well. This was something the family all cared dearly about. "Were you refugees?" Jack asked.

Bridget shook her head. "Mama and Papa had applied to immigrate before Papa died. The acceptance came through the week after the funeral."

"How tragic." He couldn't remember what age she'd said she was at the time. "You were young, weren't you?"

"I was five, and my whole world revolved around our little farm that Mama tended, and the little village where we lived. Houston was a huge culture shock."

"I can imagine."

Bridget smiled. "I want you to taste some jocote." She entered the large greenhouse, grabbed a little step ladder from the path, and put it next to one of the trees bearing small red fruit that Jack had never seen before. She picked a couple and handed him one. "I tend to peel them, but you don't have to." She showed him what she meant and then popped the orange flesh into her mouth, closing her eyes in satisfaction.

He did as Bridget had demonstrated and the flavor exploded in his mouth as he bit into it. It was a cross between a strawberry and a mango and absolutely delicious. "Wow, that's amazing."

"Isn't it just?"

He ate the rest of it and was going to ask for another one when he was distracted by Bridget licking the juice off her fingers. Heat shot straight to his groin. "Let me help you with that." He took her fingers in his and slowly sucked them.

Her eyes went dark and her mouth opened a little, her tongue touching her top lip. It was all Jack needed to lose control. He pulled her toward him and crushed his mouth to hers. She tasted like the fruit, sweet and juicy. She moaned, and he forgot where he was as he deepened the kiss.

"*Dios mío!*"

The shriek shot through his senses like a bullet and he and Bridget sprang apart. Her mother stood at the doorway, her hand on her chest, her eyes wide.

Shit. Not the best way to make a good

impression. Then he remembered how Carmen had fooled him with her hysterics over the phone and relaxed.

"Mama." Bridget's tone was a warning.

Carmen sighed and said something to Bridget in Spanish. Her expression was concerned. Bridget's answer was slow, soothing.

Carmen turned to Jack. He braced himself. "You know about the Lionel affair?"

"Mama –"

"Shush. I'm asking the man a question."

Hell. "Yes, *Senora* Flanagan. Bridget told me about it."

"So you know it almost ruined her career?"

"Yes." What was he supposed to say? He couldn't say he loved her and wanted to marry her. That would freak Bridget out.

"What would you have done in that situation?" Carmen asked.

"I would have owned up to my mistake."

Carmen nodded with approval. "My Birdy now worries too much about what people think."

"That's enough, Mama," Bridget said sternly.

He didn't want Bridget to be embarrassed, but he was curious about what Carmen was going to say. He stepped closer to Bridget and took her hand. "I care for your daughter."

"Yes, I see how much you care. You have no regard for her reputation and the gossip that will fly when people know you're together."

Her accusation hit him right in the chest. She was right. He didn't care what people thought, he wanted everyone to know they were together. "We're being careful. We have separate rooms and we've told no one how we feel about each other. They all think Bridget's doing me a favor."

"So you're embarrassed to admit the truth? Are you ashamed of your relationship with my daughter?"

Jack couldn't keep up with her, but he suspected he was digging a deeper hole for himself. "We are doing nothing to be ashamed of," he said, standing taller and looking her in the eye. "Your daughter is a beautiful person and I care for her."

Carmen squinted at him, examining him carefully. Then she nodded once, said something in Spanish to Bridget and walked off.

He let go of the breath he'd been holding. "What did she say?"

Bridget was silent, her mouth open in surprise. "She's OK with it."

Relief flooded him. He'd wanted her

mother's blessing.

"We should go back inside," Bridget said and, without waiting for an answer, she hurried out of the greenhouse.

What had got into her?

* * *

Bridget couldn't believe what her mother had said. She'd turned to Bridget and said, "I like him. Don't let him get away."

She didn't like the level of commitment the statement implied. She was relieved Jack didn't speak Spanish.

Safely inside the house, she sat on one of the sofas to chat with Carly and Zita. The other girls had made themselves scarce, with the exception of Elena, who was trying to improve her English and was listening carefully to every word.

"How many foster children have you looked after over the years?" Jack asked.

"Thirty five," Carmen answered.

"It must be hard to see them go."

"Sometimes," Carmen said. "Some are going to their families, where they are much happier, and others grow up and move out, like two of my girls have. We keep in touch." She smiled at Zita, who still lived at home.

Bridget was so proud of her family. She

remembered the day when her mother had declared she was going to be a foster parent. There had been a lot of talk about child refugees and how the migrant community couldn't afford to take them, because many were struggling themselves. Her mother had been working at a local wholesale nursery, and while she wasn't earning a fortune she had enough money to provide a bed for another child, especially since Bridget and Carly had already moved out. It had grown from there.

"That's really nice," Jack said.

Carmen nodded. "It was easier when Carly bought this property and we built the house. It gave everyone a little more space, and meant our celebrations didn't need to be held at a nearby park."

"The foster girls all come to celebrations?"

"Of course. They are my daughters as much as my own are."

Her mother had always been a nurturer.

The conversation moved to Carly and her software company and Bridget sat back, content to listen. Jack asked interesting, intelligent questions and it was comfortable, companionable. There was no tension there at all. She should be grateful.

Instead she was worried. Lionel was the

only other guy she'd brought home to her family and he hadn't fit in at all. She should have seen it as a sign, but she hadn't. But now with Jack, it was as if he'd known her sisters for years by the way they were laughing together.

Bridget wasn't ready for this, she didn't want to look more long term than this week. The whole situation with them working together was too tenuous. She was relieved when it was finally time to leave the house, say goodbye to her mother and little sister, and drive back into the city.

After they dropped off Carly, Jack said, "That went well."

She nodded. "Better than I expected. Mama likes you."

"She's a great woman. It must have been so difficult for her to move to a new country with three young children while she was still grieving for her husband."

Bridget was sure it had been. It wasn't something her mother liked to talk about. She only knew bits of what their life in El Salvador was like, the things she could remember and the stories Carly sometimes told.

"She did it for us." It was the one thing Bridget would never forget. She'd left her home country to give her daughters a better chance at life.

She didn't want to talk about her family any more. "When did your parents split up?" she asked Jack. At the party, Anna and Eric seemed on good terms, despite no longer being married.

"After Hal and I moved out," he said. "I think they wanted to give us a stable home life, but we knew they weren't happy. We were both pleased when they split, and they're enjoying life now. Dad might have a girlfriend, but he's keeping it quiet."

"It's nice they still get along."

"It is. It's so much easier at family gatherings."

Bridget pulled into the driveway and they went inside. Jack pulled her into his arms and kissed her.

"Thank you for introducing me to your family."

"If I hadn't, Mama would have turned up on the doorstep," she joked.

He frowned and she realized she might have hurt his feelings. She gave him a squeeze. "I'm glad you like them. The girls have been anxious to meet you since I first mentioned you." She brushed her lips against his and moved away. "Are you hungry?"

"Only for you."

She glanced back at him and he picked her up and carried her into his bedroom. She shrieked and then laughed as he tossed her onto the bed. He stripped off his shirt and desire spread through her.

"Come and get me then."

Chapter 19

Jack was ready for anything when he went to work the next day. He'd had a fantastic weekend, introduced Bridget to his family and met her family, and was confident they would be able to resolve the issue of working together soon.

His mood wavered when Anthony stopped him in the hall. "Have you got a minute?"

Jack nodded and followed him into his office. Anthony closed the door behind him and indicated he should sit.

"Dirk has made an official complaint about you."

Jack's mouth dropped. "On what grounds?"

"He believes he's not being treated equally and is missing out on opportunities." Anthony checked his notes. "There's a safety forum this week he wasn't allowed to go to."

Jack clenched his hands. "The forum covers high-level safety and environmental issues for managers and senior managers, which is why I'm going and taking Bridget as my second-in-command. Sally is also going because she's the environment officer. There's no need for anyone else to attend. I'll be debriefing with the whole department when I get back."

"He suggested Bridget is getting more opportunities because she's female."

Jack stared at the man in disbelief. "He's claiming gender discrimination?"

Anthony sighed. "Yeah, I know he's talking bullshit but it's my duty to investigate it anyway."

"You know what the issue is, Anthony. We discussed it last week after I disciplined him at our team-building session. The truth is, Bridget is a better team member in all regards: she's dedicated, has the respect of the technicians, has a passion to change things for the better, and she gets results. *That* is why she is getting the opportunities. Dirk is happy to go with the status quo and the guys at the plant don't like him. Neither do most of the people in my department."

Anthony nodded. "Depending on how far he wants to take this, we may have to have a session with an intermediary. I've suggested to Dirk that over the next month he records any instances where he feels he's being treated unfairly. I recommend you do the same – keep a record of whenever his work or his attitude has not been satisfactory. Then we can have another meeting to discuss the issue."

Jack ran a hand through his hair. "Sure, I can do that."

"Great. I think we can work this out to everyone's satisfaction." Anthony stood and shook his hand.

Jack wasn't sure Dirk would ever be satisfied, but he would do everything he could to protect Bridget. He walked slowly to his office. Being in charge did have its disadvantages. And putting up with jerks like Dirk was definitely one of them.

* * *

By the time the forum rolled around on Wednesday, Jack was relieved to get out of the office. It seemed like Dirk had made it his mission to be as difficult as possible. Bridget had asked him to supervise the contractors who were enclosing the relief valves, and when they were missing a single permit he'd canceled all of the work that day, instead of writing it himself. That affected the whole project plan. Jack had words with him and dutifully recorded the details in his journal. Dirk had also been surlier than normal, and Jack had received a number of complaints from his team and others on the plant.

Jack took a sip of his take-out coffee as he and Bridget walked into the hall where the safety forum was being held.

"I'll introduce you to some of the people working on neighboring plants," Bridget said. She waved to a short, dark-haired guy in his mid-forties. "Hi, Graham. How's things?"

"Same old, same old, Bridget. You still in charge over at Dionysus?"

She shook her head. "No. This is my new boss, Jack Gibbs." She turned to Jack. "Graham is the Safety Manager at the oil refinery across from us."

Graham shook Jack's hand. "Pleasure to meet you. Bridget here is a great woman."

Her eyes widened.

Jack smiled. "I know. She sure makes my job easier."

They were called into the hall as the forum was about to start.

Jack found the first panel discussion interesting. After three years working in Australia he was fascinated to note the differences in the way the two countries dealt with safety and the environment.

At the end of the panel there was an opportunity for questions from the audience. Bridget asked for further details about a particular aspect relating to process safety. It was a great question and Jack knew she was immediately thinking about how to apply it at the plant. She was always on the ball. He made a few notes of his own.

At the end of the day there was a cocktail party. Bridget introduced Jack to people she knew, and eventually excused herself to speak with someone else. A guy about Jack's age with black hair, not a strand out of place, came up to him.

"You must be one of Bridget's colleagues."

"Jack Gibbs," he said. "I'm the new safety manager over at Dionysus."

"I didn't think they'd give Bridge the job." The man's smile was genuine but for some reason it made Jack's skin crawl.

"I'm sorry, I didn't catch your name."

"Lionel Mathers. I'm the safety manager at Premium Oil."

Now it made sense. Jack clicked his fingers together. "You're the guy who messed up and then blamed everything on Bridget." The same jackass who'd made her so reluctant to be in a relationship with him.

Lionel's genial expression turned hard. "I don't know what she's been saying but it was *not* my fault."

Jack held his hands up in a gesture of surrender. "Sorry, it's just the rumor I heard. The technicians at Dionysus sing her praises and she's proved extremely competent so far."

Lionel glared at him. "I'd watch your back. She can fool the best of us."

At that moment Bridget came up to them. She completely ignored Lionel. "Jack, I want to introduce you to our inspector." She gestured to a man standing a few yards away.

"Aren't you going to say hello?" Lionel asked her with a smug grin.

She squinted at him as if he were a speck of dirt on a clean linen tablecloth and said, "You're not worth my time." She walked off.

Jack swallowed his grin and nodded to the man. "I'll see you around."

The moment he turned around his grin spread wide over his face. She was a hell of a woman.

* * *

Bridget concentrated on her breathing as Jack and Victor chatted. She'd assumed Lionel would be at the forum, and she'd prepared herself to be civil and polite. But when it came down to it, she just couldn't. The man was an insect she wanted to squash. She smiled. The shock on Lionel's face had been rather rewarding. Perhaps she should have been professional, but she didn't have it in her to feel sorry for what she said. It was actually the nicest thing she could come up with.

"Bridget, can I have a word?"

She excused herself and turned to Graham. "Sure. What's up?"

They walked a small distance away and Graham cleared his throat. "The last time we spoke, I told you about the safety projects coordinator position I was trying to get approved."

Bridget nodded. The position had sounded amazing. He'd wanted someone to solely work on projects that would improve the safety at his plant. They would have a significant budget and the full support of senior management.

"It was approved last week."

"That's excellent. I wish we could get a position like that at Dionysus."

"Well, I wanted to ask if you were interested in applying."

Bridget's mouth dropped open. "Me?" Excitement hummed over her skin at the idea of having that much opportunity to make improvements.

Graham smiled. "Yes, you. I've wanted you on my team since we first met. I can pretty much guarantee that if you apply for the position, you'll get it."

She was speechless. She blinked, realizing she had to say something. "What about the Lionel affair?"

Graham snorted. "Most of us know what an idiot he is. There aren't many who believe his story. You know that, don't you?"

Bridget shook her head. She'd thought everyone had believed him. But maybe it was just those who were willing to be vocal about it. That put everything in a different perspective. "In that case I'd love to know more. Can you send me the position details?"

"I'll do it first thing in the morning. But don't tell your new boss. He seems nice, and I don't want him angry at me for poaching his best team member." Graham winked and walked away.

Bridget took a glass of wine from a passing waiter and sipped it, trying to get her brain working again. She'd been convinced the whole industry thought she was to blame for the incident at her previous plant. It was one reason why she'd been so dedicated to Dionysus – she'd been sure they were the only company who would give her a chance, and didn't think she'd get another job if she applied elsewhere. Obviously she'd been wrong.

If she had a new job, there was nothing stopping her and Jack being together. They wouldn't have to keep their relationship secret anymore because they wouldn't be working together. That held an immense amount of appeal.

Plus she knew Graham would support her in what she wanted to achieve and senior management were behind the role as well. There wouldn't be the constant uphill battle every time she wanted to improve something. Her skin tingled with excitement.

She took another sip of the wine. Perhaps things were looking up.

* * *

The next morning Bridget checked her email as soon as she got to work. There was nothing from Graham. Perhaps he wasn't in the office yet. Slightly disappointed, she read through the rest of her emails, flagging those she needed to follow up. She hadn't mentioned the job offer to Jack. She didn't want to get her hopes up in case the position wasn't as great as Graham made it sound, and she didn't want any pressure from Jack to apply. She would make her own decision.

Her phone rang. It was Joe. "Bridge, can you come out and take a look at something?"

"Sure. Be right there."

Joe didn't generally call her unless he was genuinely worried about something. She grabbed her gear and met him at the supervisor's office. "What's up?"

"Can you shut the door?"

Bridget frowned but did as he asked and took a seat.

"We've got a line shutdown next week on the cracking unit."

She nodded. "Any problems with it?"

"A couple. I spoke with Dirk yesterday while you were off-site. Some of my crew are new and this will be their first shutdown. I wanted someone to give them a refresher on the safety systems: permits, risk assessment, that kind of thing. He said none of you had time."

Bridget gritted her teeth. The safety culture was bad enough on site without Dirk making it worse. If the shifts were reaching out to them, they had to respond. "Of course we've got time. When do you want it?"

"We're not on days again until next week, so today would be good."

"I'll fit you in. Just give me a time."

"Thanks, Bridget. I knew I could count on you."

And that was the problem. Joe should be able to count on the *entire* safety department. She had to mention this to Jack.

Joe hesitated a moment and then sighed. "There's something else. Dirk's been spreading rumors, telling the guys this new project of yours is a waste of time and will cause them extra work."

Anger stirred in Bridget's belly.

"He's saying it's management covering their asses and wasting money that could be used to make a real difference in safety."

The man was unbelievable. What he was saying was downright dangerous.

"How many are listening?" she asked.

"The usual bunch."

Bridget scrubbed at her eyes. Damn him. The usual bunch were the ones who caused them the most amount of grief because they weren't willing to change their ways – they'd been doing it for twenty years and didn't see any reason to. She was going to have to check with the other shift supervisors and ask if Dirk had been spreading these lies to them as well.

"All right," Bridget said finally, "I'll go around and catch who I can today at lunch. See if they want to vent, and then try to explain the value to them again. Thanks for letting me know."

"Thanks for caring."

As she walked back to her office Bridget's guilt began to grow. Who would people like Joe turn to if she wasn't around? If she took the job Graham offered her, would they have anyone to hear their concerns? Anyone to care whether they got home at night?

She didn't know. But it was something she was going to have to consider.

The first thing she did was call the other shift supervisors to check if Dirk had been telling them the project was a waste of time. When she had enough information she went and told Jack. She felt a little sorry for him as he made a note in his journal.

"I'll speak with them next week," she said.

"No," Jack replied. "Let me. I need to establish a relationship with these guys. I want them to feel they can come to me as well as you if there are any problems. They need to know I'll listen to their concerns."

It warmed Bridget's heart to hear him say that. He *understood* what was needed and was willing to make the time to fix it. That's what she needed from him. "Great."

"Aside from this glitch, the project's back on track, isn't it?"

"Yeah."

"Good work. I've got a few more things to finish up here. I'll see you when I get home."

He looked so tired Bridget was tempted to give him a hug. She stepped forward to do just that when someone knocked on the door. She whirled around to see Kevin. Heat rushed to her cheeks. What the hell had she been thinking? She couldn't show any affection to Jack here. Damn it, if she hadn't hesitated she would have been caught by the general manager.

Nodding at Kevin, she said to Jack, "I'll talk to you later." Then she fled the office.

* * *

By the end of the week, Graham still hadn't sent through the position description. Bridget did a quick search on the relevant job websites to see if it had gone up yet, but she couldn't find anything. She wondered if she should call him and ask, or if that would seem too pushy.

There was no point worrying about it. She wasn't sure whether she would take the job anyway. But she was glad she hadn't mentioned it to Jack.

Arriving home first, she started making dinner. Jack had worked late every night this week. Now he'd learned how the site was run and was comfortable in his position, he seemed almost more determined than Bridget to fix things. He'd had a few heated conversations with the production manager and the maintenance manager. Part of her reveled in having someone share her passion, and the workload, but the other part worried he was working too hard.

She whipped up a marinade and poured it over the steaks, setting them aside. Then she checked the pantry and decided to make a sheet cake. She hadn't done any baking in months and the chocolaty goodness was sure to cheer Jack up.

Turning on the radio, Bridget bopped around the kitchen as she measured and stirred the mixture before popping it into the oven. Finally she turned her attention to the salad. By the time she was finished it was starting to get dark.

She hadn't asked Jack what time to expect him home. She was debating whether she should call him when the front door opened. She heard his footsteps go into his room and then come down the hall toward her. He looked tired and worse yet, he looked sad.

"Is everything all right?" she asked, wrapping her arms around him.

He exhaled and squeezed her. "It is now." He rested his cheek against hers and she breathed in his musky scent.

"Do you want to talk about it?"

He released her. "No. Let's leave it for Monday. It's the weekend and I want to forget about work." He sniffed. "What are you cooking?"

"Sheet cake."

He grinned. "Smells great."

She was glad she'd decided to make it, pleased she could cheer him up. "You've got time for a shower before dinner."

"Want to join me?"

The look he gave her made her stomach flutter. "I'd love to."

* * *

It was Wednesday afternoon before Bridget finally received an email from Graham. He apologized for the wait, blaming HR for taking their time approving the position description. She closed the door to her office to give herself five minutes of peace while she read through it. By the time she finished she was grinning and all her muscles were tingling with excitement.

It was her ideal job. Every aspect of it spoke to her passion for safety and her desire to improve work practices. She had all the qualifications they asked for and more, and the company had a flexible policy which meant she could choose her own work hours.

Her inbox pinged and it was another email from Graham, this one sent from his personal email address. It contained a rough salary range for the role, which was over ten thousand dollars more than she was earning now. Part of her wanted to respond immediately with "where do I sign?" but she needed to think about it rationally.

She opened her notebook and drew a line down the middle. In the pro column she put Jack, job satisfaction, money, support and making a difference. In the con column she wrote "abandoning her colleagues".

She sighed. She did feel like she was abandoning them, that without her they would have no one to stand up to management on their behalf. Perhaps it was arrogant of her. Jack was definitely making inroads in that direction.

At a knock on the door she quickly closed the file on her computer and called, "Come in." Jack entered, looking slightly harassed.

"What's up?"

He stepped in to the room. "I need you out in the plant. The shutdown's finished and they're restarting the plant. I don't want them taking shortcuts." He glanced at her desk and frowned. "What's that?"

Bridget turned and noticed her notebook open at the pro/con column. Jack's name was at the top of the list.

"Nothing," she said and shut the book.

He stepped back, worry crossing his face. She debated for a second and then had to tell him. She hated to add further stress.

"I've been offered a job." She waved a hand toward the notebook. "I was writing up a pro/con list as to whether I should take it. You were top of the pro side."

"Oh." There was real hurt on his face. "I wouldn't have thought it was a hard decision. Not if you want to tell people we're dating."

"That's not the only thing I need to consider," she said. "There's whether I'll like the job, how much it pays, whether it's fair of me to leave the technicians without a champion."

The hurt changed to disbelief. "You'd put the technicians feelings over our relationship?"

"It's not that simple, Jack. If the guys bring their problems to Dirk, they get ignored. They *know* if they come to me, the issues will be addressed. It's something I have to factor in to my decision."

"Really? You'd let Dirk's behavior control our

relationship?"

"No." He didn't understand.

"So is the job different from what you're doing now?"

"Completely." Relieved to be on a safer ground, she said, "It's amazing. It's for a safety projects coordinator, which means I get to spend all of my day implementing improvements to the refinery."

"Sounds like your perfect role."

"It is! And it's a significant pay rise." The excitement bubbled up in her.

"So tell me again exactly *why* you're even hesitating to apply?" There was an edge to his tone.

The bubble popped. "The technicians need an advocate."

"More than we need to be open about our relationship?"

"What relationship?"

Bridget whirled around at Kevin's voice. She wanted to swear. She glanced at Jack. He was watching her, waiting for her to say something.

Holy hell.

She turned back to Kevin. It was on the tip of her tongue to tell the truth when she saw the judgment already forming on his face. No. She couldn't do this again. She wasn't ready, it was too much of a risk. She didn't have a new job yet.

"He was referring to our working relationship," she said finally.

Jack pushed past her and she flinched. "Excuse me, Kevin. I've got to get back to the plant. Bridget I expect you out there as soon as you're finished here."

He didn't look at her or wait for her response.

Chapter 20

Bridget's heart cracked, but she couldn't go after him, not with Kevin standing right there.

"I hope that's all it is," he said. "We took a chance hiring you, especially after that unfortunate incident at Premium Oil. I'd hate for you to make the same mistake and put this plant at risk."

Her cheeks warmed and anger simmered. "Of course not," she managed to say. "Was there something you wanted from me?"

"Yes. Your project has had a cost blow-out that is unacceptable."

She stared at him. "Everything's on track. Jack hired a few contractors to get things moving but aside from that we're on budget."

"That's not good enough," Kevin said.

Bridget opened her mouth to respond when a loud rumble like a freight train split the air.

What the hell was that? Her stomach plummeted. It sounded suspiciously like one of the big relief valves – the ones that vented to the atmosphere, the ones she was working on replacing.

Kaboom!

The noise was so loud her ears rang and the whole administration building shook. Fuck.

"What the hell was that?" Kevin yelled.

Bridget's pulse raced. She grabbed her two-way radio and tuned to the emergency channel. The fire alarm sounded. Jeremy was away, so she was in charge.

"Get everyone to the assembly point," she barked into the radio and seconds later another alarm sounded.

Whatever had happened was bad enough to make the building shake. She needed a head count. Her blood went cold. Jack was out in the plant.

Kevin grabbed her hand. "Shouldn't you find out the problem first?"

She glared at him. "That explosion is the problem. Get to an assembly point."

Out in the hall she caught hold of Ken. "Jack was in the plant. Check the gatehouse. If he's not there, I need you to stay there and oversee. Get me a head count, stat. I'm going out."

Ken nodded, his face pale.

Bridget ran for the exit nearest the plant, and then across to the fire station. A huge plume of black smoke billowed out of the crude unit and flames created a wall of heat. The acrid stench of burning oil filled her nostrils. The technicians were already suiting up and she did the same, making sure her radio was attached and working. "What have we got?" she yelled.

"Don't know exactly but it's the crude unit. Control tech hit the emergency shutdown," one of the fire team leaders said.

Around her the fire tender were being readied. "Everyone swiped on?" Everyone on the plant carried a swipe card so their movements could be tracked. The fire station counted as an assembly point and all the technicians had to swipe in to get an accurate head count. As she looked around they all nodded. "Any casualties?"

"Don't know yet."

She radioed the gatehouse. "Prep the ambulance." She hoped they didn't need to use it.

Jumping into one fire tender, her team headed into the smoke and flame.

The heat was hideous, coming toward them in waves, and the smell of burning oil came through her breathing apparatus. They pulled up as close as they dared and unhitched the hoses.

Bridget left them to it as she scanned the area, checking for other hazards and for people. "We got a head count yet?" she barked into the radio.

"Ten missing, Bridge," Ken said.

Her stomach was lead. She turned to the nearest man. "Go fetch the ambulance." If there were people missing they were most likely injured. To Ken she said, "Call the nearest medics. Inform them we may need transport to the hospital." He knew the drill.

"Bridget, one of the missing is Jack."

Her body froze for a split second. No. She couldn't bear that. She had to find him, had to find all of them. "Give me the names."

Ken read out the list. She peered into the destruction but the smoke and flame made it so hard to see.

"Roger that," she said, numb. "Which unit were they tagged on to?" she called over the radio.

"Four were swiped on to the cat reformer, two in the cracker and the other four were working in the crude unit."

Bridget relayed the information to her team and sent guys to each unit to search. She desperately wanted to ask which unit Jack had been tagged on to but it didn't matter. Everyone needed to be found. What had he been doing out in the plant? What would he have been checking?

"Set up a five-man fog attack," she ordered. "We've got to get the fire under control." They'd need all the fire tenders to do so.

Movement caught her eye and Joe, the shift supervisor, stumbled toward them through the smoke. She grabbed her nearest team member and ran over. He coughed as Bridget reached him.

"I've got you," she said. "Was anyone else with you?" Was Jack?

He nodded, trying to speak. It came out as a croak.

"How many more? Hold up your fingers."

He held up two fingers.

"Where?"

He pointed. "Tower," he rasped.

Together Bridget and her team mate carried him out of the smoke and into the safe zone. The ambulance was just pulling up. She left the driver to give Joe oxygen and turned to the other man. "Take a couple of guys, go up wind and find them."

He nodded, grabbed the guys and they moved around the flames into the plant.

Bridget wanted to go with them but she couldn't. She had to stay in control, to direct the response. She radioed the team she'd sent to the cracking unit.

"We've got Mike," someone said. "He's unconscious but breathing. Looks like the damn fire ball made it this far."

"I'll send the ambulance."

"Great. We're still searching for the other guy."

Bridget jogged to the ambulance. Joe was sitting inside wearing an oxygen mask. "Go around to the cracker. We've got one unconscious," she ordered the driver.

He nodded and after making sure Joe was secure, he drove off.

"Bridget, we've found three here." It was the other team at the catalytic reformer. "Two conscious but with head wounds and burns, one unconscious. I think he's broken his leg."

"Do you need a stretcher?"

"Yeah, and an ambulance. I'll keep the guys under the safety showers until it gets here."

"All right. There should be one more guy in that unit. Do you need more men to help search?"

"Yeah, send a couple."

She sent three more guys out. "Ken I need three ambulances," she said into her radio.

"We've got concussion, burns, smoke inhalation, and broken bones."

There were three still unaccounted for, including Jack. Where the hell was he? She couldn't let her fear for him take control, she had to lead the response.

Four people emerged from the smoke. She frantically scanned them, looking for the familiar face. Her heart fell. They were the responders she'd sent with the men who had been with Joe. They were disoriented but unhurt. There was a truck nearby and Bridget checked there were keys in it.

"Take them to the gatehouse for first aid." The gatehouse was also the medical center and the security guards were all trained medics. The injured were loaded into the truck and sped to the plant entrance.

Still no Jack.

Her heart raced but her mind was clear, focused on the task at hand. She had to find the remaining men and get them to safety, and she had to protect her team.

"We're going to need some more fire tenders," she radioed to Ken. The men she had on the hoses were not making much progress. "Put a call out to our neighbors."

There were other oil refineries in Houston and they had a mutual aid agreement to help each other out in an emergency. They were going to be needed.

Her radio barked to life. "Bridget, what the hell is going on out there?" It was Kevin.

"We've got the mother of all fires," she said. "We can't get close enough to determine the cause yet. I've got men hosing it down to stop the spread and others searching for our three remaining missing people. Anyone know what work they were doing?"

She rattled off the names of the missing. Only silence in reply. She swore.

"Bridget, Jack might be at the sleeping hut." Anthony came on the radio. "I told him he had to close it today."

"What sleeping hut?" There wasn't such a thing as far as she knew.

There was a pause before one of her team said, "I know it. I'll check."

Bridget didn't have time to hope. She continued monitoring the fire, checking in with her team members and praying like mad.

The ambulance arrived back with Joe and Mike on board. She sent them straight to the gatehouse. Mike was now conscious and could be checked there before going on to the hospital. She was still waiting for the other ambulances. "Ken, where are my ambulances?"

"Two offsite ambulances have arrived."

"Send both straight to the catalytic reformer and order another two. We've got three missing still. Get the guys in the truck to show them where to go."

Her biggest concern was the unconscious man and her three missing people. "Found anyone else at the cracker?" she called through the radio.

"No, Bridge. Area's all clear. No one else is here."

"Hell." She needed to set up a bigger search. If the man had been foolish enough to cut through the alkylate unit he could be in serious trouble. The unit was full of hydrofluoric acid and no one was supposed to enter it without a hazmat suit.

Bridget grabbed five team members she knew worked in the alkylate unit. "Get in full hazmat suits. I need you to search the alky unit."

They nodded and jogged away.

She turned to check her remaining numbers. "We've got three missing men. We've got to do a methodical search, starting from the cat reformer and working back to the crude unit." It was too hot and dangerous to start near the fire and there was still one operator unaccounted for in that unit.

"Yes, ma'am," they said and headed out.

Bridget turned her attention to the fire. It was not abating.

"Bridget, the fire trucks have arrived."

"Direct them my way," she said.

"Bridget, we found one. He's in a bad way, major burns. Need an ambulance to the north side of the alky unit."

"Who is it?" Bridget's heart stood still.

"Chris. We've got him under the safety shower. He's unconscious and his breathing is weak. He must have been walking back to the control room when it happened. He's been knocked into the alky unit but I can't see any signs of acid burns."

Hydrofluoric acid would eat through skin and bone quickly and if the man had fire burns, the acid burns might be hidden. He needed to get to the hospital immediately.

"Ken, you got that?" Bridget called.

"Yeah. Another ambulance just arrived. Directing it now."

She breathed out deeply. She couldn't worry about one person. There were still two more. Two more people to find and one of them was Jack. He had to be unconscious, because he knew to get on to the closest emergency channel to let her know his position.

Her skin tightened and for a moment the

fear threatened to overwhelm her. She fought it back. Jack would be fine. He knew how to protect himself. He had to be all right. She wouldn't consider the alternative.

The fire trucks pulled up and Bridget directed them to where they were needed. Then she stood back and scanned the unit, searching, trying to find some sign of Jack and the other missing man. He'd said he wanted her to monitor the startup but he hadn't said what he was doing. It was her fault. She'd not had a chance to ask him, not after he'd been so angry at her denial of their relationship.

She shaded her eyes, looking up, and radioed her team. "What's your status?"

"Chris is in the ambulance. We're making our way closer to the flames."

"Was there no one at the sleeping hut?"

"I'm here, Bridge. A piece of steel is blocking the door," one of the guys said. "I think I can hear someone inside."

She didn't let the hope take over. She needed to focus. "What do you need to move it?" Bridget asked.

"We might need a crane. Give me a minute, I'll let you know."

"Get confirmation someone's in there."

"It's noisy as hell here. All I can hear is knocking."

The whole damn unit was creaking and groaning and the roar of the fire was above it all. Bridget waited impatiently, straining to hear any message over the radio. She paced up and down. The tenders' engines purred and the plant still hummed.

"Control room, when is this plant going to be down?" she asked.

"We're under orders to only do the emergency shutdown on that unit," came the reply. "The others are doing a controlled shutdown."

White hot anger seared through Bridget. "Who the hell ordered that?"

"Kevin."

She knew he was listening in to the radio feed. "Kevin, there are men's lives at risk here. ESD the whole damn plant. It looks like a goddamned warzone out here. A pipeline could burst at any moment."

"You're not qualified to make that judgment." Kevin snarled.

"Like hell I'm not. I'm looking into a wall of flames and the metal is groaning in protest. You don't shut down this plant and you could kill all my team and the firemen who have come to help, not to mention cause an explosion the whole city will feel."

Bridget took a breath and directed her next

comment to the control panel technician. "Do an emergency shutdown, Tim."

"Yes, ma'am."

"You order that and your job is gone, Bridget," Kevin spat out. "You're not in charge."

A calm settled over her. "Check your emergency response procedure, Kevin," she said, still watching her team. "I'm in charge until the emergency is over, and it ain't over."

"Plant shutting down," Tim said.

One of the other control panel technicians said, "Copy that. We've hit the ESD too."

Bridget breathed a sigh of relief. The alky unit nearby creaked and groaned but that was normal for an emergency shutdown.

"Guys, how's it going with that beam?" she asked.

"It's too heavy, Bridget. We're going to need a crane."

"Nothing in the area?" she asked.

"It's damaged."

"Who's got their crane license?"

One of the guys on the fire hose said, "I do."

She walked in and took the hose from him, being careful to keep it pointed at the flames. "Someone tell me where the nearest crane is to the hut," she called over the radio. After a moment the reply came. "On the south road."

The crane driver headed in that direction. "I need someone to take over this hose," Bridget said. "And confirm how many are inside the hut."

A few minutes later one of her team members replaced her and she moved north of the unit to see where the search team was.

"Bridge, I think they're both in there," the searcher said over the radio.

Bridget hoped to God he was right. Spotting the men, she moved into the crude unit toward them. She had to see for herself. She had to know where Jack was.

It was hot as hell and it was going to be an awkward lift, but they couldn't rush this. She had to keep her team safe. The "hut" was hardly more than a half-sized steel door. "Could two people fit in there?"

"It'd be a squeeze but it's possible."

The steelwork around her screeched, the heat from the flames was intense. Puddles of oil had formed, probably from the relief valves venting. If it got hot enough those puddles would ignite. They had to do this fast. It was getting hotter by the minute.

"We only need one person to attach the chain to the steel," Bridget said. The metal needed to be lifted high enough to open the door. It wasn't much. "I can do it. I want the rest of you to clear the area."

The two men looked at her. They knew the risks.

"Move," she yelled. "Get me a fire tender to the east side of the crude unit." The area needed to be foamed. She glanced up and noticed the oil streaks ran all the way down the tower. Had the relief valves closed or were they stuck open? If the flames got into the tower the explosion would kill them all. She couldn't even calculate the blast zone.

The technicians moved away and Bridget turned her attention to the steel and the crane. She had to be quick.

The crane jib moved toward her, the chain dangling from the edge as it inched its way lower. Grabbing on to it she gave the driver the signal to stop and hooked the chain around the steel, making sure it was secure before motioning for it to be lifted.

The steel lifted slowly, inch by inch, until it was clear of the door. Bridget flung it open as the chain slipped, causing the steel to fall onto the open door. It didn't matter, it was open.

All she could see was a pair of pants and boots. "Get out," she called as whoever it was started to crawl backward.

"Get out of here," she radioed to the crane operator. "It's not safe."

The fire tender hadn't arrived yet and it was getting hotter. She hoped they'd clear the area before it heated to ignition point. She stood back to give room to whoever was crawling out so he could stand. It was one of the operation technicians. He reached back in and started to drag someone else out.

Jack.

Bridget's heart pounded heavy in her chest, almost in slow motion. His head was covered in blood and his arm was at an unnatural angle. He was unconscious.

Now was not the time to panic. "Help me stand him up," she told the technician, who was a little unsteady on his feet.

They got Jack to a semi-standing position and Bridget picked him up in a fireman's lift over her shoulders. Goddamn, he was heavy. She shifted him a little, hoping she wasn't doing further damage, and nodded toward the safe zone. "Go!" she ordered the technician.

The fire tender arrived and started spraying the whole area.

Gritting her teeth she moved as fast as she could, following the technician out of the bund as metal creaked and groaned around them. She climbed the small flight of stairs, her muscles screaming. One step in front of the other. She couldn't stop now.

"You're almost there, Bridge," someone called encouragement over the radio.

She grunted. With every step, Jack seemed to gain five pounds. They hit the road and Bridget nodded. "That way."

Next to her a spot fire ignited.

Chapter 21

She moved with a burst of speed, willing her legs not to fail her. Her pants were soaked with foam as someone dowsed the flames near her. A couple of men ran forward to help the technician who was struggling, and to take some of Jack's weight.

She reached the ambulance and the medics took Jack off her shoulders and laid him onto a stretcher. She spun around to check how far away they were from the plant and the flames. The fire officers had saturated the whole area in foam and the spot fire was out.

"We've got Jack and Roger," she yelled through her radio. "Is everyone accounted for?"

"Yeah, Bridget." Ken told her. "That's everyone."

Relief swept through her and all her breath

seemed to leave her. She turned back to Jack. He was being loaded into an ambulance. She raced over.

"How is he?"

"He's critical," the paramedic said. "No burns, but that gash on his head is serious. We'll keep you informed."

Before she could check him herself, they shut the ambulance and drove away. She turned to the technician who had been with Jack.

"How are you?"

"All right. Jack took the brunt of the impact. I was behind him."

Bridget couldn't spend time finding out what happened now. She waved to one of her team members. "Take him to the gatehouse, make sure he gets checked."

She turned back to the burning plant and spoke into the radio. "Fire teams give me a status update."

One by one they reported in. The fire was contained but it was going to be a long time before it was out. She breathed a sigh of relief. What was next?

"Anthony, you need to call the families of all the injured and let them know what's happened. I want all non-essential personnel to go home. We need to clear the plant. Send twenty at a time. I don't want a traffic jam in the parking lot."

"Anthony's already doing it," Ken said.

That was one less thing to worry about. Over in the plant the plume of smoke was thick and black, reaching far up into the sky like a mushroom cloud. The repercussions of this were going to be felt for a long time.

"Control room, what have you got for me?"

"The whole plant is in shutdown, but there are some alarms that need checking."

"Tell me who you need."

The last thing she needed was an incident in another unit. When they gave her the names she sent the relevant operation technicians to check the alarms.

She had to regroup. She called each fire tender leader to her and reviewed their plan of attack. They set up one team to form a perimeter to make sure the flames didn't spread and another team to keep the temperature of the surrounding areas cool and wet. A further team was set up for dealing with spot fires and the rest concentrated on the source of the fire.

They worked for hours. At some stage Ken radioed to say the site was clear except for the managers who were in crisis management mode and the technicians who were dealing with the alarms.

Bridget's thoughts constantly strayed to Jack. How was he? How bad were his injuries? Was he already stabilized? She shook her head. She had a job to do. The teams had to be well hydrated and they needed to take breaks – she had to make sure they weren't exhausting themselves.

At some time close to dusk, she was taking over a fire hose from a technician going on a break, when her radio squawked.

"The cavalry have arrived. Time for a shift change?" It was Jeremy.

Bridget closed her eyes briefly. "Haven't you been at the competition all day?"

"No. Ken called me up when it happened. Told us to go home and rest up."

She wanted to bless Ken for thinking of it. "How many have you got?"

"Two shifts. We can replace this shift and some of the neighbors. Where are you?"

She gave him her location, and not long after he arrived. She handed the hose to one of his men and took Jeremy some distance away to run through a handover.

When she was finished he let out a low whistle. "I'm impressed, Bridge. You handled yourself well. That's some major shit you've dealt with."

"Did you catch whether there's any news on the injured?" She was desperate for news of Jack.

"No, didn't ask. The crisis management team want a debrief though."

Bridget groaned. She couldn't remember exactly what she'd yelled at Kevin in the heat of the moment but she was not likely to be popular. "We're going to need to send a report to the authorities too." Had anyone thought to do that yet?

"Good luck. I'll take over here."

She hugged him and called to her team. "It's home time, guys. You've done a great job."

She spoke to each of her team members before they left, making sure they were all right to drive and telling them she'd call with an update. Then when there was nothing left to procrastinate over, she went into the administration building and found where the managers were holding the crisis talks.

Knocking before she entered, she went straight over to the HR officer. "How is everyone?"

"Most are under observation for another couple of hours," he said. "Those who were unconscious are being kept overnight."

"What about Jack?"

Before he could reply, Kevin strode over.

"Who the hell do you think you are?" he bellowed.

Bridget was too tired to deal with him. "I'm the only emergency response coordinator who was on site today. Have we notified the authorities about the incident?"

"We'll deal with the paperwork later. Right now I want to know why you thought you had the right to shut down my plant."

Bridget walked over to the nearest computer and brought up a document. "We have a legal obligation to inform the authorities of an incident on site within twenty-four hours."

She pressed print, walked over to the printer, and picked up the document. Scrolling through, she found the section she was looking for, grabbed a pen and circled it.

"This is why I had the right to shut down the plant." She handed Kevin the document, and turned back to the other managers. "You need to arrange a roster for the fire fighters. That fire is going to keep burning for a while yet. I recommend keeping everyone off site until next week. The regulators are going to be crawling all over the plant as soon as it's safe to do so."

"This document is ridiculous," Kevin spluttered, having finally read the section about the emergency response coordinator taking full control in an emergency.

"Then you shouldn't have approved it," said Bridget.

"You don't expect me to read everything put in front of me?" Kevin demanded.

She shrugged. "It's entirely up to you." She turned to the production manager. "Crude unit one is ruined. It's not going to be up and running for months. It's too soon to tell how much damage has been done to the second crude unit."

"This is your fault. That damned safety project of yours must be the cause of it," Kevin said. "I should have known better than to hire you after that last incident."

Her fury released like a shark scenting blood. "You don't know shit," she cried, ignoring the gasp from someone behind her. "The previous incident wasn't my fault and I'm damned sure this one wasn't either." She prayed she was right. "I don't know what caused the initial fire but those relief valves venting to atmosphere sure added fuel to it. If you'd approved my project three months ago, they'd have already been replaced. So if it's on anyone's head it's yours." She walked toward the door. "Don't forget to submit the report to the regulators," she said. "I'm going home."

The second she sat behind the wheel of her truck she started to shake. The convulsions wouldn't stop. Her teeth clattered together and her heart pounded in her chest so hard she thought it was going to burst through. She hung on to the steering wheel to stop herself from shaking apart.

Ten men. She'd nearly lost ten men today.

It could have been a lot worse, she knew, but ten badly injured men were bad enough. There were ten men who weren't going home in the same state as they'd left it. Ten men who had been injured on her watch.

And one of them was Jack.

* * *

Jack's first thought when he woke was that he must have had a great night out, because his head was throbbing and he couldn't remember a thing. As he cautiously opened one eye he heard the blip of a machine, and as he focused he realized he was in a hospital bed.

What the hell had happened?

Carefully he moved and pain shot through his arm. He moaned.

"Oh honey, you're awake. Don't move. Let me get a nurse." His mother's face appeared in his line of sight for a second before disappearing again.

A moment later she returned with a nurse in tow.

"How are you feeling?" the nurse asked, shining a light in his eyes.

He blinked and squinted. "I'd be better if you didn't shine that thing at me."

The nurse chuckled. "Good. Can you tell me your name and what day it is?"

"Jackson Gibbs." Hell, what day was it? "Wednesday?"

"Great. Just squeeze my hands for me," she said, holding out her hands.

He did as she asked.

"Are you feeling any pain?"

Now that he was becoming more alert, every muscle in his body ached. "My head is the worst."

"We can give you some medication for that. Anywhere else?"

He mentally scanned his body. "My shoulder." The rest of his body just ached.

"You've dislocated it, but the meds will help that as well."

Jack turned to his mother and noticed his father behind her. "What happened?"

"You had an accident at work. They wouldn't tell me anything more."

Closing his eyes he tried to recall. He remembered the unit starting up again, remembered going to ask Bridget to supervise because he'd overheard the technicians sounding stressed. He'd been in her office and seen a list with his name at the top. He remembered the hurt when she'd told him she was only considering the new job, remembered the feeling of not being good enough for her ... remembered storming out.

Then what?

Anthony had discovered some of the technicians had crammed a bed into a little hut in the plant so they could get a few hours' sleep on night shift. He wanted it immediately removed and Jack had to make sure it was done safely. He'd gone into the crude unit with Roger, one of the technicians who had been trying to convince him there was no harm in the guys getting a bit of shut-eye on night shift. It wasn't good for them to be working fatigued.

When Jack had seen the tiny space, right next to some of the most dangerous lines on the plant, he hadn't believed it. As he'd turned back to Roger, there'd been a loud roar and Roger had shoved him inside. He'd hit his head on the opposite wall as the plant shook.

Shit. Something had gone seriously wrong at the plant.

Bridget! He'd sent her out to supervise. His heart raced and he tried to sit up. "Is Bridget all right?"

"I don't know." His mother put a hand on his shoulder. "You need to lie down."

"I need to know she's all right."

"I'll find out for you. Take the pills from the nurse."

The nurse had returned and was holding out two white pills and a cup of water. He grabbed them and swallowed them down. "The HR manager is over there." The nurse pointed past the partition where Anthony was talking to Mike.

"Tell him to come here," Jack said to his mother. If anything had happened to Bridget he'd never forgive himself.

A minute later Anthony was at Jack's bedside. He looked exhausted.

"What happened?" Jack demanded.

"We don't know all the details yet. There was an explosion in the crude unit. We have ten injured, none killed."

"Bridget?"

"She's the incident controller. When I left she had everything under control."

Jack let out the breath he'd been holding. "How bad are the injured?"

"You're one of the worst," Anthony said with a small smile. "It's mostly smoke inhalation, a few broken bones, and some burns that should heal well. We've only got one guy with major burns. He's in surgery now."

Even one was bad enough. "Are all the injured here?" He nodded toward the curtains and winced at the pain. They must be in an emergency room.

"A couple have been discharged already."

Gingerly, Jack tried to sit up. "I need to talk to them." He wanted to check for himself they were all right.

"You shouldn't be moving yet," Anthony said, and Anna nodded.

He ignored them both. It wasn't until he slowly swung his legs out of bed that he realized he was wearing a hospital gown that wasn't done up at the back. He paused.

"Let me get that," his mother said, and walked around behind him to tie up the gown.

When his feet touched the ground, Jack had to wait to allow the wave of dizziness to pass. With his father's help he walked over to Mike's bed. There was a wolf whistle behind him.

"Nice legs, Jack." Roger was in the bed next to him, fully clothed.

Jack flipped him the bird and he chuckled.

He turned to his parents. "Why don't you take a break? Grab a coffee." He wasn't sure how long they'd been there and they looked tired.

His father nodded. "All right."

When they were gone he spoke with Mike, and then went around to each bed, slowly putting together the story of what had happened. Finally he stopped at Roger.

"What do you remember?" Roger asked him.

"Everything up until you pushed me into the hut. Why did you?"

"That hideous roar, like a damn rocket taking off, was the relief valves on top of the crude tower venting. We were about to be showered in hot crude oil. I just reacted, pushed you into the hut and then jumped in after you. There was an explosion and a piece of steel blocked the door so we couldn't get out."

Jack wasn't sure how they both managed to fit in that tiny space but that didn't matter. "What happened next?"

"It took about twenty minutes for the emergency response team to find us. I thought we were going to roast before they did. They had to get a crane to lift the steelwork. By the time they got it off, the whole damned unit was like a furnace. It wouldn't have taken much more for the oil to ignite. I pulled you out of the hut and Bridget picked you up in a fucking fireman's lift and carried you all the way out to the cold zone. She was amazing. There were spot fires igniting the whole time we were running out."

Jack blinked. Bridget had saved his life.

"We're both lucky to be here."

Jack nodded, his legs a little unsteady.

"You need to get back into bed," the nurse ordered.

He did as she said without arguing. Fatigue suddenly swept over him as he laid down.

"Go to sleep," the nurse said. "It will help you heal."

Jack closed his eyes, and almost instantly fell asleep.

* * *

Bridget took a deep breath, swiping at the tears pouring down her face. She had to see Jack, she had to see for herself he was all right. She'd asked the security guard for the details of the hospital where the injured had been taken, and getting her shakes under control, she drove straight there.

When she arrived, she was directed to his cubicle in the emergency room. She slowly pushed the curtain back to find Jack's parents beside the bed.

Anna's mouth dropped open. "Bridget? You look like you've been in a war."

Bridget hadn't considered how she looked, or smelled. "It's been a rough day." She glanced over at Jack. His eyes were closed, his head was bandaged, and his arm was in a sling.

"How is he?"

"He's just gone to sleep," Eric said. "He dislocated his shoulder and got knocked on the head. The doctor's confident he'll make a full recovery."

The relief washed over Bridget, almost drowning her. She stumbled under the weight, and then straightened again. "That's good. When we couldn't find him ..." She broke off as his mother paled. Of course she hadn't been told the full details.

"You were out there?" Anna said. "What happened? They didn't tell us anything aside from he'd been injured at work."

Bridget shook her head. "I can't give you details yet. I don't know Jack's side of the story. There was an incident, and when we did the head count we had ten missing. Jack was one of them."

"And you searched for him?"

She nodded. "I was the incident controller. When we found him he was unconscious so I carried him out."

Before Bridget could say anything else, Anna hugged her tightly. "Thank you. Thank you for saving my son."

Uncomfortable, she pried herself away. "It was nothing. Just doing my job."

And if she'd done her job properly and been able to convince management of the importance of the project sooner, none of this would have happened. She'd almost killed Jack. She couldn't look at him. She needed to get out of there before she broke down. "I'd better get home."

She turned and left immediately.

* * *

As Bridget drove home news of the incident was all over the radio, so she switched it off. Pulling into her driveway she found Carly on her doorstep. Her sister raced down the path to her car and the moment Bridget climbed out, she flung her arms around her.

"Thank God you're all right. We didn't know where you were."

It was enough for all of Bridget's walls to come crumbling down. Her body shook and her vision blurred as the tears she'd been holding back came thick and fast.

"I almost lost him," she sobbed.

Carly pulled back. "Lost who?"

"Jack. He was missing after the explosion. We couldn't find him."

"Oh, *mi niñita*. Let's get you inside."

She took the keys from Bridget's numb hands and opened the front door, leading her into the living room. Bridget collapsed onto the couch, buried her head into her sister's chest, and cried.

* * *

Sometime later when she'd cried herself dry, Bridget sat up. Carly brushed her hair off her face. "Do you want to tell me what happened?"

Bridget nodded. Slowly she recounted what she remembered from when the alarms had first sounded.

"You risked your life to save him," Carly said, her tone a little angry.

"Of course I did! I'd risk my life to save anyone I love." She shut her mouth with a snap.

She *did* love him.

She loved him, and to hell what anyone thought. She'd been so stupid, so caught up in worrying about what people would say. But that didn't matter. She'd been foolish to let anyone stand in the way of admitting her feelings for Jack.

Carly gave her a small smile. "You look a little dazed."

"I didn't realize. I've been so blind, and he's so mad at me right now." She could

Claire Boston

understand why he was so hurt. "I'm not sure if he'll forgive me."

"I'm pretty sure saving his life will earn you some brownie points." Carly patted her arm. "If you're feeling a little better, you need to call Mama. She was frantic until I told her I'd spoken to someone at your work and you were fine."

Her conscience pricked. "Of course." She hadn't considered her family's reaction, she'd been too focused on the plant. "It must be just like Papa for her. I should have thought." Bridget reached for her phone.

Carly frowned. "What do you mean, like Papa?"

"An accident at work. Papa not coming home."

Her sister shook her head. "Papa didn't die at work. He was murdered on the way home."

Bridget froze, staring at her sister.

"I thought you knew."

She shook her head. "Mama never spoke about it. I just assumed … Who murdered him?"

"No one knows. He got caught in the tensions in the aftermath of the civil war. Mama always blamed herself for not leaving El Salvador sooner."

Bridget sat back down, phone in her hand.

347

All this time she'd thought her father had died at work. No wonder her mother didn't want to go back to El Salvador. She shook her head. She couldn't deal with this now. It was something she'd have to ask her about later. Right now she needed to tell her mother she was all right.

It took a while to convince Carmen that Bridget didn't need to go to the hospital and didn't need her mother to come and stay. In the end Carly promised to stay the night and Bridget was able to hang up the phone.

"Go take a shower. I'll make you something to eat," Carly said.

"I'm not hungry," Bridget said as she walked to the bathroom, relieved to finally have a chance to clean up. She ran the water until steam clouded and then stepped under the scorching spray. The heat scoured her skin. She slid to the ground, allowing the water to beat down on her and wash her clean.

Exhaustion smothered her. Her body was heavy like lead. She wasn't going to move ever again. Her brain began a slow-motion replay of all the events of the day, and every possible worse outcome. Everyone had been so very lucky.

Now it was over she couldn't quite believe she'd taken control the way she had, that the emergency response team respected her enough to follow her commands without question, and that she'd spoken to Kevin that way.

She couldn't find it within herself to regret it. Kevin wasn't happy with her, but it didn't matter. If Graham still wanted her after this, she was going to accept the job. Today had shown her it wasn't possible for her to keep everyone safe. They had to take responsibility for their own actions and look out for themselves as well.

Plus she was endangering the technicians more by staying where Kevin didn't trust her. If he hadn't countermanded her orders and delayed the project, the incident might not have been so bad. But that wasn't *her* fault. It was Kevin's. The realization was a relief. She'd done everything she could to improve the safety on the plant.

Bridget would move to a company that valued her advice and her expertise, where she wouldn't be ignored by senior management and where she could actually make a difference.

Slowly she climbed to her feet and shut off the water.

That way she could be with Jack.

If he still wanted her.

Chapter 22

If the explosion had been hell, the next day started out as purgatory.

Bridget had fallen into bed the night before straight after her shower and had slept solidly until her cell phone woke her at five.

It was a journalist from the *Houston Age* wanting to know what had happened at the plant. She gave him the number for the media coordinator at Dionysus and hung up. It was then followed by three more phone calls in quick succession, the last from Dionysus's contact at the Occupational Health and Safety Administration.

"Bridget, why haven't I received an incident notification in my email?" Victor asked.

Bridget swore under her breath. "They didn't send it?"

"Not that I can find."

She got out of bed and began pulling on some clothes. The notification should have been immediate as a matter of courtesy, and they now had only six hours to get the initial report in. She gave Victor what information she knew. "I'll get the rest to you as soon as possible. I'm heading to work now."

"I'll be on site at nine. You can give it to me then." He hung up.

Bridget strode into the kitchen to find Carly making coffee. She'd forgotten her sister had stayed the night. "I'm sorry, did my phone wake you?"

"I was awake," she said. "You need to eat something before you leave." She handed her a mug.

Bridget didn't bother to argue. She called the hospital for an update on Jack. He'd been moved to a room overnight and the nurse said he'd had a good night's sleep and should be discharged later today. Bridget breathed out a sigh of relief and hung up.

"All good?" Carly asked, buttering toast.

"Yeah. He should be home today." Bridget wasn't sure what she was going to say to him, but that didn't matter. What mattered was he was all right. She took the toast Carly handed her. "Are you going to eat?"

"I'll buy something on my way to work,"

Carly said, grabbing her purse.

Together they walked out of the house. Bridget hugged her sister tightly. "Thanks for being here."

Carly smiled. "Any time, little sister."

* * *

When Bridget arrived at work the fire was still burning. She stopped at the gatehouse.

"Who's here?" she asked the security guard.

"The technicians on the new shift have arrived and are gathered in the crisis management room for handover. We've got a couple of big wigs from corporate office who have pulled an all-nighter trying to put a spin on this, and the rest of the managers are in there."

"Thanks. Can I get the full list of names of those who were injured? I need them for my report."

The guard photocopied a document and handed it to her. She thanked him and turned to go.

"Bridget?"

She turned back.

"I heard what you did yesterday. They should give you a medal."

She smiled. She doubted very much that was going to happen.

Her aim on entering the administration building was to avoid the crisis room and go straight to her office to organize the report for Victor. Unfortunately Kevin walked out of the room with the CEO Bob Randall as she walked past.

"Bridget." Kevin's voice was a command. "You need to come with us."

She stopped and forced a smile to her face. "I'm just going to write the incident report for OSHA. Victor is arriving at nine and it appears it hasn't been sent yet." She didn't hide her disbelief.

"It can wait. Bob wants an explanation of yesterday's events."

She nodded to Bob. "I'm sure you don't want us in any more trouble with the regulators than we already are. Can you give me half an hour to put together the report?"

"No. Now," Bob demanded.

Bridget swallowed her anger and followed him into the general manager's office.

She wasn't offered a seat, so she stood. "Where would you like me to start?"

"From the alarms."

Bridget took out her phone and set the record function. She wanted this on record. She could use it to build her own report later. Slowly she went through what she could recall of the events. She answered Bob's questions and defended her decision to shut down the plant. The Chemical Safety Board would be on site as soon as it was safe to start their investigation, and Bridget was certain they would agree with her decision when they'd examined all the facts.

An hour later they'd finished grilling her. With leave to go, she stalked out and headed straight to her office. The corridors were deserted, a sure sign something bad had happened.

She shut the door and turned to her computer. There was a sticky note on the screen from Sally: *Sent verbal notification to the EPA. Will be in tomorrow to write report.* She breathed a sigh of relief. That was one less thing she had to do. She fired up her computer and began writing. As soon as she was satisfied she had the detail OSHA wanted, she printed the document and delivered it to the crisis management team for their approval, before heading out to the plant to talk with the fire team.

Bridget made her rounds, making sure they had enough to drink and were in reasonable spirits. With a promise she would be monitoring the radio channel should they need her, she went back to her office to write up her version of events.

Her phone rang as she was halfway through. It was the gatehouse.

"Victor and his team are here."

She checked her watch. Nine o'clock. "Can you let Kevin and Bob know we'll be in meeting room one?" They would need to be present for this.

At the main gate she greeted Victor and the two other men with him, who he introduced as investigators. She led them to the meeting room. Kevin and Bob arrived and after the introductions were made they settled down to business. Bridget handed Victor the report she'd written and when the explanations were done, they proceeded to tour the plant.

In the bright light of day it looked like a warzone. Smoke still lingered, thick and acrid in the air, and the blast zone from the explosion had cleared a large area. Buckled metal was lying all over the place. Bridget hadn't taken in the level of destruction while she'd been searching for people and trying to get the fire under control. It was a wonder no one had been killed.

"What was the cause of the fire?" Victor asked.

"We're not certain," Bridget replied. "When the fire is completely out, we'll be able to do a more thorough investigation."

"And what do you expect to find?"

Bridget had spoken to a couple of the fire officers who had told her it looked like liquid had got into the fuel gas main due to a sticking level transmitter. It was the same transmitter she'd told the plant to fix several weeks ago.

But she couldn't say that. "I'd rather not guess on such a serious matter."

Victor looked at her for a long moment and then nodded. They both knew she had a fair idea of what caused it. It took another couple of hours before Victor was satisfied he had enough information to start with. Kevin and Bob walked him to the gatehouse and Bridget went to continue recording her recollections of the event.

Her phone had half a dozen messages on it, so she listened to them. The trainers both wanted updates. The rest of the department was on site, already doing the initial incident investigation. Bridget called both men back and updated them on the plant and on the people who had been injured. Anthony had mentioned that all but the burn victim were due to be released today.

Graham had called expressing his concern and Bridget debated for a moment before calling him back.

"Bridget, how are you?" he asked.

"Tired," she said. "But everyone's safe and alive, so that's the main thing."

"The rumors are already flying. What happened?"

She hesitated. "I can't tell you yet." It was speculation until they'd done a proper investigation and she didn't want to add to the rumors. When the investigation was completed the report would be in the public domain anyway.

"Yeah. All right." He paused. "This is probably a bad time to ask, but have you read the job description?"

Hope flickered. "I have." She took a breath. "Do you still want me?"

"Of course."

Bridget let out the breath she was holding. "Then I'm going to apply."

"That's fantastic news. I realize you'll be snowed under for the next couple of weeks with the investigation, so get your application to me whenever you can."

"Great. Thanks Graham." She hung up. She would make it a priority.

Sally knocked on her door. "Rough morning?" she asked, handing Bridget a take-out coffee.

She took it gratefully. "Yeah, thanks.

Where'd you get this from?"

"I pinched a couple of cups from the crisis room. Nick and I have finished the initial environmental report. I figured you had enough on your plate, so I gave it to Kevin."

Sally was as passionate about the environment as she was about safety, so Bridget knew it would have been thorough.

"Is there anything else you need to do?" Bridget asked.

"Nothing we can do until the fire's out. We're going to head home."

She nodded. "Good idea. We'll all be putting in extra hours over the next few weeks. Take it easy."

Sally left and was soon replaced by Ken.

Bridget stood. "You did an excellent job yesterday," she said. "Thank you."

Ken shook his head. "I hardly did a thing. You got all those people out safely."

She wasn't comfortable with the praise. "The information you kept passing to me was invaluable," she said, and then noticing he wasn't any more comfortable with the praise than she was, she asked, "What have you been up to this morning?"

"I did a round of the plant. Made sure everything else was in order, just in case we missed something in the excitement."

"And?"

"It was all good. The control panel technicians shut everything down properly."

Trish walked into the room.

"Trish and I are arranging interviews,' Ken said. "We figured the sooner we write down what happened, the better."

"Any news about Jack?" Trish asked.

"He should be out today," Bridget said.

Trish stepped forward and hugged her, as Ken slipped out of the room. "You were amazing yesterday. The way you barked out orders, it was clear you had everything under control. You impressed all the managers."

Bridget didn't care who she impressed. "Thanks. Call me if you need a hand with the interviews."

"What are you going to do?"

She wasn't sure. She suspected she needed to report to the crisis room and see if they needed anything from her, but she really didn't want to. In Jack's absence she was supposed to be the Health, Safety, and Environment representative on the crisis team. "I'll check in with management. Has anyone seen Dirk?"

"Last I heard he was with the crisis team. He's the HSE representative after you and Jack, isn't he?"

Bridget swore. He was. The last thing she

needed was him stirring up trouble. "I'd better go check."

Trish gave her a sympathetic smile and walked out.

Bridget grabbed her notebook and a pen and walked back to the crisis room. She heard the raised voices down the hall and picked up her pace. As she entered the room Dirk was pointing and waving his finger at Jack.

Jack! Her heart swelled to see him there, to see him standing, to see him alive and conscious. Her eyes roved over him checking for injuries. His arm was in a sling and there was a dressing on his head. He really shouldn't be here. He should be resting at home.

No one had noticed her walk in, and she was about to speak but Jack beat her to it.

"She saved my life." His voice was rough and his eyes were red.

"How would you know? You were unconscious when you left here," Dirk said.

"I spoke with Roger at the hospital last night. He told me how Bridget carried me out."

"Like she'd be able to lift you," Kevin said. "The men are protecting her."

Bridget gasped. After all she had done, he still refused to believe her. She wasn't going to spend a minute longer than necessary here.

The sooner she completed her application, the better. "I can demonstrate if you'd like."

All eyes turned toward her and Kevin's face went red. She ignored him and looked at Jack. "I'm glad to see you up."

She wanted to run to him, to fling her arms around him and hold him tight, to convince herself he was all right.

The hell with it. No one could think any worse of her than they already did.

She crossed the room and wrapped her arms around Jack's neck, being mindful of his arm in a sling. "I thought you were dead," she whispered, holding him close.

His free arm came around her, hugging her back.

Somewhere behind them Kevin made a grunt of outrage but Bridget ignored him. "I'm sorry for making you think you weren't good enough, for not trusting what we have. I'm sorry my baggage made you so unhappy." She stepped back and looked him in the eyes. "I love you. When I thought I might have lost you –" That was as far as she got before he covered her mouth with his and kissed her.

When he stopped he rested his forehead against hers. "I love you too."

"Do you see what I mean?" Dirk's disgust was clear. "She's sleeping with him. She's probably been filling his head with lies since he started. I'll bet you it was her stupid safety project that caused the incident."

"Shut up, Dirk," Jack snapped, turning to him but keeping his good arm firmly around Bridget's waist. "I know my own mind and I know safety. From what I've heard about the incident there could be a number of causes, but those relief valves venting to atmosphere caused Roger and my injuries."

Kevin's face went red. "Dirk told me the project was unnecessary." He glared at Dirk who turned pale.

Bridget's eyebrows shot up. That was information she hadn't known. She couldn't prevent the smallest hint of satisfaction going through her, but she needed to make a point. "We were very lucky yesterday —"

"*Lucky?*" Bob's voice was incredulous. "Half the plant is ruined and we're going to lose millions of dollars."

Bridget stared him down. "We're lucky we didn't *kill* anyone."

He pursed his lips and she continued. "The burns were bad enough. It's time this site took safety seriously and started listening to the *experts* they've hired when they tell them something is wrong."

"Fire's out ..." Jeremy's voice trailed off as

he walked into the room and noticed the tension.

Bridget smiled at him. "What's next?"

"There's a bit of mopping up to do but it should be clear within the hour. We'll need to get some structural engineers in to check the stability of the area and then we can start the investigation." He nodded to Jack. "Good to see you up, boss."

Bridget turned to him. "About that ... you should go home and rest."

"I feel fine. I've had ten hours' sleep and have some great painkillers for my arm. I want to sit in on the interviews."

Bridget turned to Anthony to back her up.

"He's been cleared to work," he told her with an apologetic smile.

Jack kissed her again. "I'm fine. I promise. Now I need to speak to you alone for a moment."

He took her hand and led her out of the room, past an unusually silent Kevin, to his office. He shut his door and turned to her, pulling her close with his one good arm.

"I've accepted Graham's job," she said. "I need to officially apply, but as soon as it's confirmed I'll hand in my resignation."

Jack kissed her deeply. "I don't care. All I care about is that you're safe. When I woke up and remembered the explosion I was so scared something had happened to you. I made Anthony come straight over and tell me. Then afterward, when I was talking to everyone who was injured, your name kept popping up. It sounds like you saved the day."

She shook her head and stepped back. "I just followed procedure. I was the only emergency response coordinator on site. I had to take charge."

"By all accounts you were amazing. Thank you for saving my life."

"It was in my best interests," she said, blinking back tears and swallowing the lump in her throat.

"I'm sorry for the way I acted." He squeezed her hand. "I was selfish, not thinking about what you wanted, but expecting you to change jobs so we could be together. All I could think was you didn't love me the way I love you."

Bridget smiled at the thrill his words sent through her. He loved her. "The only thing stopping me from accepting it right away was my sense of responsibility for all of the guys at the plant. I didn't want to let them down. But after what happened, I've realized everyone is responsible for their own safety, and management doesn't want me here. I'm probably more a hindrance than anything.

You'll be able to make progress where I wasn't able to."

"I wish it wasn't that way."

Her smile was a little sad. "Me too. But wait until you see the job description – you'll be jealous," she teased.

He laughed. "Come on. We need to get back to work."

Yes. She took his hand. "Safety first," she said and smiled.

Epilogue

"Here's to Bridget: heroine of the plant. Long will she be missed." Jeremy raised his glass, and around him people echoed his sentiments.

Bridget smiled her thanks, raising her glass of wine. Her chest was full of emotion but luckily she didn't have to speak. The people who surrounded her now were the ones who had supported her the whole time at Dionysus. These were the people she was going to miss.

She'd given two weeks' notice when she'd handed in her resignation. She'd made sure the incident investigation was well under way and Jack would be able to ask her any follow-up questions.

Now she sat in a bar not far from the plant, with people who wanted to wish her well on her final day. Her heart warmed as Jack squeezed her hand.

The last couple of weeks had been difficult, but as they uncovered more details about what had happened, Kevin had gone from openly hostile to quietly subdued. She hadn't expected an apology from him, nor did she get one, but they were both aware he'd been very wrong about her.

The company's vice-president of safety, health and environment had praised her efforts during the incident when he'd returned from leave, and had done everything he could to convince her to stay with the company, but as far as Bridget was concerned it was too late. She was excited about the next stage in her career and felt she was going to make a difference.

"Hey, Bridge!" An arm came around her neck and Tanya kissed her cheek. "I thought I'd come and celebrate with you." She waved to Jack.

"Hi. You know a few people, don't you?" Bridget said, gesturing to Sally and Trish.

"Sure do. I'm going to grab a drink. Do you want another?"

Bridget nodded. She was going to relax and celebrate.

When Tanya was gone, the vice-president approached her. "Are you sure I can't convince you to stay?"

She smiled at him. "I'm sure." He'd been involved in the investigation and she'd got to know him over the past few weeks.

"It's a shame, but I guess we let you slip away."

She nodded. Tanya returned and handed Bridget a drink before finding a seat next to Trish.

Taking a sip, Bridget glanced at Jack. The few days following the incident had been difficult with them both having to answer questions about their relationship. Kevin's ire vanished as soon as they discovered the cause of the explosion – the sticking level transmitter Bridget had told production to fix. The thinning pipeline Mike had identified had also played a part because the explosion had caused it to rupture as well. They were both things that could have been avoided if Bridget had been listened to.

But she didn't feel vindicated, she felt sad. It was better for her to leave the company. After her run-in with the CEO she doubted the company's other oil refineries would be any better than the one she was on.

Jack squeezed her hand again. "You OK?"

"Yeah."

He leaned over and kissed her and Bridget

closed her eyes, savoring the moment. She loved that Jack could kiss her in front of all her colleagues now and she wasn't the least bit perturbed. It was incredibly freeing. She'd let her experience with Lionel affect her life, had given him far more power over her than she should have. But all of that was in the past.

She and Jack were together. The day after the incident she'd moved her things into his bedroom, which was the bigger of the two, and the following weekend they'd moved the rest of his things out of storage. Her mother kept asking when he was going to put a ring on her finger, but Bridget wasn't in any rush. She was content to be with him, to have him safe and by her side. They'd started searching for a place to buy together and for Bridget that was commitment enough.

"I love you," Jack murmured in her ear.

A warm shiver of pleasure went through her.

"I love you too."

She smiled as the pleasure welled up inside her, making her feel like she could burst with happiness. She was moving to her ideal job, she had Jack by her side, and she was surrounded by friends.

Life couldn't get better than this.

Acknowledgements

There was a lot of research that went into this book and I want to thank the following people; Pete for all his information about oil refineries - brainstorming all the things that could go wrong was quite fun (and a little scary!), Anne for her information on unaccompanied child refugees, Carmen for checking all the Spanish and giving me some details about El Salvador, and my beta reader Michelle for spotting all those Australianisms which keep sliding their way into my stories.

I also want to thank the team at Momentum; Joel, Patrick and Ashley for all their hard work, plus my editor Dianne for helping me make the book better. Though Momentum weren't able to publish this book in the end, I appreciate the support they gave during its development.

Change of Heart

The Flanagan Sisters #2

Software billionaire Carly Flanagan has an abundance of everything except time.

With everyone wanting a piece of her, or more accurately, her money, she spends her days trying to live up to her company's motto of Community, Sharing, Support. Having always been so focused on responsibility, success and supporting those less fortunate than her, Carly's forgotten to consider what she wants for herself in life – until she meets Evan.

Evan Hayes is an artist and free spirit, and when they meet at a local art exhibition, he is immediately intrigued by Carly. He sees through her public persona, realizing she is not the person she portrays. Evan's the type of man who doesn't have a lot, but is perfectly comfortable with who he is. A man who knows what he wants – and he wants Carly.

Carly is sure Evan wants something else from her. Everyone does. All Evan is asking is the chance to get to know her, but will Carly let him in? Or will a lifetime of protecting herself prove too hard to overcome?

Blaze a Trail

The Flanagan Sisters # 3

They're from the opposite ends of town but they're worlds apart.

Zita Flanagan wants more. She wants to help more Central American refugees and make more of an impact. But her family comes first and fulfilling her own dreams seems impossible.

David Randall leads a privileged life and knows nothing about refugee issues. When he meets dynamic, sexy Zita, it seems like the perfect opportunity to learn. Zita's passion for helping those less fortunate and her selfless devotion to the girls her mother fosters brings David's life sharply into perspective.

Zita soon realizes that David is so much more than a rich boy. She begins to trust him with her foster sisters' stories, and her own hopes and dreams. But when David's father announces he's running for governor and the focus of his campaign is the 'refugee problem', Zita has grave concerns for her sisters' safety. Then David's betrayal exposes secrets, and it becomes a race against time to save lives.

Can David convince Zita to trust him again, or will his mistake put the life of the woman he loves in jeopardy?

Place to Belong

The Flanagan Sisters #4

Sean Flanagan has spent a lifetime alone and rejected, constantly hiding who he really is.

With a father who deserted him and a mother who despised him, Sean didn't think things could get much worse … until he was kicked out of home for being gay. Now he's discovered he has three half-sisters on the other side of the world. This might be his last chance to find people who will love and accept him. But he's terrified that if they find out who he really is then they'll reject him like the rest of his family.

Sean arrives in Houston and is stunned by the warm welcome he receives from his sisters. He begins to hope that maybe this time things will be different. That's when he meets Hayden Johnson. To follow his heart means risking everything with his newfound family.

Hayden is tired of endless dating. He's looking for a man to love, someone to spend the rest of his life with. His boss's new brother ticks all the boxes on the attraction scale, but there's just one problem – he's not gay.

Will Sean let his fears rule him, or will he let in the chance of love and find a place where he belongs?

https://www.claireboston.com/books/the-flanagan-sisters/

CPSIA information can be obtained
at www.ICGtesting.com
Printed in the USA
LVHW090344300419
615920LV00002BA/226/P

9 781925 696301